THE GIRL NEXT DOOR

A.J. RIVERS

PROLOGUE

"Mr. Burke, I'm sorry to have to do this at a time like this…" Travis Burke shook his head, fighting the stinging of tears in his eyes.

"Ask me anything you want. Anything you think might help."

The officer nodded and gestured for him to stop pacing across the room and come sit on the couch. He sat but couldn't bring himself to rest back against the cushions. Instead, he perched at the edge, his muscles ready to bring him back up again in an instant. His hands flattened on the upholstery beside him, and his thumbs brushed against the slightly rougher texture of the roses against the cream background. Mia loved those roses. It was the only thing in the furniture store she loved. After nearly an hour of wandering through all the displays, testing the couches, staring at them and wondering how they would fit into the rest of the house, this was the one she chose. Her face lit up the second she saw it, and when she sat down, he worried she wouldn't get up long enough for them to deliver it.

He didn't love it then. He thought it was gaudy and belonged better in the house of a great-grandmother, ready to drape it in doilies

1

and fill it with the smell of coordinating rose perfume and cookies, rather than that of a woman in her mid-thirties. Five years later, it still hadn't grown on him much, but that night, he knew he'd never look at it the same. Every time he looked at it now, he'd see that glowing smile on her face. He still didn't love it, but maybe now he would learn to.

"When was the last time you saw your wife?" the officer asked.

He didn't know the officer's name. Either she hadn't told him yet, or he wasn't paying attention when she said it. She sat on the dark blue easy chair Mia only relented to him adding into the living room because she said it brought out the dark blue accents scattered among the roses.

"Um... two days ago," he answered.

The officer looked down at the pad in her hand like she was consulting notes she hadn't taken. He tried to catch a look at the front of her uniform. The least he could do was be able to refer to her by name. Her uniform stretched tight over a bulletproof vest and contorted her name tag. Travis could only see the first few letters of her name.

"Two days ago?" she asked. "Is it unusual for you to go that long without seeing her?"

He could be offended by the question. In his situation, anyone would be. But he wasn't. They'd been asked it a dozen times. He knew people didn't understand. But that didn't matter. It never had. They were the only ones that mattered, they always told each other. All that mattered was what they felt and how they looked at each other and their marriage. Who cared if anyone else thought it was unusual? Who cared if they thought it was strange?

It never mattered what anyone else thought.

But now it did.

"No," Travis told her, shaking his head. "It wasn't. Mia sometimes does that."

"Does what? Leaves?"

"Yes, but not in the way you mean. Mia is an artist. She's incredible." He gestured at the nearest wall, where four of Mia's paintings hung in sequence. "And like most artists, sometimes she just needs to be in her own head. She needs to be able to dig into her thoughts and drag them kicking and screaming out of her head and onto the canvas, as she likes to say. Having another person near her, even me, could stop her flow. So, she goes to her studio."

"Her studio?" the officer asks.

"It's just an apartment across town. Appropriately, I guess, a studio. Just big enough to have her supplies on one side, a bed and some clothes on the other, a kitchen for when she decides to come to the surface to breathe, and a bathroom. Streamlined and basic, but that's exactly the way she wants it."

He rubbed his hands along the couch cushions again. Her two worlds were so different in so many ways.

"And she just goes there for days at a time?" the officer asked.

"Yes. Sometimes. Sometimes it's only for an hour or two. Sometimes over the weekend. Sometimes an extra day. But she keeps in touch. She calls and texts. Sometimes she sends me pictures of what she's working on." He pulled his phone out of his pocket and pulled up the last image Mia sent him. "This is one of her most recent paintings. She sent it to me yesterday."

"Lovely. So, you did hear from her yesterday?"

Travis didn't like how dismissive her tone was. She was pushing his words away like there was no value in them, like she already understood the meaning and wasn't willing to sift through for any further details.

"Yes. You asked when I last saw her. That was two days ago. But I heard from her yesterday."

"And why do you think she's missing?" the officer asked.

"She didn't come home when she said she would. I went to her studio to check on her. I even brought her favorite Indian food in case she was so wrapped up in her work she didn't think about the time and was hungry. It's happened before. She gets so invested in a project, it's like it takes over her soul. She'll go all day without stopping to eat and then gets sick. But she didn't answer the door. I let myself in to look for her."

"So, you have a key?"

The officer was hiding a lot in that little word, 'so'.

"Of course I do. Why wouldn't I? The apartment isn't her escape from me."

"What did you find when you went in?"

"Nothing. That's the problem. She wasn't there. She wasn't at home, she wasn't there, she wasn't answering her phone or texts. Her car was still sitting in the parking lot. I called two or three dozen times. I left voicemails until the inbox wouldn't accept anymore. I sat outside waiting, thinking she might have gone for a walk, until it got dark. Then I came back here and waited for another couple hours before I called you."

"Would you bring us to the studio and let us look around?"

"Sure. Just try not to touch too much. When she comes back, I don't want her to be upset someone has messed with her art."

CHAPTER ONE

HIM

One by one, the fires started. They were small at first. Exactly how he designed them. He wanted them to take hold and gain strength behind their burn before they were noticed. Fires that spread too rapidly call attention too quickly. That means people are more likely to get out of the building and there would only be a loss of structure.

That wasn't his intention.

He wanted each of the blazes to burrow into the carpet, find fuel along the walls, and creep through the electrical wiring and ventilation systems. By the time these fires would be discovered, people would be surrounded. Fire would be everywhere, bursting from within the walls themselves, covering the doors, raining down on them. He didn't mind if some escaped. It was inevitable that they would. But he wanted them to have to work for it.

He wanted the fire department to scream down the streets and throw themselves into the blaze. He wanted hearts beating at speeds so intense they could simply give out at any minute. He wanted broken windows and flights of desperation, soundbites of goodbye calls filling the airwaves. He wanted the news to chronicle the gracious sloping lawns scattered with bodies, exhausted survivors, collapsed firefighters, ash, and glass.

More than any of that, he wanted to make sure the trail was there. It wouldn't be obvious. It wouldn't glare out at anyone who looked or call attention to itself. He didn't plan on using skywriting or taking over the lights of a marquee. No, this trail was subtle, encrypted in everything he did. That, too, was by design. The more subtle the trail, the more likely it was to be believed. No one would think someone brilliant and devious enough to create something like this would then drop breadcrumbs leading to themselves.

It had to be just a trace, just a whisper. An imprint more than an announcement. A heavy hand could push his target over the edge and possibly into a net. But a light touch could weave the ropes that bind for eternity.

The men he sent into the building came out casually through different exits. They were skilled now in the art of looking disconnected from anything happening around them. People always want to believe it would be obvious to identify someone willing and capable of doing something like this. Administrators of terror are solemn-faced and wear grungy clothes, black hoods to cover their faces, and gloves to disguise their fingerprints. They slouch and slither, scuttling away from their crimes. It's easy to tell who they are because they couldn't possibly be normal. Normal, like the rest of them. For most people, it's unfathomable to believe they are as familiar as looking in a mirror.

But that isn't reality. Chaos comes wrapped in tailored suits and expensive haircuts. Expensive jewelry and well-kept hands. They don't run from the tiny newborn burns strategically placed throughout the building. They ride elevators that would soon be inoperable and linger in the lobby to chat with security guards. They flirt with receptionists who, in moments, would feel the heat on their backs and stroll out into the parking lot talking on their phones and carrying briefcases. Every one of them had legitimate business there. Every one of them had their faces on cameras and etched into minds. They were so obvious, they were invisible.

Custom silk and hand-stitched cotton covered the leviathan tattoos on their backs.

CHAPTER TWO

NOW

"Play it again," Eric says.

I reach around him to start the short clip over again. It's the Richmond station again, just minutes before the deadly attack. Just minutes before the explosion rippled through, killing over a dozen and ruining the lives of dozens more.

And for some reason, my ex-boyfriend Greg Bailey was there, carrying something suspicious.

Eric and I both listen as he slides something across the desk toward the woman behind it and leans forward.

"Give this to Emma Griffin," I say right after Greg does. "That's what he says. He says to give whatever it is he's handing over to me. By name."

"Yeah," Eric nods. "That's definitely what it sounds like."

"That's not what it *sounds like*, Eric. That's what he says. How many other words are there that can be easily confused with 'Emma Griffin'?"

He shakes his head.

"Probably none." He scans back through the footage again and zooms in as close as he can on Greg's hand. "I wish I could figure out what he's handing her. He's holding it in such a weird way I can't tell what it is."

"I've been trying to figure it out, too. Maybe it's a note?" I suggest.

"Or the key to the locker he stashed whatever he had in that bag in," Eric points out.

"What's going on here?" a deep voice demands from the doorway. I turn and see Creagan bearing down on us, his eyes dark and angry. "Griffin, what are you doing here? You have no active cases you are working on right now."

"I know, sir. But I might have uncovered new evidence in Greg's disappearance, and possibly the bombing at the bus station," I tell him.

"I thought I made myself very clear your consultation on that case was over, and you were no longer to be involved."

"Yes, but if you will just hear me out," I attempt.

"She got an anonymous message containing a piece of video from just before the bombing," Eric cuts in. "Greg Bailey is in it."

Creagan furrows his brow, then stomps up to the desk and peers at the computer screen. Eric repeats the video clip I sent to him two days ago, when I received it during game night with Janet, Paul, and Sam. I watch my supervisor out of the corner of my eye as he watches the clip. Rather than showing interest, his expression gets more tense and angry.

"Where did you get this?" he demands.

"Eric told you. It was sent to me directly by a number I don't recognize. It didn't have a name or any other information on it. It just said 'listen carefully' and had this video attached."

"That woman is Mary Preston, one of the victims of the bombing," Creagan points out.

"I know. She was a vlogger. She must have recorded this video on her phone while making one of her videos. She didn't know what she was recording behind her."

"That phone was taken from underneath her body and processed into evidence. None of the content on it has been distributed to the public, and no one should have access to it. Except for those who are working on the case," Creagan sneers.

Eric looks at him, obviously offended by the accusation.

"I had nothing to do with this, if that's what you're implying. I haven't even seen this footage. There are other people working on processing everything they can get from the electronic devices gathered at the scene. I haven't gotten anywhere near Mary's or any other phone," he tells him.

Creagan ignores him and turns to face me.

"Listen to me carefully, Griffin. This is not your case. Neither one of them. You are not to be involved in any way. You are not an active agent, and you are not a consultant. You do not have clearance and are not privy to any further information. You will have no further part in either investigation. Do I make myself expressly clear?"

I draw myself up, hoping the deep breath I pull in is enough to quash the angry outburst trying to work its way up my throat. Finally, it settles enough for me to respond.

"Yes, sir."

"Good, because I don't want to have to deactivate your access badge for the building and remove you from duty entirely. Eric, get her out of the building."

He turns and storms out of the office. I know he's going to lurk nearby, out of sight, but still watching to make sure I leave. Eric and I exchange glances. He shakes his head slightly before gesturing for me to walk out first.

I leave the headquarters building and pull my jacket around myself as I head for the parking deck. The temperature is dropping, but most of the chill came from Creagan. My head's tucked down, and I'm going over everything that happened in the office as I approach my car.

"I take it that didn't go as planned?"

I look up and see Sam leaned back against the hood of the car, his ankles crossed in front of him, and his arms over his hips casually.

"Not exactly." I walk around to the passenger side, feeling like I'm probably not in a place to take the responsibility of a vehicle in my hands right now. "But at least you didn't have to wait too long."

"I'd have waited as long as you needed me to," he says, cranking the engine.

I smile at him. There's a big difference between the last time I came to headquarters to talk about Greg and this time. Last time, just a couple of months ago, I came alone. I didn't know if Sam was even going to be a part of my life anymore. I thought we had come back to the same crossroads we already did seven years ago. When I left Sherwood and him behind to focus on my FBI training and the career ahead. This time, he's right beside me. He came along for support, and I'm even happier to have him than I thought I was going to be.

"I know," I sigh. "Did you get anything done?"

I glance back into the backseat at the stacks of folders he brought along, filled with paperwork for him to do while I was inside. Without security clearance, he wasn't able to come into the office, so his plan was to hunker down in the car and take care of some of the administrative things he doesn't particularly like but are an unavoidable part of his career as sheriff of Sherwood. It doesn't look like any of the papers have been moved.

"I got kind of wrapped up in the book I was reading," he admits.

I shrug. "That's productive, too."

"So, are you going to tell me what happened up there?"

We pull out of the parking deck and start toward my house. I didn't relish the idea of taking on the drive between Sherwood and the Bureau headquarters twice in one day, so we're going to stay the night. It's only a few hours, but after the amount of travel I did with the last case Sam and I handled, I'm still going through road trip and flight detox.

I let out an aggravated sound and drop my head back against the headrest.

"Creagan. Creagan happened," I tell him. "He stormed into the office and threw a complete fit over me being there."

"Even after you told him about the video?" Sam asks.

"Even after we showed it to him. Mary Preston's phone was put into evidence, and no one should have been able to access that video to send it to me. He all but accused Eric and me of stealing it."

"And still no word on who sent it?"

I shake my head. "Eric traced the number, but it came from a burner phone. There's no way of knowing who's attached to it."

"Is Eric going to keep looking into it?" Sam asks.

"I think so, but I can't have anything to do with it. Creagan essentially told me if he finds out I'm still sniffing around Greg's disappearance or the bombing, I'll lose my job," I say. "Or at least, not be a field agent anymore."

"How do you feel about that?"

"What do you mean?" I ask.

"What are you thinking about your future with the Bureau? You've been on leave for a few months now. You're going to have to make a decision eventually," he says.

It's the question I've been anticipating and dreading. When I went on leave after a particularly harrowing case with Sam during the summer, it was open-ended. I knew I needed some time to piece myself back together, and I was still recovering from the case before that one and the emotional trauma it dragged me through. Creagan agreed, along with the therapist he strong-armed me into seeing for a few weeks and gave me his blessing to take all the time I needed. There was always the assumption I would be available for consultations while I was gone, and at some point, I'd feel back to normal and head back to my regular life.

But things have changed. My life isn't the same as it was a few months ago and now the answer isn't so clear.

"It's not like I've really been on leave," I answer, diverting attention away from what he's really asking.

It's true. It didn't take long for me to realize I'm not good at just sitting around not doing anything. In addition to reacclimating myself with my hometown of Sherwood, I've been helping Sam with investigations and cases that come up, including an intense one a month ago.

"Which makes me wonder even more what you're doing," Sam says. "Are you going to go back full time? Or keep going like you are?"

CHAPTER THREE

I'm still thinking about the question when we get to my house. There's a lot to unpack in it. Despite how simple the words sound, Sam isn't just asking about my work hours. He's asking about all elements of my future, including his involvement in it. Being on leave means staying in the house where my grandparents lived, and where I stayed during my stints in Sherwood when I was younger. It means living a totally different life. It means being with Sam. Every day. Him swinging by for breakfast some mornings before work. Popping into the station to bring him lunch. Dinners together. Game night with Janet and Paul across the street. Curling up on the couch to watch movies. Things we couldn't do if I came back to Quantico.

Coming back into full duty would mean leaving Sherwood again. I would move back here to the house my father left me when he disappeared and immerse myself once again into the world of the Bureau. I may see Sam on weekends or the occasional longer visit, but it would be a totally different life. One I don't know if either of us could handle. It's the exact reason I walked away from him when I went into training. I didn't want to have to choose every day or wonder where my thoughts would be, so I made that choice once and forced my mind to stay on just my career. That choice meant leaving Sam behind.

And now that choice is back in front of me again.

"Have you thought about doing both?" Sam asks a few minutes later, once I've changed into stretch pants and a cozy sweatshirt and we're perusing menus to order a late lunch.

"What do you mean?" I ask.

"Not coming back here full time," he says. I look up at him, and he shakes his head, his eyes dropping to the menus as he sifts through them like he's trying to look distracted from the topic. "Never mind. I'm sure this isn't what you want to talk about right now."

"It's fine," I shrug. I sit back against the couch and let out a long breath. "I actually have thought about it. It might be possible for me to step back from being fully active duty and take on more of a consultant role. They could call me in for the investigations they really need help on or for undercover work that would benefit from someone who isn't in the field all the time."

"And the rest of the time?" he asks.

I shrug and look over at him.

"That might be up to you."

Our eyes meet.

"I could use more help around the station," he admits. "You've been invaluable in the last couple of cases. If you had the time, I could hire you for a more permanent position than just deputization."

Deputizing me during our first case together granted me the powers of the department and allowed me to work on the case, including gaining access to information not available to the public. But it wasn't an official position.

"It's definitely something to think about."

A few minutes later, after we've settled on what we want to eat for lunch and ordered it, Sam is walking slowly around the house with a look of nostalgia on his face.

"It's strange to be back here," he says. "It's been a long time."

He only came to the house a few times during our college years. The house has changed a lot since then, but I can still see him standing in the living room talking to my father. They got along well in those brief interactions. They picked up from the time we spent together in Sherwood.

We grew up alongside each other in a fractured path. Sam was always the consistent and steady one. The one friendly face I could always count on no matter what. I popped in and out of his life unpredictably. He never knew when I'd be there or when I would leave. I'd be gone for weeks, months at a time. Years, even. But every time I came back to Sherwood, back to him, it was like nothing had ever changed.

"It has," I confirm.

"It's weird. It's like I'm walking through the past and seeing part of your life I never got to at the same time," he comments, tossing a rueful smile over his shoulder at me.

I made a lot of changes to the house after my father went missing. As soon as the deed to the house showed up with his signature shifting ownership and control of the property over to me, I knew everything had changed and would never be the same again. So much of me wanted to just stand still. I didn't want anything else to change. I wanted to keep it exactly as it was, so when he came back, he would fit right back in as if he'd never left. But at the same time, I couldn't let myself do that. Hovering and waiting, refusing to take a step ahead for fear of leaving my father behind, was only leaving myself behind. There was so much more to do, and I had to change my surroundings to fit that new life.

There is one room of the house I barely touch any more. Sam wanders close to it now. The door stands shut, almost never opened. He hovers beside it, looking at the doorknob like he can see my father's hand turning it for the last time.

"It's still his office to me too," I explain, even though he didn't ask the question. "I couldn't bring myself to change it to a guest room. It still feels like his."

"You never have to," he tells me. "It's isn't hurting anyone to have it there."

I've often wondered if that's really true, but I don't say it. We walk around the house, sharing memories, talking about the few bits of art I have on display, and thumbing through the books I still have on my shelves years after the classes they belong to ended. The sound of the delivery driver knocking on the door stops our debate over a section in my worn Introduction to Criminal Justice text, and I hand the book over so I can go claim our Thai food.

Before opening the door, I steal another glance at him. I agree, it's a little strange to have him here after the rift. For some time, I never thought he'd step foot near me again. But it also feels like he's settling into an open space, like he's what's been missing from the house for all these years.

I open the door and take the heavy bag the driver holds out to me. Something over his shoulder catches my eye. I look over toward a car parked across the street. There is a man standing behind it. My heart squeezes in my chest, and my palms sting with tiny pricks. As soon as I look at him, he hurries to climb into the car and disappear behind the tinted windows. I'm still staring even after he speeds down the road.

"Ma'am?"

The delivery driver trying to get my attention makes me jump, and I look back at him. He's holding the credit card receipt out toward me with a pen and looking at me with expectation in his eyes.

"Oh. I'm sorry." I take the receipt and pen, scribble my name, and shove it back at him with several folded bills as his tip. "Thanks."

I dart back inside, closing the door behind me. I flip the lock and take a second with my back pressed against it.

"Are you alright?" Sam asks, coming toward me. "What's wrong?"

"I saw him again," I tell him.

"What do you mean? Saw who?"

"Remember a few weeks ago when I told you I thought I saw my father in my neighborhood? He was at the house next door a couple times?"

"Yes," Sam says, his voice drawn out slightly to express his reluctance to fully accept what I'm saying I saw.

"I think I just saw him again."

Sam takes the bag of food from me and wraps his other arm around my shoulders so he can guide me to the couch. He sits me down, sets the bag on the table, then comes to sit beside me.

"Emma, it wasn't him. You know it wasn't him. Right? Why would your father be lurking around your house, both your houses, and not come in or say anything to you?" he asks.

"I don't know," I admit.

"Remember what we said before. Your brain wants to see him. It's been so long, and you haven't heard anything about where he went or how long he's been gone. You miss him. You've been through a lot and you want to share it with him and get his input. It's normal for you to think you see something when you want it that much."

I nod and try to push the moment aside. Maybe this is just a wall in my path to fully moving on with my life. I've started living outside the bubble of the Bureau. Outside the life I crafted around my CIA father and the world I entered after my mother's murder. Maybe seeing him is my brain just trying to drag me back.

I can't let it.

CHAPTER FOUR

HIM

He drove away fast enough to get away from her curious eyes, but not fast enough to draw any more attention. The last thing he needed was to get pulled over and have to hover nearby her house for any longer than he already was. Especially if that meant the cop who was there at the house with her would come sniffing around. That's the thing about police officers. They're all the same. Every one of them. Anything another officer was doing is their business, too. If they see something happening or a crime being committed, even if it was already being handled, they proudly come puff up their chests and offer their assistance.

That was definitely something he needed to avoid. He couldn't let Emma or the sheriff get any closer to him. He already didn't know why they were there at the house. It was a shock to show up and see the car sitting in the driveway. It was even more of a shock to stand at just the right angle to peek through the front window and see their silhouettes in the living room. When Emma opened the door to the food delivery driver, he wanted to just stand there and look at her. It had been a while since he got a glimpse of her. Pulling back and staying away was one of the hardest things he had to do, but there was no choice. He couldn't keep risking it, being so close to her. He knew she saw him. A couple times now, she'd locked eyes with him and stared at his face in a way that couldn't be accidental.

She never said anything. He didn't know what he would do if she did.

He didn't come to the house that day to see her. If he had known she was going to be there, especially with the sheriff, he wouldn't have come. The whole purpose of coming was to slip inside unnoticed. The police had long since stopped their continuous surveillance of the house. For several weeks they were there twenty-four hours a day, watching every inch of the perimeter, focusing on the doors and the windows, not allowing anyone or anything anywhere close. Except for Bellamy. She was able to slip past and go inside whenever she pleased.

It was torturous having to stay far beyond the surroundings of the house, only able to stare at it, knowing he couldn't get inside again. A single step onto the lawn would have gotten him arrested and everything would be over in an instant.

The house itself would have been so easy, but for this. Locks were nothing to him. Security systems were easy to move past and manipulate. Only the barrier of the police kept him back.

There were times when he watched Bellamy go inside and wondered if she might be his way inside. He could convince her to allow him to slip inside. He could make it so she left a path open for him. It wouldn't be the first time he took the people in Emma's life into his hands and twisted them to his own uses.

But he held himself back. She was too close. For now, he had to keep her in reserve. If the time came, he would use her, but that time wasn't now.

Over time, the police became less insistent about being at Emma's house all the time. Nothing happened. Of course it hadn't. He was all that would happen, and he wouldn't get near the house. They watched, day after day, as nothing affected the house. No one got near it. There were no incidents to seem like she was in any danger or under any threat. Eventually, the frequency of the patrols lessened and lessened until they just went gliding past in their patrol car every few days, just to make sure nothing had happened while they were gone.

It made it safe for him to test them. He got closer and walked across the grass. He touched the doors and tested the windows. When no one came to stop him, he made plans to come back after his next job. It would be the perfect time. He would have more to bring into the house and deftly plant among her possessions. Not where she would easily find them. He didn't want Emma to come into the house and know anything was different. He wanted the papers and tiny, almost inconsequential details to sift down in among everything else in the house, so it was like they were always there.

That was critical. They couldn't stand out. The bits and pieces of another life he wanted to graft onto the life once lived within that house had to be almost unnoticeable. They had to seem like something that was there all along, so when it was found, it fit seamlessly. That would be the only way to convince her and everyone else who were watching that it was real.

He was chipping away at what they thought. Breaking down their view of reality and rebuilding what he wanted them to believe a little bit at a time. It would take patience, but that was a skill he honed long ago. So many years. So much time lost. But he could take it back. He could make up for it. All this would be worth it soon.

He just wished he knew why she was there. He hated when something didn't make sense to him. When he didn't understand what was happening and control slipped away from him.

They couldn't be staying long. Sherwood couldn't be without its sheriff. Not now, when it was still fragile from the horrors it already faced and still holding its breath to see if tragedy really did come in threes.

And maybe it would.

CHAPTER FIVE

TWO WEEKS LATER

"Are you alright? You look exhausted."

Sam runs his hand down the side of my face as he sets the chair down in the middle of the living room. We've been emptying the storage unit containing possessions my grandparents and father left behind in the house before it became a rental in the weeks since we found out about it. There wasn't much inside, to begin with, but I didn't want to just bring it all over in one fell swoop and overwhelm myself. Instead, I've taken it slow. An occasional transaction.

All around the house now are the things put into it before it was first rented out. More generic, store-bought things. The kind of decor the management company thought would make it more appealing as a furnished home in a fairly sleepy town. There are still a few signs of my family. I found them when I first came back here over the summer to help Sam with a case that was confounding and terrifying him. I had thought then that it would only be for a few days, and I walked into the house almost like one of those new renters. I saw the house as temporary, even with eyes that saw memories in every floorboard and tile and wall and door.

Gradually the memories took over. The realization that the house is truly mine—not a rental, not something offered to me to borrow for a time—settled in. It's more my home every day. That means I want to strip away the generic touches and replace them with what belonged there all along.

So I make my transactions. I take away something I'm not familiar with or that I don't feel any connection with and bring it out. It goes to the Goodwill or another donation center or sometimes sits on the grass just beyond the sidewalk in front of the house to draw the attention of a new owner. So far, everything I've put there has been scooped up and brought off to its next life. Once something is out of the house, I feel better about bringing something else in.

Today, it's the chair that was sitting at the back of the storage unit with the stack of boxes in front of it. When I first saw it, I didn't remember it from my grandparents' house. It didn't look familiar the first few times I saw it. It wasn't until I realized it was recovered at some point over the years that I remembered it used to sit in the corner of the back room my grandmother used as a sunroom. She liked to sit in there and read or quilt, and when I got older, we would drink tea and talk. This was the chair I always sat on. Her chair is still sitting in that room, and now this one is going to go back to join it.

Thank goodness I have Sam to carry it for me. I don't feel like testing my limits by lugging it all the way into the back room.

"I haven't slept well the last few days," I tell him.

"You didn't sleep well when we went to Quantico, either," he notes. "What's going on?"

I shrug and rub the back of my neck. My nightmares haven't found me again. They've stayed away and haven't tried to invade this house, which I'm thankful for. But something stops me from keeping my eyes closed for more than half an hour or so at a time, staggered throughout the night. It doesn't stop me from waking up at dawn like I always have, but by the middle of the afternoon like it is now, the tiredness starts to drag on me.

"I don't know. It's just been happening the last couple of weeks," I tell him.

"Maybe you should lay off the coffee a bit," he teases.

"The coffee is the only thing that keeps me off my face in the middle of the afternoon some days," I say. "But I have committed the ultimate sin of switching to decaf after five."

"Blasphemy," he chuckles. He leans forward and gives me a kiss. "You really do look tired, though. I don't want you to get sick."

"I'll be fine. It can't last but so long. I just have a lot on my mind."

"I know. Any news?" he asks.

I let out a sigh. "I'm not officially allowed to know anything, but Bellamy told me Eric mentioned Creagan tried to figure out who took the phone out of the evidence locker," I tell him.

"Playing telephone?"

"Something like that. He figured I was entitled to at least that information, and he can tell her about it because she has been given some clearance. She wasn't in the room when Creagan said I wasn't allowed to know anything, so she isn't held by his requirements," I say.

"That's a little shaky," he says.

"A little, but I'm willing to be a little shaky for this."

"Valid. So, what did they find?" he asks.

"Nothing," I sigh.

"Nothing?"

"Nothing. There is absolutely nothing on the evidence locker. The only people who went in are working on other investigations and have specific things they were looking at. None of them have any reason to take out the phone. They don't even know what it is or what's on it."

"Then how did whoever sent the message to you get access to it?" Sam asks.

I throw up my hands in exasperation. "That's the big question. I can't stop thinking about the whole thing."

"Well, it just so happens I might have something that will help take your mind off it," he says.

I lift my eyebrows at him. "Oh?"

"The annual police department fundraiser."

I blink. That is not what I expected him to say.

"The annual… police department fundraiser?" I ask flatly.

"Yes," he says with a bright smile. "You probably remember some of them from when you were here. Every year the department has some sort of fundraiser to…"

"Raise funds? Yeah, I'm familiar with the concept," I quip.

"Then you're already ahead of the game."

"What game?"

"I think you should head up the fundraiser this year," Sam says, tossing himself down into the chair and grinning at me.

"Excuse me?" I raise an eyebrow.

"Well, not head it up completely. Help me do it," he says.

"You want me to help you plan a fundraiser for the department?" I ask slowly, clarifying what he wants.

"Yeah. It'll be fun. We can come up with a theme together, find vendors. It'll give you something to think about other than people going missing or buildings blowing up. I know that's a strange concept for you, but I suggest you give it a try. You might like it."

"Very funny," I mutter.

He laughs and reaches for me, taking me by the hips and bringing me down to sit on his thigh.

"I don't know, Sam. I'm not a party planner."

"I know you aren't the extravagant, highly experienced event coordinator I am, but I believe in you," he teases. I shoot him a glare, and he laughs. "Come on. It's a fundraiser. I'm not asking you to plan the Inauguration. Just help me plan it and let people know about it. It could be a fun way to spend some extra time together."

He knows how to wear me down. I let out a sigh.

"Alright," I relent. "Just give me my clipboard and my headset."

"No headset," he says.

"No headset?" I ask in mock horror. "Now, what kind of extravagant, highly experienced event coordinator are you if we don't get headsets?"

"Is that a yes?" he asks.

"Yes."

"Perfect. Alright, now that I've made your chair delivery, I have a Girl Scout Troop to go talk to about bike safety."

"You're such a good sheriff," I grin, giving him a quick kiss.

"I know. Sherwood is lucky to have me."

He pats me on the hip to get me to stand up.

"I'll see you for dinner tomorrow?" I ask.

"Absolutely. I'm looking forward to hearing what treasures you find in the other box from storage."

I glance over at the box I brought over today, trading it for a set of lamps I haven't liked looking at since I first came back. There's a hint of anxiety mixed with my anticipation. As I've learned from the first couple boxes I've already opened, I have no idea what I'm going to find in there.

"I'll let you know if it's anything important," I say.

We walk to the door, and I wave goodbye as he climbs into his truck and drives off. He'll head home for a shower and put on his uniform before going to the school for the Girl Scout meeting. He often volunteers his time to help the little girls earn their badges and, while I haven't witnessed it, I'm sure he's a sucker when cookie season rolls around. He has a tender place in his heart for children, but especially little girls, I think he sees his future daughter in.

As he drives away, I glance across the street. The house next door to Janet and Paul's has been vacant since I came back, but now the door of the garage door is standing slightly open. Someone must be moving in. It's nice to see someone coming to the quiet little neighborhood. And with its double-sized lot, large back deck, and flowerbeds ready to be filled in the spring, it will be a wonderful home.

It will be so nice to have new neighbors in town.

CHAPTER SIX

FIVE YEARS LATER

"It's been two weeks. Why haven't you been able to find anything?" Travis demanded.

The officer stared at him, emotionless. He knew her name now. Phillips. Officer Phillips. She never bothered to mention her first name. Not like the men who occasionally called to check in or scoured every inch of the house. They introduced themselves and shook his hand. They talked to him like a husband who was terrified because his wife was missing, not like he just another name on a list of interviews to have.

She should have chosen a different career. Something that wouldn't require her to interact with people and make assumptions about them she would need to act on.

"I'm sorry, Mr. Burke. We're doing everything we can to find your wife," she said.

"I find that extremely hard to believe. You manage to find people who break into cars within twelve hours, but a decent, beautiful woman disappears, and after two weeks, you haven't found out anything?" he asked.

"That's a crime, Mr. Burke. It's a different situation," Officer Phillips said.

"Why? Because that person did something wrong? Is that the only reason you want to find them? The only reason you put any effort into finding them is because you want to be able to hold them accountable for doing something wrong?"

"That's not what I'm saying," she tried to clarify.

"That's exactly what you're saying. All that matters to you is ticking off cases on a list. You like tying up things with a neat bow. Mia has never done anything wrong, so you have no use for her."

"That's not it, Mr. Burke. I know you're upset, and I know this is really bothering you, but it's important for you to stay calm and coop-erate with us."

"Cooperate with you? I've done everything I can possibly do. I've turned over my financial records. I've given you access to Mia's studio even though I know you destroyed the work she's been doing. I've let officers crawl all over my home, invading every corner and inch of my privacy to find anything that might be helpful. And none of it has done any good."

"The reality is, that might be by design," she said.

"What do you mean by that?"

"Your wife is an adult woman. She doesn't have to get permission to do anything or go anywhere. It may be uncomfortable for you to think about, but that's something we're going to have to consider."

"Consider what? That she just… left?" Travis asked.

Officer Phillips nodded.

"Yes," she said matter-of-factly. "You haven't heard from her or seen any sign of her. Clothing and personal items are missing from your home."

"I told you; she went to her studio to work on her new art pieces. That's what she does. When she is planning on being there for more than just a few hours, she brings along clothes and toiletries. I don't understand your fixation on that. If you are planning on going some-where overnight, don't you take things with you so you can take a shower or change clothes the next day?" Travis asked.

"Of course, I do, Mr. Burke, but we're not talking about me," Officer Phillips said.

THE GIRL NEXT DOOR

"Maybe we should be. What if someone you loved went missing? Wouldn't you want the police to do everything they possibly could to find them?"

"Yes, Mr. Burke, but..."

"And if you were missing, if something happened to you and you were possibly in danger, wouldn't you want to think your family would do everything they could to find you? And would insist the police do the same?" Travis continued, his voice getting more intense with every word.

"Mr. Burke, I understand you're upset. This isn't an easy situation, and I can't honestly tell you how I would react if I was in it, because it's never happened to me. But you need to think clearly and really evaluate what's happening, so we have the best chances of finding your wife," Officer Phillips said.

Travis took in a deep breath and let it out slowly to settle himself.

"What do you need me to evaluate?" he asked.

"Like you said, you gave us access to everything, so we've been able to fully investigate your wife's movements in the days leading up to her going missing."

"Yes."

"And we noticed several withdrawals from her bank account over the last three weeks."

His eyes narrowed, and he shook his head at her.

"There haven't been any withdrawals from our bank account over the last three weeks. We make all our payments with our debit cards," he frowned.

"No, Mr. Burke. Not your bank account. Hers."

"I don't understand."

"While investigating your personal financial information, we uncovered an account in your wife's name. You are not on it," she said.

He blinked a few times.

"In my wife's name? Mia had her own bank account?" he asked.

"Yes. She opened it approximately three months ago and has made steady deposits into it since. Over the last three weeks, she withdrew nearly all of it in several transactions. I take it you weren't aware of her bank account?"

His eyes burned into hers.

"Do I sound like I knew about it?" he asked fiercely.

"We also searched your home and the apartment studio. There were no clothes or toiletry items at the apartment, though they are missing from your home by your account. Yet, you found her car at the studio."

"What are you getting at?"

"I think it's time for you to consider the possibility she was preparing to leave for some time, and is not missing, but left on her own accord. With someone."

"Excuse me?" he sputtered. "You're suggesting my wife left me? My wife who made dinner every night and who I'm planning a trip to Miami with for her birthday in three weeks?"

"It might not make sense to you right now. Often the partner being left feels blindsided by the decision and is confused, thinking the relationship was going well, when in reality, the other partner was unhappy but going along to maintain peace as long as necessary to ready themselves for the split. Your wife might have maintained her usual behavior and even seemed happier in the weeks leading up to her disappearance. That's because she was putting the steps into place to extricate herself from the relationship and didn't want to create an unwanted situation."

"Cut your psycho-babble bullshit. You're not here to lull me into a sense of complacency and guide me into an understanding of my new lifestyle," he said in a slow, mocking tone. "You're here to find my wife. Do I make myself fucking clear?"

Officer Phillips stood and straightened her uniform.

"If you can think of anything else, Mr. Burke, you know how to get in touch with us," she said.

"And if you start doing your job and looking for my wife rather than coming up with some half-assed story, you know how to get in touch with me."

Travis followed her to the front door and slammed it firmly behind her, glaring through the glass after her until she drove away.

CHAPTER SEVEN

NOW

I f I scrape and gather up all the stray minutes I slept last night, I might be able to smash them together into a total of four hours. A hot shower perked me up a little, so I took advantage of the slight spike in energy to stuff myself into my favorite leggings and tank top, top it with a sweatshirt, and head out for a jog. I haven't been nearly as active recently as I'm used to being. Heading to the gym a few times a week, martial arts classes, and regular jogs were all normal parts of my week when I lived near headquarters. I just considered it part of my job. I'm not a lot of good as an agent if I'm not in good enough shape to take down suspects.

My theory, and hope, is that my brain is fogged and my sleep is disrupted because I've been neglecting my exercise. If I just get back into my groove a bit, I can clear my mind and start sleeping again. It's worth the first shock of cold when I head out and the fact that I didn't eat beforehand. The neighborhood is in that odd time of day when it's awake, but little is happening. Early mornings mean people getting ready for work and sending children off to school, my older neighbors gardening and pampering their already pristine lawns, and the one young stay-at-home mother near the end of the street whisking her son off for a day at the park, library, or whatever else she fills her days with. The late afternoons and evenings are for people coming home, relaxing outside when the weather is nice, and taking strolls along the sidewalk. The time in the middle often feels like it's just me when I'm home.

Fall is settling into the neighborhood, and I'm starting to see hints of reds and yellows where there you used to be green. I turn a corner and a breeze picks up. It brings the scent of someone burning leaves in the distance. I'm enjoying the crispness of the air, the colors of the leaves, and the smells of fall around me so much I don't notice the woman walking up the walkway to my front porch until I'm about to turn onto it myself. She looks unsure, and I get an immediate hint of concern. It's rarely a good thing when a stranger walks up to your front door.

"Hello," I call out to her, pulling my earbuds from my ears and raveling them up to shove them away in the pocket of my sweatshirt.

The woman turns around and smiles. She looks to be in her midforties, maybe a couple of years either way, with a pleasant face and a severe black bob to her chin. The floral dress she's wearing almost looks like she wasn't aware of the season when she got dressed, and she tugs her sweater closer around herself as she takes a few steps toward me.

"Hi," she smiles. "Do you live here?"

"Yes," I tell her.

She points with both thumbs toward the house to the side of Janet and Paul's across the street.

"I'm your new neighbor," she says.

"Oh. I saw the garage open a little last night and thought somebody might be moving in." I extend my hand to her. "I'm Emma Griffin."

"Ruby Baker. It's nice to meet you."

"You, too." I glance at my house, then back at her. "Um. Is there something you needed?"

She smiles a little wider and glances at her feet like she's embarrassed by the question.

"No. I'm just not a particularly social person, and I know if I didn't get around to meeting my neighbors soon, I'd just hole up in my house like a hermit. And that's exactly why I've been looking for a fresh start. So, I've been walking up and down the street, introducing myself to everybody." She leans slightly toward me and lowers her voice to a conspiratorial hush. "Does that make me sound really creepy?"

I laugh. "No. I think there are plenty of things these people have seen that are creepier than someone coming to introduce themselves."

"That's good to hear," she says, then seems to think about what I said. "I think."

Ruby grins, and I gesture toward the front door.

"Do you want to come in for a cup of coffee?" I ask.

"I'd love to, but I actually have to run. My brother took my truck to go grab some things at the store, then we have to do another run from the storage unit full of," she lets out a big sigh, "pretty much everything from my old apartment. Another time?"

"Sure."

"Great. I'll see you soon."

Ruby waves as she backs down the sidewalk, then turns and jogs across the street, ducking down to slip under the garage door.

I go inside and head directly for the shower. When I get out, my phone is glowing. I pick it up and find three missed calls and a message from Bellamy to call her back.

"Everything okay?" I ask when she picks up.

I tip to the side to let my hair fall free, so I can rub it dry with a towel.

"Where did the magic of our relationship go?" she starts. "When did you stop trying?"

I laugh. "I'm sorry. Hi, Bellamy. How are you doing?"

"I'm good. How are you?" she asks, all the sappy morose notes gone from her voice.

"Just got out of the shower after a jog."

"Sounds fun. So, Eric asked me to look into a few more things for you," she says.

"About Greg?" I ask.

"No, about the things you asked him to look into before he got wrapped up in the bombing investigation," she explains.

"Oh. You know, B, I love you, but anything you can do to look into those things, I could do myself. I asked Eric to do it because he has more skills and better equipment," I tell her.

"That's true. However, I do have something you don't."

"What's that?"

"Outside perspective and distance, which lets me make better decisions," she deadpans.

"I won't argue with that," I relent. "What did you find out?"

"I wanted to find out more about the necklaces," Bellamy says. "They've been bugging me."

"Me, too. Especially after seeing the picture of my mother and me wearing them when I was a little girl," I nod. "But all I have is the necklaces. Nothing else. Not even a hint of when we got them other than when it was when I was really young."

"Ah, see, there's my point. You're only thinking about what the necklaces mean to you. I thought about them just as they are. Which led me to looking them up. I have pictures of them, and I scanned them in, then searched images for them. It took some time and fancy internet footwork, but I managed to track down the craftsman who made them," she says.

"Are they still making jewelry?" I ask.

"Yes."

"Then how can we be sure these are actually the necklaces that belonged to my mother and me and not just ones that look the same?" I ask.

The thought deflates me. It's strange and unsettling to not remember the necklaces and to not have any idea how one of them ended up in a box stuffed in my couch cushions and the other brought by a man who then died on the front porch of the cabin I stayed in while undercover. But strange or not, it's something. It gives me a connection to my mother and a clue about what might have happened in my past. If the necklaces aren't the actual ones we owned, it has much less of an impact.

"I spoke to the artist myself. She said they are a unique design, like everything else she makes, and they are the only two she ever made. In her workshop." Bellamy pauses. "In Florida."

"In Florida?" I ask.

"Yes. Long before you could just hop on someone's Etsy shop and buy something online. She only sells in her physical shop in Florida. Which means…"

"Which means we spent time in Florida while living in Iowa," I connect the dots.

"Exactly."

"And she remembers the necklaces? You're absolutely sure she remembers them and not just something like them?" I ask.

"She has a website now. It's not for sales, it's more of a gallery and lets people request commissions. But she has pictures of things she's made in the past, but that aren't available for recreation or sale. Your necklaces are in those pictures. I asked her about them, and she said she loves those necklaces. She very clearly remembers them, but doesn't remember who bought them," Bellamy says.

"Well, it's not much. But it's definitely something," I say.

"And it's not all," she continues.

"It's not?"

"Nope. I also looked into the house in Iowa. I went over the ownership records and identified exactly when your parents owned it after your grandparents, then when they sold it," she tells me.

"Who bought it?" I ask.

"That's the interesting thing. It wasn't a person. It went to a company," Bellamy says.

"What company?"

"It was called Spice Enya."

"Spice Enya? What the hell is that?"

"I have no idea. I have searched everywhere, and I can't find anything about it. There's nothing. No website, no references in any news. By all rights, it doesn't exist and never has."

Spice Enya. I strain, but the name doesn't ring a bell. Unless an

Irish singer has started a culinary company to boost her brand decades after her '90s relevance, I have no possible idea of what it could mean.

But this company is connected to my parents. Somehow.

CHAPTER EIGHT

I'm officially stumped. With all my investigative skills and experience, this is one I just can't figure out.

Why the hell are there so many different kinds of tickets for carnival games?

When Sam said I'd be helping him with the fundraiser, he more meant he was going to tell me there was a fundraiser, pick the theme, and then occasionally call in to see how I'm doing planning it. Honestly, it's probably better this way. Streamlining the planning means not debating things like the merits of a funnel cake vendor versus a doughnut vendor. Funnel cakes win, clearly. But it also means not having much input when I get stuck on details. Like which of the damn tickets to choose. Large or small? Booklets or in a wheel? Is red too aggressive?

We went with a carnival theme because it seemed approachable and traditional. Everyone loves a carnival. Only now, I'm getting a glimpse of what goes into putting together a carnival and think I'm probably going to need to call in reinforcements. I've just made the executive decision to switch from choosing tickets to working on my vendors list when someone knocks on my front door.

I toss the rest of a carrot stick in my mouth as I head to the door.

It's not Sam. He has a key, and I almost always know when he's headed over, anyway. It might be Janet. The last time Eva got sick at school, Janet came here to ask if I could keep an eye on her while she finished up a last bit of work before bringing her to the doctor. But when I peek through the peephole, I see it isn't her, either. It's the woman I met yesterday.

"Hi, Ruby," I say as I open the door.

She's gripping a glass measuring cup and looks at me sheepishly.

"Hi, Emma. This is so incredibly cliché of me, and I can't believe I'm doing it, but... can I borrow a cup of sugar, neighbor? I thought I lugged some with me from my old place, but I guess I didn't," she says.

I laugh and step back to gesture for her to come inside.

"Absolutely," I tell her. "Come on in."

"Thanks," she says.

Her eyes fall on the scattering of flyers, catalogues, and sample tickets on the coffee table. I flutter my hand in its direction.

"I'm planning a carnival," I tell her.

"Oh, that sounds like fun," she says enthusiastically.

"Maybe," I reply with a laugh. "I think I might be just a bit too wrapped up in the details to really have found the fun in it yet."

Ruby looks confused.

"Doesn't that make it difficult for you as an event planner?" she asks.

I laugh and shake my head. "I am definitely not an event planner. This is a brand-new experience for me. I'm actually an FBI agent." I glance at the table and shrug as I look back at her. "Who knows, though? Maybe I'll catch the bug and it will inspire a new business."

"You're an FBI agent?" she raises her eyebrows, sounding surprised.

"I am."

"That's amazing!"

I don't want to get into the usual conversation that follows that kind of response, so I point toward the kitchen.

"Let me get that sugar for you. Can I make you a cup of coffee?" I ask.

"That sounds really good," she says. "Thanks."

We walk into the kitchen, and she sits at the table, still gripping the glass measuring cup between her hands even when she sets it on the table. I'm drawn to the whispers in her eyes. Everyone with a story has them. They cloud the color and darken the edges. Hers are there, and I find myself wanting to hear them.

"Where are you from originally?" I ask.

"A little town called Crozet," she tells me.

I nod. "Oh, I know Crozet. Nice place. What brings you to Sherwood?"

I reach into the pantry and pull out the bag of sugar. One of these days, I'll be like my grandmother and pour the sugar from the bag into a canister when I get home from the grocery store. Maybe I'll even keep it out on the counter next to the flour and coffee. But that's a step into settling into a place I haven't fully taken yet.

"Looking for a fresh start," she says.

She said the same thing yesterday but didn't elaborate. I set the bag on the table beside her so she can pour the sugar into the measuring cup herself.

"Chasing a new career?" I ask.

It's extremely unlikely. Sherwood has a lot to offer, but a booming job market isn't exactly one of them. People living around here can stay comfortable, but it's not a place people come to chase a dream. The question fulfills its purpose.

"I wish," Ruby says with a short, mirthless laugh. She stares at the cup in her hands for a few seconds before she straightens and reaches for the bag of sugar. "I'm actually running away from a bad relationship. I guess I shouldn't put it like that. It makes me sound like a sullen teenager."

"No, it doesn't," I assure her. "Problems with your ex-husband?"

"My ex-husband is a pocket protector-wearing CPA with the intimidation factor of a bowl of vanilla pudding. And not even the French kind. Just plain, jiggly yellow. No, this is Frank. He never got so far as the husband status. But he definitely causes problems," she says. She smooths off the sugar, then looks at me with an embarrassed expression. "I'm sorry. I shouldn't be telling you all this. We just met."

"No," I smile, shaking my head. "It's fine. Go ahead."

The machine finishes spitting out the first cup of coffee, and I slide the mug across the table to Ruby. Reaching into the refrigerator, I bring out the container of cream, then get a spoon out of the drawer for each of us. She scoops a spoonful from her measuring cup into her coffee and stirs absently.

"Frank is the classic example of why women my age don't want to date. He seemed perfect when I first met him," she starts.

"That should have tipped you off," I comment, swirling a thick ribbon of cream into my coffee.

She chuckles. "Probably should have. He was so sweet and caring. I was still getting over my divorce, which I guess I didn't even realize. It's not like my ex-husband, and I had some dramatic, passionate affair, and it consumed us or anything. We had a very quiet, very monochrome marriage. Eventually, I just wanted a bit more color. The split was quick and clean. We literally signed the papers during his lunch hour, and he helped me move into my new apartment that evening, then we had pizza together. It wasn't until a few weeks later that I really started to notice him not being around. Isn't that strange? We rarely did anything together, and I thought we were totally disconnected. But then I was reading one night and found a line I thought was funny. I turned to the other side of the bed to tell him about it. And he wasn't there. That's when it hit me. Does that sound ridiculous?"

"No," I tell her, shaking my head. "Sometimes you're so used to something that even when it's gone, you don't really notice it as long as you're doing different things. Then it's a totally mundane moment and it all hits you. That happened with my father. I thought I had processed he was gone, but then it was pizza night. He wasn't there to order it, and I completely fell apart. I sat in the living room by myself and cried for hours."

"I'm sorry to hear about your father," Ruby says.

I start to correct her, to tell her my father isn't dead, but I stop myself. I just met her. I'm not going to get into that much detail about my past right now.

"Thank you," I smile.

She takes another sip of her coffee and lets out another long sigh.

"So, after the incident with the book, I got into a really dark place. I didn't think I was going to struggle with not being married to James. I thought I was going to be so much happier. But I was sad and lonely, and felt like a failure. Like somehow, he couldn't be an exciting husband because I wasn't a good enough wife. Maybe there was something I needed to do more of, or better, to make him a better husband. Then I met Frank. He made me feel wanted and beautiful. He hung on my every word and always wanted to be with me. It was intoxicating. Then it changed."

"What happened?" I ask.

"It wasn't anything major at first. He would get upset if I wasn't available to have plans with him. He was jealous when other men talked to me. He started commenting on what I was wearing and suggesting I choose something more modest or flattering. Then it just progressively got worse. He became controlling, then intimidating. The first time he hit me, I wasn't even surprised. I hate to admit that. I should have been shocked and horrified, but I wasn't. It's like he'd needled me and needled me until I was just willing to accept anything from him. It took me months to get strong enough to get out."

"I'm glad you did," I tell her, reaching out to squeeze her hand. It's strange—I barely know this woman—but I feel a kinship with her. I am always glad to be there for any woman who has gone through what she has.

She manages a smile.

"Thanks. How about you? Anyone special in your life?"

Just as she asks, my phone rings. I excuse myself and go back into the living room to find it and smile when I see Sam's name on the screen.

"Calling to tell me you have the fundraiser all planned, and I don't have to pick a ticket style?" I ask.

He laughs. "Not exactly. I just wanted to make sure we're still on for dinner tonight."

"Absolutely."

"Good. I'll call ahead of time and reserve our usual table," he jokes.

"It's so impressive you can always get us the best spots."

"Anything for you. I've gotta go. Apparently, someone went for a joy ride in a stolen car last night and hit a few things along the way." I can practically hear the roll of his eyes through the phone.

"That's going to be fun," I say, walking back into the kitchen. "I'll see you tonight." I hang up and notice Ruby watching me. I wave the phone back and forth. "Speak of the devil. That was Sam, the man I'm seeing."

"Oh," she says, giving me a smile that says she is ready for some good old-fashioned girl talk. "What's he like?"

"Pretty amazing. I've known him most of my life. He's actually the local sheriff."

"Wow," she says, looking slightly deflated. "Sounds wonderful. You must feel so safe."

I sit down across from her and take a long sip of my coffee, pondering her words.

She's right. I should.

CHAPTER NINE

HIM

The empty room sent a cold chill down the back of his neck. It shouldn't have been empty. Just hours before, Finn was there. He'd put him there himself. Ensured he was in place and unable to leave. Finn had been too loud recently. Saying too much, pushing back too much. Simply too much. He was going to change that. He would make sure he had the loyalty and devotion the tattoo on Finn's back required.

But now he was gone. Somehow Finn slipped away and now was loose, unrestrained, and among outsiders. There was no telling what he was going to do. He had to stop him. To find him and ensure he remembered his place.

Storming out of the room, he went to where the others gathered, the ones still there. Some were out on missions, serving him the way they should be. But most were there. Most stared at him reverently when he stepped into the room and leaned closer to him as he walked past, hoping to catch his attention. They hoped to be chosen by him. They wanted him to show them favor. But that wasn't why he was there. Not that night. None in the room had gained his trust. Not yet. But they could. The chance was there if they wanted it.

"Where is he?" he barked. "Where is Finn?"

Every eye in the room locked onto another. They searched each other. They dug past the surface, burrowed into each other, tried to find the information. Even if the one who held it wasn't going to speak, someone might see it. They might catch sight of the secret flitting across their vision and reach out to grab it so they could present it to him like an offering. People carried whispers in their eyes. He'd heard that. A long time ago.

Someone in this room carried that secret. Someone knew how Finn had got out of that room. He couldn't have done it alone. Someone knew how he got out and where he was now. All he needed to do was draw it out.

He could smell their desperation to please him. It filled his lungs. There was a time when that devotion was heady, almost dizzying. He loved the way it felt to have them right on the tips of his fingers, easy to manipulate. The best part was that none of them were weak. He had his fill of weak, moldable people. People who didn't have spines of their own, so they needed his words and validation to hold them up.

Not these men. These were among the strongest, most intense men he ever encountered. They were willing to offer themselves to his service not because they had nothing else to fulfill them, but because they believed in what he said. They wanted to uphold the same truths he did. They were fearsome and calculating, each intelligent and skilled in ways he could use for his own devices. It made his ability to control them more satisfying. When they looked to him for instruction, it wasn't because they didn't know how to do it, but because they were striving to do it the way he wanted them to. When they sought his approval, it wasn't because they didn't believe in what they were doing, but because they craved knowing they shared his thoughts. That in that moment, they were aligned.

He enjoyed being able to gather the thoughts of those who could think for themselves and mold them into his likeness. It means more to harness wild mustangs than to lead a flock of sheep.

The men searched each other's eyes, scoured memories to find each other. They were piecing together a puzzle in hopes of finding what he wanted. He waited. He watched them interrogate each other silently. But none of them said anything. Some gave up and looked back at him imploringly. They were waiting, too. Waiting for him to tell them what to do next. Waiting for a hint or a clue they could use. Waiting for anything that would take away the helpless feelings that came from not being able to follow, even when they wanted to.

"None of you?" he asked. "Not one of you will tell me where he is?" He took a step closer to them. "He should not have been able to get out. But he did. I don't know where he is or what he might be doing. That should be a concern for all of you."

"What do we do?" a man kneeling in front of him, with barely the outline of a sea creature on his back, asked.

He lifted his chin, his shoulders square to them.

"Find him."

CHAPTER TEN

The door opens while I'm upside down over the back of the couch. With my ass in the air and my head almost crushed by the wall, I'm not exactly in a position to defend myself if there's an intruder. Fortunately, I know it's Sam.

"What are you doing?" he asks.

"Rethinking my spatial awareness," I tell him.

"What?"

I wriggle backwards.

"I didn't move the couch enough, and now I think I'm stuck. I can't move my head enough to get back upright."

Sam laughs and crosses the room. I feel him come up behind me, and suddenly, the couch moves. He takes my hips and helps me back down. I land on the cushions with a gust of air from my lungs.

"Why were you upside down? And where have you been? I've been calling you," he says.

"That's why I was upside down," I explain. "I can't find my phone. I have no idea what could have happened to it. I just had it."

"When was the last time you used at?" he asks.

"Yesterday, when I talked to you. I could have sworn I put it down in here on the charger. But it's definitely not there. and I can't find it anywhere. I even used a landline to call myself, trying to figure out where it was."

"I still can't believe you still have a landline," he teases. "What's the point of it?"

I toss a glare at him. "For when I can't find my cell phone."

Sam laughs. "It worked out really well for you, didn't it?"

"You are not being helpful."

I head back into the kitchen for the third time. I already searched the counters and under the table and even in the trash can. Now I'm resorting to digging through various bags of snacks to make sure I didn't somehow drop it in during a late-night binge I don't remember. Which brings up its own whole set of questions.

"I'm sure you'll find it. Come on. We need to get going," he says.

Closing the pantry door, I head for my bedroom to get a sweatshirt. I take one last look through my room for my phone, then join Sam in the living room. He's eating an apple as he peeks under the throw pillows on the couch.

"Now I get to ask you what you're doing," I say.

"Being helpful," he offers.

"Don't you think I looked under the pillows?"

He shrugs and takes a bite of his apple.

"You also looked in a bag of tortilla chips, so I figured it wouldn't hurt to do a quick once-over."

I laugh and tug the sweatshirt down over my head.

"Let's go. We have a fun festive carnival to plan."

Two hours later, I still feel completely disconnected from the world without my phone, but we're making progress on the carnival. It's been decades since Sherwood had its own county fair, but the small fairgrounds still stand near the outskirts of town. The current owners weren't easy to get ahold of, but once I did, they agreed to let us use the grounds for the fundraiser. There's just one catch. We have to whip them into shape by the time we want to use them.

The threatening cold announces winter is definitely on its way. That makes it harder to imagine. It won't be until the spring, but getting the plans in place now means not having to contend with the chaos of the holiday season while searching for vendors. When the time comes along to put the finishing touches on the event, we'll already be way ahead.

But that means actually doing all the work by then. That's where Sam's big overachieving plan shows its cracks. It's not easy getting people excited for an event so far into the future, and the sheer volume of work necessary to get the fairgrounds ready is daunting enough without the cold. I can't even imagine what it's going to be like when the actual winter weather hits. But Sam believes in his vision, so I'm doing my best to be supportive.

A few people are already at the fairgrounds by the time we get there. One car in particular catches my eye.

"Lionheart Property Management?" I ask, glancing over at Sam. It's the same company that has been managing my grandparent's house all these years.

"Apparently, there are a couple of structures on the grounds the company manages. The owners haven't let go of their big dreams of selling the land to a theme park developer," he tells me.

I'm waiting for there to be some sort of joke attached to that, but there isn't.

"Seriously?" I ask.

He nods as he turns off the ignition and releases his seatbelt.

"They think Sherwood could become a tourist destination if there was a theme park here. Roller coasters. Maybe a water ride or two. I listened to their entire spiel when I finally talked to them about using the grounds for the fundraiser."

"So, they weren't able to keep up with having a fair once a year, but they're sure a theme park would just do massive business?" I ask.

"There was a documentary," he nods, as if that completely explains it.

"If Lionheart manages the property, why is it in such bad shape?" I ask.

"Not much of a budget, I'm assuming. They keep the buildings up to code and are ready at the waiting if a potential buyer shows up, but that's about all they can do."

"That's why they let us use it. Free labor and marketing."

Sam winks at me. "The American Dream."

He gets out of the car, and I shake my head at him.

"I don't think that's actually how that works," I comment, getting out and following him toward the small cluster of people waiting for us. Most are off-duty officers and their families or members of the local volunteer club. But one face stands out. "Oh, fantastic."

"Good morning, Sam," Pamela Welsh nearly purrs. Her eyes slice over to me so hard I'm surprised the pupils didn't detach and stay in place. "Emma. I'm surprised to see you here."

"Why is that?" I ask. "I'm organizing the fundraiser with Sam."

"Oh," she says, cocking her hip to the other side. "I just mean, after everything, you know, I'm surprised you're out and about. Do you really think you're up to this?"

"What the hell is that supposed to mean?" I ask. Sam takes me by the arm and pulls me away. "No, seriously. What the hell does she mean by that?"

"Let's just get to work. There's a lot to get done and these people have come out to help us," Sam says.

Doing my best to ignore Pamela, I stand close beside Sam while he does his pep talk for the group. We go over the list of tasks to be done that day and assign everyone to different areas of the grounds. With nearly everyone else ready to collect trash and start fighting back the areas of overgrowth, I make my way to the first of the scattering of buildings. Today I get to be the sweeper. I'll check through the buildings making sure there aren't any squatters or wild animals. With any luck, it will be a fast and easy jaunt. The footsteps and somewhat shrieking voice behind me dash that hope pretty quickly.

"I have to be with you!"

I don't stop but glance over my shoulder to watch Pamela try to scurry across the overgrown grass in heels that were a ridiculous choice for the occasion. I truly do not understand that woman. She's always been like this, even back in high school, when she got it up in her head that she and I were rivals for Sam's affections.

"Why?" I ask.

She makes her way to me and glares from under her heavy eyelashes.

"Why do you think I'm here?" she asks.

"Because Sam is?" I respond.

Her arms cross over her chest so hard they threaten to pop her cleavage right out of the top of her shirt.

"I'm here because Lionheart Property Management is responsible for these grounds. We're under instructions from the owner to give you people permission to access and improve it for your fundraiser, but it's in our best interests to make sure nothing happens to the property," she tells me.

"Are you suggesting I might do something to the building?" I ask.

"We would just hate to see someone get trapped or a fire start or anything," she says, her lips curling into a cruel smile.

I refuse to feed into her. She's taunting me, trying to push me off the edge she thinks I'm standing on. Instead, I just keep walking, forcing to the back crevices of my mind the horrific memories she just brought back to the surface.

The first building used to be a funhouse and looks essentially like a tall, narrow tower with cutouts covered with boards. The door at the entrance looks much newer than the rest of the building, like it was added to the front when the attraction closed. Pamela follows me to the door and hovers close behind me like at any second I'm going to yank the doorknob off the door and start smashing things.

"Is it locked?" I ask.

"It shouldn't be," she says. "These buildings don't have traditional locks. If you don't see a padlock, it's open," Pamela tells me.

"Doing a bang-up job with the security."

It's nowhere near as fun going through a funhouse with only the light from a pocket flashlight, and on constant lookout for what is about to go terribly wrong. Fortunately, we make it out the other side without incident. Next is a building that used to be a small restaurant. Other than a pile of discarded containers, there's little inside, and I quickly move on.

The third building looks like a small, fairly deep house. I wonder if it's been standing there since before the land was the fairgrounds. It looks like it could have been a farmhouse at some point. The little porch across the front would be perfect for sitting in a rocker and looking out over crops waving in the evening air. At this point, those crops are crabgrass and dandelions, so it's not quite as picturesque. But for what they are, they are flourishing.

I'm surprised when I open the door to see the building in fairly decent shape. Considering how long it's been since it was used, I was expecting much more disarray. There's dust and some debris piled in corners, but I'm taking the lack of bodies and drug paraphernalia as a bonus.

Sweeping through the first floor is quick, but that all goes to hell when I get to the second floor. This is where the house is hiding all its secrets.

Every room on this floor is stacked nearly to the ceiling with boxes, broken wood, tarps, and unidentifiable items. I prod through what I can. So far, I don't see anything overtly dangerous, but it's going to take some serious work to make this place usable for much of anything.

There's one more room at the end of the hall. By the placement in the house, I would guess it's a master bedroom. Unlike the other rooms, the door is fully closed. Ingrained instincts and training immediately make me suspicious of the room. The hair on the back of my neck pricks up, and I prepare myself for what might be just beyond the door.

I reach for the door handle and push the door open away from me, keeping myself as far in the hallway as I can. Before I can take a step toward the room, something tumbles down from above the doorframe.

The light from my small flashlight hits it, and my stomach turns. It's a noose.

CHAPTER ELEVEN

I gasp, stumbling back from the rope dangling from the doorframe. I push past it into the room beyond, but it's nearly empty. It's as if someone took most of what was in the room and stuffed it into the others.

"What's that?" Pamela asks behind me.

I don't bother to answer but force my way past her and down the hallway back to the stairs. I take them two at a time and rush out of the building that suddenly feels hot and close. Sam is only a few yards away, cutting down the overgrown grass. He looks up and furrows his brow as I hop down from the porch.

"Emma?" he calls. "Are you okay?"

He doesn't wait for my response before dropping the tool in his hand and jogging toward me. My mouth feels dry, and my mind races with stark images from only weeks ago. I only saw the pictures, but I remember every detail. And those details brought me back to the backseat of a speeding car and a cold, stone cell.

"There's a noose," I tell him.

"What?" he asks.

"A noose. There's a noose hanging inside the house. Someone went in there and put up a noose."

"You mean this?" Pamela asks, coming out of the house with the rope draped between her hands.

"Pamela, you shouldn't have touched that," Sam tells her. "The whole point of sending Emma into the buildings was to make sure there wasn't anything potentially dangerous happening inside. Abandoned buildings can attract serious criminals."

"The building isn't abandoned. Lionheart has been managing it."

"Without a lock on the front door," I point out.

"It wasn't locked?" Sam asks.

"It's just an unused building," Pamela protests.

"Do you know how many times I've gone into supposedly unused buildings and found what was left of people who were tossed into rooms or stuffed under the floorboards?" I ask.

She rolls her eyes, but Sam reaches for the rope and examines it.

"It's not new," he mutters. "There are wear patterns on it like it was used, and there's something dark embedded in the frayed fibers. It could be blood."

Pamela scoffs. "You're starting to sound like Emma, Sam."

"You can't just ignore things like this, Pamela. It could mean something," he says.

"Yeah, like it held up a mannequin covered in fake blood."

"Excuse me?" I ask.

Another roll of her eyes makes me wish she would go just a bit too hard and topple herself over on her self-righteous ass. But I'm not that lucky. She stays upright and cocks her hip, flipping her hair back over her shoulder like she's forgotten she's a grown woman supposedly working.

"Didn't you bother to look at pictures of this place when it was still fairgrounds?" she asks.

"We did," Sam says.

She licks her lips, a smug look coming over her face like she is just enjoying this too much.

"So, you realize that isn't actually a real house. It's a set. That was a haunted house attraction when this was a fair," Pamela explains. "The noose was a prop. Some kids probably snuck in there to prove how big and bad they were to each other. They found some props and thought it would seem edgy if they put one of them up again. It's really not that serious."

She tosses a glare at me, then glances back at Sam. "Maybe you're spending too much time with her, Sam. You're not thinking straight."

"What's that supposed to mean?" I ask again. My irritation is through the roof with this woman.

Sam takes hold of my wrist and guides me back, so I'm slightly behind him.

"Everybody get back to work," he says to the group that has filtered in from the various points throughout the grounds to watch the growing confrontation. He looks directly at Pamela. "I'm going to look into this, Pamela. I suggest you let Derrick know."

She bristles, but nods. I think even she understands how little her manager would appreciate knowing something like this happened in a building they were supposed to be managing.

"I think I can search through the rest of the buildings by myself," I tell her. "Feel free to wait out here, and I'll let you know if something happens."

I don't give her the chance to answer. I know full well I'm under no obligation to have her with me anywhere on the grounds. The owners gave us complete permission to use the property. Tolerating her was a courtesy, but I've reached my absolute limit with the way she looks at me and talks about me.

It's obvious she thinks something's wrong with me. I'm not far enough removed from our confrontation in the Lionheart Property Management office a few weeks ago to forget her talking about the rumors. Evidently, my triumphant return to my hometown wasn't so triumphant after all. Even helping with the devastating case that lured me back here apparently wasn't enough to keep the abundantly healthy grapevine from passing along stories of my delicate mental health.

The ladies who lunch, or more appropriately, the ladies who knock back wine, were whispering that the only thing that brought me back here was my time in the FBI chipping away at my sanity, and I bet anything Pamela is the ringleader of it all.

I don't care so much about rumors floating around about me. When you are perpetually the new girl in town and have a tendency to leave without a word, people talking about you is just something that happens. For the most part, the things made up about me are nowhere near as exciting or as complex as my actual life. It's them tracing my break with reality and questioning my integrity that grates on me. Pamela's persistent perception of me as a romantic rival despite barely being a blip on the radar of my past doesn't help.

None of the other buildings scattered around the old fairgrounds present any trouble, and I clear through them quickly. Sam looks at me with raised eyebrows that communicate his interest as I walk toward him from the last.

"Anything?" he asks.

"Some old school fair props that collectors would probably have a fit over, but that's it. We'll want to choose which of the buildings we want to use for the fundraiser so we can concentrate our efforts on those, and find effective ways to secure the other ones," I tell him.

"Sounds good," he nods. He pulls me toward him to kiss my forehead.

It's a sudden show of affection, but I know him well enough to know it's more than just wanting to get in a quick peck. The dirt and grit of the buildings can't make me that appealing. Sam is thinking of the same images, working through the same memories as I am. The lingering pain in his legs and still-fading scars on his shoulder and hip won't let him forget.

We stay at the fairgrounds for another couple of hours before a heavy rain cloud collapses down on the area, bringing with it a damp chill that soaks us to our bones. I rub my hands together in front of the heater in Sam's car as he waits for the rest of the crew to drive away before us.

"I think that was a pretty successful day," he comments. "With the obvious exceptions."

I nod. "If it wasn't Pamela, I would have thought to ask if Lionheart worked with my new neighbor."

Sam looks over at me as he starts driving away from the grounds.

"What new neighbor?" he asks.

"You know the house across the street? The one beside Paul and Janet?"

"With the extra lot beside it?"

"Yep," I tell him.

"Someone moved in there?" he asks. "I didn't hear about that."

"Well, you're getting the news now. Hot off the presses, too. She just moved in a couple of days ago. Her name is Ruby," I say.

"What's she like?"

I shrug as I sit back from the heater, my hands sufficiently thawed.

"Seems nice. I haven't spent a lot of time with her. She was just getting settled in, but she was going along the street meeting everybody, then she came by yesterday to borrow some sugar."

"Seriously?" he asks with a laugh.

"Yes. And that's not a euphemism. She actually walked out of my house with a measuring cup full of sugar," I tell him.

"At least that explains why you were searching your baking ingredients for your phone this morning," he points out.

"Yeah. That's still bugging me. I don't understand what could have happened to it," I tell him. "I talked to you, then later I realized the battery was low, so I plugged it into the charger. But this morning, I couldn't find it."

"I'm sure you just moved it at some point without thinking about it. You'll find it somewhere you didn't even think about," he reassures me.

"I hope so. What if Eric or Bellamy call me?"

He laughs. "They'll call me."

I nod. "It's not the same."

CHAPTER TWELVE

FIVE YEARS AGO

Travis Burke paced around the outside of the cabin, staring deep into the trees for any sign of eyes staring back at him. Somehow, he knew he'd be able to feel them. They were so familiar to him now. They'd been on him for so long, watching him. He would know if they were there, hiding among the stark trees, not wanting to be seen, but wanting to see everything. He didn't feel them on him. His skin didn't prick, and the hair on the back of his neck didn't stand up. Those eyes weren't there, so he kept walking.

He made his way around the cabin, then found the entrance to a path leading into the woods. It was overgrown, vines and tangled weeds from either side creeping across the foot-beaten trail like it was trying to cover it up, trying to atone for the sin of it being there. Travis crushed them down with his thick-soled boots. They clung to him, trying to keep him there. It was as if they knew what was going through his mind. They didn't want him to go down the path to venture deeper into the trees. But he kicked them aside. The eyes were there, staring back at him. He had to go further.

His feet knew the path so well he could have walked along it in the pitch blackness and they still would have found the same steps. Much of the path was made by those steps over the years. Sections of the dirt cutting through the trees were deeper than others, sinking further into the ground because of his weight pressing into them again and again over the years. He followed those same spots carefully, paying attention to the rest of the dirt at his feet. He'd recognize changes on the ground, notice other footprints or places where the invading plants were trampled or cut to make space.

When he didn't see anything and could no longer perceive the shape of the cabin in the distance, he stopped. He took the phone from his pocket and dialed, hanging up after two rings. Checking the time, he stuffed it back in his pocket and continued further into the woods. Several minutes later, he heard an alert on the phone and took it out again to open the text. It didn't matter what it said. It wasn't to him.

Several minutes later, he repeated the call, but this time set the phone on a nearby stump and left the path. His boots flattened the undergrowth, but he was careful not to break any of the low-hanging branches. He ventured down an incline, following memory. It brought him to a mound of rocks that concealed a small cave carved out of the side of the hill. No one would know about it unless they spent a considerable amount of time exploring the land. Few ever had the opportunity to do that, leaving the cave unknown even to those who might wander onto the land without realizing it.

Travis ducked behind the rocks and into the cave. He took off his backpack, removed the contents, and hid them in the furthest back corner before climbing out again and returning to the phone. It went back into his pocket, and he left the woods, returning to his car and driving home.

———

The next day, a truck pulled slowly up to a lot at the edge of another piece of land. A section of grass had been cleared, and a rectangular hole cut into the hardened ground. Several feet away from the edge, two large storage containers waited along with tools. Travis got out of the truck and lowered the tailgate so he could reach inside and drag out large, heavy bags of cement mix. Opening one of the storage containers, he got out a bucket and containers of water. It took several minutes to mix the cement and pour it into the hole. He smoothed the surface and went to the other storage container. He didn't need to open it.

It took more effort to pull the container than it did to get out the cement, but he got it to the edge of the hole and pushed it over, using all the strength he had to counteract the rapid fall so it eased down into the wet cement. When it was down, he walked around to the other side of the hole and lay down on his stomach, so he could reach into it and grab onto the handle on the other end of the container. He inched backward, dragging the container further into the center of the hole. It brought some of the cement with it, and when it was in place, he used the same tool to maneuver the cement again. Satisfied, he went back to the truck to drag out more bags of cement. He went through the process of mixing the cement again, then tipped it into the hole. Two more rounds covered the container.

She was fully encased now, thick layers surrounding her on all sides. No one would see her again. No one would know where to look. They thought they had it figured out. Every time they looked at him, their eyes dug into him. Those looks were meant to chip away at him, sand away the layers and find what they thought they were searching for. They didn't know he anticipated those looks, that he covered himself in thick, false layers that shielded him and deflected those stares. They would think she had run. To them, he was never even close.

Part of him wanted to sit in his truck and watch the cement dry. He wondered how much pressure it would put on the storage container. If the plastic would crack as the stone dried. He wanted to watch as his plan unfolded in front of him. Even the smallest details were a thrill. The way the cement surface changed color as it dried. The way the blades of grass tamped down by the storage container gradually rose back up to conceal that anything was ever there. But he knew he couldn't linger. Staying too long in one place might throw everything off track. He needed to go back to the woods, back to the cabin, but still needed to make it home in time for the officer to show up at his door and find him drinking bourbon and poring over newspapers.

Travis had his reasons for going with this plan. There were other ways he could have handled the situation, sure. There were other things he could have done or other decisions he could have made. There were other decisions she could have made. But this was the path he chose. It might not seem to make much sense at that moment, but it would. When it all unfolded, it would.

CHAPTER THIRTEEN

NOW

I should really get into a better habit of glancing out the window at my front porch before opening the door. Or at least take Sam up on installing one of those video doorbell things he wants me to have. But I'm so confused at the moment that when I hear the perky knock on the door, I just walk up to it and open it without a second thought.

"Emma?"

My eyes snap up and see Ruby standing on the other side of the storm door. She looks for all the world like a clipping right out of a 1950's ladies' magazine in her floral dress and pale pink cardigan. She's even holding a covered cake plate.

"Hi," she says cheerfully, but her smile fades quickly. "Are you alright?"

"Oh," I say, coming back into reality and shaking my head as I push the door open. "Yes. Come in. Sorry."

She comes into the house and looks at the phone in my hand.

"Get an upsetting phone call?" she asks.

"No. I actually just found this. It's been missing since yesterday morning," I tell her.

"Well, that's good. Where'd you find it?"

"In the laundry room. It was wedged in the space between the washer and dryer."

She smiles again. "I've heard of the dryer eating socks, but not phones."

"It must have fallen out of my pocket when I was switching the loads," I muse.

Only, I still don't remember taking it off the charger.

"At least it didn't fall into the washer while the water was on. I've done that before, and it was terrible. All the rice in the world can't save a phone from the wash cycle."

I laugh. "That's a bad day for technology. What's really strange is the charge."

"The charge?" she asks.

"I realized I couldn't find it early yesterday morning. I just found it. But it still has almost a full charge. Wouldn't you think it would have run down the battery? Even if it was just sitting there?" Ruby stares back at me with a strained smile like she has reached her quotient for my cell phone conversation. I shove it in my pocket. "I'm sorry. You didn't come over to hear the saga of my phone. How are you doing? I love your outfit."

"Thank you," she says, looking down at her dress and pulling her skirt out to the side to display the pattern. "My ex never liked when I wore dresses. He said it brought too much attention to me."

"So now you wear them whenever you have the chance?" I ask with a smile.

"Exactly. Oh." She holds out the cake plate. "This is actually why I came over."

I take the plate and lift the lid. The smell of rich dark chocolate tempts me to not even bother with a fork and just lick the frosting. I restrain myself. I still have company.

"I told you I was just borrowing the sugar. See? Brought it back," Ruby says.

I laugh and start toward the kitchen. "It looks incredible. Want to have a slice with me?"

"Actually, I have to head out. I know that seems to be my M.O. Duck and run. But I'm still working on settling in, and there always seems to be something else I forgot or didn't think about needing. My brother is on his way to get me for another trip to the hardware store. Apparently, I have a lot more books than a normal house is meant to hold. He's going to build some shelves into my living room walls," she tells me.

"That will be nice. Thank you for the cake. Come by when you have some more time," I say.

"I will."

Ruby waves and walks out of the house. As soon as she's gone, I head into the kitchen and cut myself a chunk of the decadent cake. Bringing it with me into the living room, I curl up on the couch and scroll through my prodigal phone. There are a few missed calls from Sam and a text from Janet asking about our upcoming game night. The charge on the battery is baffling. Despite being asked several times throughout my career, the FBI does not provide me with a phone equipped with futuristic technology not available to the regular public. The battery drains just like any other phone. Yet here I am, staring at ninety-eight percent charge after it's been off the charger for at least a day and a half.

I down the cake while I'm still going through my phone, and I force myself into workout clothes to stop myself from slicing off another piece. Spandex is only forgiving up to a point. I would hate to have to explain to my jogging pants that the reason we can't spend more time together is chocolate cake.

I channel my training and run for the next hour and a half. The endorphins kick in quickly, and when I get back, I'm feeling energized. Sam responded to my kidnapping a few weeks back by filling a spare bedroom with exercise equipment and weights. I'm sure part of the motivation was to keep me from actually going out jogging by myself, but I'm not going to hide. I will, however, take advantage of the equipment and build my strength.

After another hour of working out, I'm sufficiently sweaty and reward myself with a long shower hot enough to sting on my skin. My phone is ringing when I finally force myself out, and I wrap myself in a towel before running through the house to get to it.

"Hello?"

The word bursts out of me, but there's no response.

"Hello?"

Still silence.

I glance at the screen and see a number I don't recognize. I'm heading back into the bathroom when it rings again. This time I catch it on the third ring, but again there's only silence.

———

The strange calls are still sticking with me hours later, when my sleeplessness has me up making a cup of peppermint tea. I hope it will combine with my exertion from earlier and help me get at least a few more hours of sleep tonight. Enjoying the feeling of the warm mug wrapped in my hands, I roam into the living room. It's the usual path I wander at night when I can't sleep, which is why the strange difference in the light catches my attention.

The large front window in my living room looks out over the peaceful street, giving me a clear view of Janet and Paul's house to the left and Ruby's house to the right, with the large empty lot attached to Ruby's yard creating a buffer in the center. Every other night there is only darkness beyond the curtains on the window. Tiny porch lights and the glow from distant streetlights make up all the illumination that filters into the room. But tonight, there's more light than usual. It draws me up to the window, and I push aside the curtains to look out.

Bright yellow light comes from the front window on Ruby's house. It looks like she might struggle with insomnia, too. With what she's told me about her ex, that would make sense. She might wear pretty floral dresses and joke about her addiction to books during the day, but when the night comes, her ex closes in again. Just as I take a sip of tea, the front door to the house across the street opens. Light splashes out onto the lawn, and the silhouette of a person appears against the glow. I can't see them clearly, but the size doesn't seem right for Ruby.

Too tall. The light goes out, and they step out of the house. When they turn, I realize they're carrying something large in their arms.

I shift my position to see them walk to the driveway and adjust the object in their arms so they can open the door. The object goes into the backseat and the figure climbs behind the wheel. The engine roaring awake sounds too loud in the silence of the night, and the car disappears down the street.

By the next morning, I've remembered Ruby talking about her brother. He was going to build shelves for her, which means he was probably at her house and would have supplies and equipment with him. I feel silly for letting myself be suspicious about something so mundane. Not wanting to always be the neighbor opening the door, I decide to go check on her progress settling in. I slide the rest of the chocolate cake onto a platter, wash the cake plate, and head across the street to return it. I knock on the door and step back to wait. After several seconds with no response, I knock again. My third and final try is ringing the doorbell, but after another few minutes, she still hasn't come to the door.

The front of her house has a similar window to mine, and I notice there aren't any curtains yet. Curiosity draws me over to it, and I peek inside. This would be a terrible moment for her to come down the stairs or up from the basement and notice me. Fortunately, she doesn't. The house looks pretty much like I would expect. Boxes and other stuff take up much of the front room and spills into the room beyond. The sweater Ruby wore yesterday hangs on the post at the end of the banister.

I bring the plate back across the street to my house and set it on the kitchen counter. Maybe I'll bake her some cinnamon rolls to return on the plate. I'll double the recipe and have the extras for game night. Multitasking at its best.

CHAPTER FOURTEEN

My phone rings the next day, just as I'm coming back from spending the morning at the fairgrounds. Sam only had a few hours this morning to work on the grounds before going back to his usual work, but we made good progress. I answer as I kick off my shoes and head into my bedroom for a change of clothes.

"Hey, Eric."

It's been several days since I've heard from one of my two best friends, and I assume he's just calling to check on me. He and Bellamy haven't coped well with me relocating to Sherwood. When I first came back, we all thought it would only be for a few weeks at the most. Now it's been months, and I'm still here with no set plans on returning.

It's not that I don't miss them or my house. It's not that I don't miss my life in Quantico. It's just that being in Sherwood has simply been what's right for me while I'm on leave. I'm still deciding what I'll do next, but until that decision comes, here I am. Which means I anticipate my regular calls from the two of them, updating me on what they consider the real world. If I can convince them to come for an actual visit rather than them constantly trying to lure me back, maybe I can change their perception.

"I have an update," he starts.

"An update?" I ask, surprised by the matter-of-fact declaration.

"About Greg," he says.

"I know you're not supposed to be talking to me about this," I tell him. "I don't want you to get in any trouble."

Even as I say it, I hope he'll ignore me. I can't stand being forced to stay on the outside of this investigation. I should be right in the middle of it. I already am right in the middle of it. Greg Bailey was my boyfriend right up until just shortly before his disappearance. I spent more time with him and knew him better than anyone else in the bureau. Creagan calls it a conflict of interest, but I think of myself as a resource.

"I know that," Eric says. "We'll just have to be clandestine."

"And you're all right with that?" I asked.

"Some things are worth shaky ethics."

"Alright," I shrug. "What did you find out?"

"It turns out the video didn't require Mary's phone at all. It wasn't sent to you directly from her device. At least, it didn't have to be. The video automatically uploaded to her cloud. So, it could be accessed from any device using the internet. It had to be accessed by password but could more easily be opened using a saved access on a device she used frequently. Which brings up the significant and prevalent problem with people not properly securing their devices and utilizing passwords that are easily cracked. I can't even believe there are still people in this day and age who use the same password for every single account and device they have access to. All it takes is one person to figure out the right combination of words and numbers, and they can get to absolutely anything in that person's life. And the people who use their names or their pet's names or their favorite activity? It's so beyond sanity, and I can't even wrap my head around it," Eric rants.

I close my eyes and nod my way through his jabbering. It's not the first time I've heard it. There's a woman who favors the same pizza shop I used to frequent nearer my other house who is likely still recovering from the dressing-down Eric gave her when he inadvertently found out she used her birthday as her debit card pin. Some people have religion. Some people have politics. Eric lives and dies on cybersecurity.

"Eric, there's really not much we can do about the password situation right now. Can we detour away from proper virtual self-protection methods and find our way to your point?" I ask.

He lets out a huff of frustration.

"Yes. Sorry. My point is, Mary Preston's phone being in the evidence locker and no one getting near it since the bombing doesn't really matter. Whoever sent you that file didn't do it from her phone, but from the cloud," he says.

"How could that have happened?"

"Well, that's where we hit a bit of a speed bump. I'm not sure how it was done. Her family would have no reason to go into her computer, find that video, and send it to you. They don't know you or your connection to Greg. Besides, she didn't live with them, and the chances of them knowing her passwords are slim."

"Even though poor password creation and security is rampant?" I ask.

"Even though. But here's the thing. We haven't been able to find her laptop. It would make sense she would have it with her. She takes her videos with her phone but would use her laptop to edit and post them. Her previous videos said she was taking the trip so she could make videos about it, so it would make sense she would have her computer with her," he explains.

"But no one knows where it is?" I ask.

"No. We assumed it was destroyed in the blast," he tells me.

"Was the area around her searched thoroughly for it? If it was there during the explosion and was destroyed, there would still be pieces of it around her," I point out.

"Unless it was completely destroyed and mixed in with the rest of the debris," he counters.

"It was a computer, Eric. Not a sack full of packing peanuts. A human body is a lot more susceptible to being blasted and burned to unrecognizable bits by an explosion than a computer is. Especially if it was kept in a case. Not that I would expect it to be sitting there intact, but there should be some sign of it near her."

"The official findings of the search didn't identify any elements of a laptop," Eric insists. "So, it was either completely destroyed there at the bus station when the bomb went off, or it wasn't with her and no one knows where it could be. Her family has already gone to her apartment and completely cleared it out. There was no sign of a computer. They even went back through everything they took out of there. It was still in boxes in their spare bedroom. They didn't find a computer, a tablet, anything like that."

"Do you know if they found a laptop charger?" I ask.

"A charger?"

"Yeah. You said they didn't find a computer or tablet when her family went through the apartment, but do you know off the top of your head if they found a charger?"

"I don't know. We asked them to do an inventory. I'll check it. Why do you want to know?" he asks.

"Because a charger means a device. Most people would use a laptop for more significant activities like editing and loading videos, but have you seen some of the phones these days? I'm fairly certain a few of them are just tiny transformers and could turn into full-on servants if they got enough gumption. Mary very well could have one of the more advanced phones and be capable of doing everything she needs to do for her videos right from it. I watched a few of her other videos, and none of them were terribly advanced. But if her parents found a computer charger in her apartment, that means she definitely did have a laptop," I explain.

"And if she had her computer with her when she was at the bus station, most likely the charger would be with her, too. So, if they have a charger, the computer was still at her apartment when she went, and someone must have taken it before her family got there to remove her belongings," Eric realizes.

"Exactly."

"I'll look into it, and I'll let you know. How has everything been there?" he asks.

He doesn't want to say it outright, but I know he's making sure the frightening events that started happening earlier in the fall haven't continued. The feeling of someone being in my house still slithers along my spine and occasionally makes me stop and listen to insignificant sounds a little longer.

"Everything has been fine," I tell him. "There's a new neighbor moving in across the street. We've voted Trivial Pursuit for game night this week. They still won't go for Twister. I'm still working on that fundraiser. There. You are now updated on the news."

"Riveting. I don't know how you stand the excitement of living there."

My mind wanders back to the noose hanging in the building at the fairgrounds.

"I get by."

CHAPTER FIFTEEN

Even standing on her front porch with the open cake stand
flagrantly displaying a fresh batch of cinnamon rolls with
enough cream cheese frosting to pool on the ceramic doesn't
bring Ruby to her door later that afternoon. The other half of the
dough went into the freezer so I can let them rise slowly tomorrow
and bake them up for game night. But these really should be eaten
today while they're still fresh. I try not to let myself worry throughout
the rest of the afternoon and evening. This woman is almost a
stranger to me. If I scrape together all the minutes we've spent talking
since the first time I laid eyes on her, it would add up to less than an
hour. That's not exactly a deep emotional investment.

Yet I can't stop my mind from going back to her. And what she
told me about her ex. It's a story I've heard too many times before.
Even saying that feels like a cliché. It's a horrifying reality that virtu-
ally everyone has someone in their life who is or has been affected by
abuse. But many would never know it.

Most people suffering at the hands of an abusive partner or family
member don't want to advertise it to the world. Whether out of fear of
making the situation worse, or guilt because of their misguided view
that the abuser's reprehensible, cowardly behavior is somehow their

fault, or sheer, basic humiliation, they keep the reality of what they're going through close to them. Some overcompensate by acting happier and more energetic than before, while becoming fiercely protective of their relationship. It can make it extremely difficult to sift out the truth.

Ruby is a woman who has reached her breaking point and decided this time she wasn't just going to stay and be broken even more. She swept up the pieces of herself, pieced them back together in the most convincing semblance of the person she once was, and left. She feels confident and comfortable enough to start talking about the past that made her run, but she's still ready to run again if she needs to. I'm under no delusion she told me everything. That was only a small glimpse into what she went through with that man. But it was enough to keep me glancing out the window and waiting for her to show up again.

———

Late that night, I'm jolted awake by an echoing thud. I'm not exactly sure what it was, but it sounded like it came from across the street. Maybe Ruby is moving those boxes in her house.

I try to fall asleep again, but the sound repeats. Louder this time. I sigh and embark on what has become my nightly nocturnal stroll through the house, trying to convince myself to sleep.

My feet bring me back into the living room. Relief washes over me when I see the same light across the street I did last night. The front window of Ruby's house glows brightly, and I immediately feel better, and perhaps a little silly, for being so wrapped up in my new neighbor.

Both feelings are short-lived, though. I've only been standing at the window for a few seconds when two shadows appear somewhere deep in the house. The figures come closer to the window, and it takes me a few seconds to realize they are indistinct because semi-sheer curtains have been put up over the glass. I can only make out the shapes of the people, but it's enough to see they're locked in a fierce confrontation. The larger of the two figures grabs onto the smaller one, who I can only assume is Ruby. The man shakes her and slings her to the floor before coming down on top of her.

I instantly burst into action. Running to the back of the house, I grab my phone from my nightstand and yank the drawer open. The emptiness inside it gives me a sinking feeling. When I left FBI headquarters to officially take leave for my mental health, Creagan ordered me to leave my Bureau-issued firearm. It's a standard safety precaution I've seen several times before during my time as an agent. Anyone going into a non-active status for an extended time, particularly those with reasons related to mental health, have their guns secured for them until their return. Most of the time, I don't think about it. But there are moments, like this one, when I feel naked without it.

Running to my closet, I take the next weapon that comes to mind, a small stun gun I bought recently, and dart out of the house. The figures are gone from the window, but the light still intrudes on the dark of the night. I scan my surroundings, bracing myself, and get closer to the house.

In the glow of the light, I see the door is standing open a few inches. There's a streak of something across it. Another step shows it is glistening wet and red. Blood. I rush up to the window and peer inside.

There on the floor, among the move-in chaos, is Ruby's body. Most of her is concealed by the scattered boxes, but I clearly see her legs, bare except for steaks of blood and a dark blue robe tangled around them. The tips of her fingers are visible just beyond one of the boxes.

I want to go inside. My instincts push me to kick the door open and rush in to check on her. My memories and training remind me I am alone. The rest of the street is sleeping, and no one knows I'm out here. It was only a matter of moments from when I watched the assault from the window and ran outside from my bedroom. That means whoever hurt Ruby is very likely still close by. I'm by myself in the darkness, at a disadvantage because I don't know where he is, with only a stun gun to defend myself with.

I hear something behind the house, something rustling that sets my feet moving. Taking my phone from my pocket, I dial Sam and run back to my house. He answers in a groggy voice as I slam the door closed and lock it behind me.

"Emma?"

"Sam, I need you to get up," I hiss.

"Emma? What the hell are you doing? Do you have any idea what time it is?" he asks.

"Yes, I do. I need you to get up and get to my house. Bring your squad car."

"What's going on?" he asks, sounding slightly more awake as the panic in my voice cuts through the sleep and burrows into his brain.

"I think I just witnessed a murder in the house across the street. My new neighbor," I tell him.

"Where are you, Emma?" he asks.

The sleep is gone from his voice, and the scuffling sounds tell me he's already getting dressed.

"I went back to my house," I tell him.

"Thank goodness. You stay put there," he tells me.

"What's that supposed to mean?" I ask.

"You know very well what that means. Stay put. Don't go outside. Don't open the door. Stay away from the window. Wait for me. I'll be right there."

He disconnects before I say anything. The temptation to go to the window is strong, so I go into my bedroom to resist it. I want to watch what might be happening out there, but Sam's right. I need to stay securely inside and away from where I might be seen. Whoever did that to Ruby is not someone I want to know I was watching him.

My front door opens a few minutes later, and I rush out to Sam, meeting him in the hallway.

"You startled me," I say. "I didn't realize you got here."

"I didn't do lights and sirens. If this guy is still around here, I don't want to spook him and make him run," he explains. "Now, tell me exactly what you saw."

I relay the entire event to him, and he listens silently. When I'm finished, he nods his head slowly.

"How were you able to see what was happening inside the house?" he asks.

"I told you, from my living room, there's a clear view of Ruby's house. The light on in her living room lights up the window like a TV screen. She must have just put curtains up because they weren't there yesterday, but I couldn't see everything going on because they were blocking them," I tell him.

"The living room light isn't on," he says flatly.

"What?" I frown. "Yes, it is. It was on when I looked out the window and when I got across the street."

"I just looked at the house before I came in here. It's dark," Sam points out.

Giving him an incredulous look, I push past him back into the living room. I don't even have to get all the way to the window to see there is no glow. The house across the street is completely dark.

"It was on," I insist, pointing toward the window. "That light was on. He must have still been in the house when I was over there."

Sam takes his gun off his hip, and I take a step toward the door, but he holds up his hand to stop me.

"You stay right here. Lock the door behind me but be ready to open it. I'll be right back."

I reluctantly lock the door as he walks out of the house. I want to be out there beside him. It feels like another way I'm just being sat on the sidelines when I could be helpful, but I have to keep down my arrogance. Sam is the one in a uniform and badge right now.

I pace up and down my hallway for what feels like the rest of the night but was likely only a handful of minutes. The door opens, and I run out to the living room. Sam shakes his head.

"Is she dead?" I ask.

"There's no one there, Emma," he says.

"What?" I practically shout, incredulously. "Did you go inside?"

"I couldn't. The door was locked."

"It was open when I left. There was blood on it."

85

"There was no blood. The door was perfectly clean, shut, and locked. I knocked, but no one answered. I shined my flashlight in the window and didn't see anything."

"Nothing?" He shakes his head, and my ears start ringing. "I don't understand. I was there. Not ten minutes before you got here. The light was on, the door was open, there was a smear of blood across it, and Ruby was dead on the floor."

"Emma, calm down," Sam says, resting his hands on my shoulders. "I know you haven't been sleeping well. You probably had a nightmare or were sleepwalking. It's perfectly normal."

"This wasn't a dream, Sam," I insist. "I know what I saw."

"Sleepwalking can seem very real. I've seen it before. Come on. Let me tuck you into bed so you can get some rest. I'll sleep on the couch tonight to help you feel safe. How does that sound?" he asks.

I want to protest, to tell him to stop infantilizing me, but the sincerity in his eyes stops me. He's not trying to talk down to me. He genuinely wants to take care of me. And to be honest, the thought of him taking up residence in the front room, if just for tonight, sounds fantastic.

He brings me into my room and waits while I slip between the covers. He kisses me goodnight, then turns out the light. I listen to him walking around the front of the house and hear the thud of his boots hit the floor, then his slight groan as he settles onto the couch. Knowing he's there helps me relax, but I can't sleep.

I know what I saw.

CHAPTER SIXTEEN

Exhaustion must have taken over at some point, because my eyes snap open, my heart already beating hard in my chest. What happened last night presses down on me. I can still feel the panic, the horrible feeling of watching the attack, and the dread of getting to Ruby's house too late. The sound I heard behind the house is still with me. It was just a rustling, not identifiable as any specific thing. But with Ruby lying dead in the living room and the short time between me seeing the blood on the door and it being gone, the only thing it could have been was the person responsible, running off to escape.

My blood runs cold at the thought of being so close to the killer, and him slipping away. Everything in me says I should have chased the sound. I should have gone after the person as soon as I heard them moving around behind the house. But I've forced myself to become more cautious. I can't fling myself blindly into situations the way I used to. During my time as an active agent, being fearless in the face of uncertainty and danger was an asset. It meant I went into situations others wouldn't. I hunted suspects down and overcame obstacles to carry out my missions. But it wasn't without its risks. It got me in trouble with Creagan. It put my life in danger. It was that same determination to do what needed to be done and unwillingness to wait around for others or follow a rigid protocol that slowed me down, that put me in several tight, dangerous positions over the last year.

I honestly can't say I'm totally reformed. My experiences haven't suddenly transformed me into the type of person who is going to watch every step and always make the decisions others want me to. But it stopped me last night. It kept me from running into the backyard to find out who was there and forced me back across the street to my house to wait for Sam rather than taking it on myself.

I know it was the right thing to do. The logical part of my brain reminds me this person just murdered a woman and being on leave means being willing to rely on the police in situations like this. But there's still a voice in the back of my mind. It reminds me of the open door and the blood glistening in the light. If I had gone after him, he wouldn't have had the chance to eliminate the evidence of him being there. I could have stopped them from getting away.

The thought of Ruby still lying in her living room makes my stomach turn. She doesn't deserve that. A woman who has been through everything she told me, has already been made to feel like she doesn't matter. She has been ground down and peeled away bit by bit. But she dragged herself out of it. She overcame what so many don't and tried to escape with her life. Now she was being made into even less. She was tossed aside like trash and left to be ignored and neglected again.

I won't let that happen. Getting dressed as fast as I can, I rush across the street to Ruby's house. Just like Sam described when he came back to my house last night, the door is closed, and the smear of blood across the front was washed away. I hurry up onto the porch and tug on the door, but it doesn't move.

I head over to the window. The first thing I notice is there are no curtains. I was sure there were sheer curtains hanging over the glass last night. It obscured the people and made it so I couldn't see the details of their faces. But now the glass is completely open. Cupping my hands around my eyes, I press them to the glass and look inside.

The house is empty.

It isn't just that Ruby's body is no longer lying where I saw it. Everything in the house—all the boxes that were scattered on the floor, the belongings placed on tables and shelves, the sweater hanging from the banister—is gone.

My heart clenches in my chest, and my head feels hot. I don't understand what I'm seeing. Yesterday the house was full. It was the mess of a woman just moving in and finding places for everything she brought from her old life and what she bought for her new one. The house was becoming hers, filling with life and energy. Now it was cold and still.

Back home, I call Sam.

"Hey," he answers happily. "I was just about to call you. Did you want to grab something to eat before game night with Janet and Paul tonight?"

"She's gone," I say.

"Janet? What happened?" Sam asks, sounding startled by the announcement.

"No, Ruby," I tell him. "Her body is gone."

"Emma, we talked about this last night." The surprise is gone from his voice and has been replaced by caution. "I know you think you saw something, but you were having a dream."

"No, Sam. I wasn't dreaming. I saw it happen. I saw her body. But it's all gone. The house is completely empty," I tell him.

"I'm sorry. I want to talk to you about this, but I have to go. We're rounding up warrants today and this one could get a little tense. I'll see you when I got off work. Okay?"

"See you tonight," I say with a sigh.

I try not to let it upset me that Sam didn't call to involve me in the warrant cases today. That's something we have been doing together. Now deputized into the department, I've had a chance to be a part of Sam's work. I've enjoyed the chance to help him. But the more invested I get, the more he seems to pull back. He doesn't want me to push too hard, and he worries about what I've been through. He doesn't talk about it, but I know the thought of me going back to my other house and returning to active duty in the Bureau is never far from his thoughts.

Another long jog brings me back by Ruby's house. I stare at it, wanting to see something that will tell me what happened. I look at the attached garage. The door is pulled down tight, suddenly reminding me of her brother's car sitting in the driveway. The first time I noticed activity at the house, the door was slightly open, but there was no sign of a car inside the garage. I've never seen any vehicle other than her brother's, or what I assume was her brother's, the night before last. I don't know what it means, but it bothers me.

A fruitless call to Bellamy and lingering over boxes from the storage unit now sitting in my attic take up the middle of the day. Finally, it's an hour before Sam should be showing up, and I get the cinnamon rolls out to warm to room temperature so I can bake them. The house fills with the intoxicating scent of cinnamon and hot yeast dough as the rolls rise and brown in the oven. A thick ribbon of decadent cream cheese frosting is cascading over the rolls, filling the crevices and pooling between them when the front door opens.

"You made cinnamon rolls," Sam almost groans with pleasure as he comes into the kitchen.

He comes up beside me and dips his finger into the frosting, sucking it away before he dips his head to kiss me.

"I see that the frosting got precedence over me," I comment.

He grins and goes in for another dip, bringing this one to my mouth so I can sample the creamy sweetness.

"What do you say we turn off all the lights, close the curtains, and watch movies tonight. Just the two of us," Sam offers.

"You and the cinnamon rolls?" I raise an eyebrow.

He shrugs. "You can come, too, if you want."

I start transferring the rolls onto a dish to bring with us.

"Janet and Paul live across the street, Sam. I think they'll notice your squad car sitting in front of my house."

He gives a dramatic sigh.

"Trivial Pursuit it is, then. I'm going to go change really fast. Be ready in a minute," he says.

Sam takes his black duffel bag into my bedroom and emerges a few moments later wearing civilian clothes instead of his uniform. He picks up the rolls, and we head over to Janet and Paul's house. Like we do most weeks, we settle in to dig into the evening's snacks before actually getting into the game. We listen to a few stories about their week at work and the accomplishments of Eva, the ten-year-old granddaughter they are raising. It's good to hear she's thriving after the trauma she went through over the summer. The case she was involved in was what brought me back to Sherwood. There was a time when we were terrified we wouldn't find her alive. Now she's growing fast and enjoying a new, stronger bond with the father who missed much of her early life but has returned, dedicated to being there for her.

They finish, and as I reach for a wedge of pita to dip in Janet's amazing spinach artichoke spread, I glance over at them.

"Did you notice anything strange at Ruby's house last night?" I ask.

"Emma," Sam hisses under his breath.

I look at him with widened eyes, trying to quiet him. I don't plan on giving them the full detail of what happened, but I need to know if they noticed anything.

"Ruby?" Paul asks.

"Who's that?" Janet asks.

My eyes snap over to her.

"You didn't meet her?" I ask.

"No," Janet says, peeling off some cinnamon roll. "Should we have?"

"She moved in next door a few days ago," I explain.

"Really? I didn't realize anyone was moving in," Paul says.

"You didn't see her? Or the lights on in her house?" I ask.

He shakes his head. "The only room in the house with windows toward that house are in our bedroom. They have blackout curtains on them, so we don't see any light coming in from anything," he says.

"But you haven't seen her there or her brother bringing things to the house?" I ask.

Both shake their heads.

I'm still reeling from the revelation when Sam walks me home a few hours later. He's crowing in victory after collecting all his little pie wedges first, but I'm too confused to celebrate with him.

"I don't understand," I say when we get into the house.

"That I'm magnificent at trivia?" he asks, puffing his chest out playfully.

"That they didn't meet Ruby. That they didn't even know someone was moving in," I clarify.

He sags. "Emma, please. Don't start on that again right now."

"She was there, Sam. She was in my house. I had conversations with her."

"Just like you said, Janet and Paul never met her and didn't even know someone was moving in," he points out.

"Are you suggesting I created all my interactions with her in my head?" I ask defensively.

"I'm just wondering how you explain them not knowing anything about her."

"I don't know. They both work a lot during the day. When they aren't working, they are taking care of Eva and helping Jimmy get back on his feet so he can be a good father. Maybe they've been so busy they just didn't notice. They missed her," I offer.

Sam looks at me suspiciously, but I'm not backing down. She was there. I spoke to her. We shared stories. She baked me a cake.

Then I saw her body. I can't just put her behind me and pretend I never knew she was there.

CHAPTER SEVENTEEN

HIM

They took so much from him. His past, his name, his future. It was all gone, shed from him so easily they acted as though it never even happened. It was easy for them, and that's what made it taste so bitter sliding down the back of his throat. They didn't understand. They never would. All that mattered to them was what they saw. Their lives were sketched out for them. Paint-by-number representations of what was, rather than what was possible.

Only he knew there was more. Only he could see what could be.

They had taken so much from him, and every minute they just kept taking more. There wasn't as much to take now. He had already lost so much. Nearly all the most precious things in his life were gone. But he would keep going. What he did have was enough to keep him going.

One thing they couldn't take from him was his memories. They could force him away, blot him out, make him as though he had never been. But what resided inside him was his, and there was nothing they could to do take it. No matter how they tried, they couldn't split him apart and gut him. They couldn't scrape away his inner being. He may no longer exist to them, but fragments of all they once were, were still embedded in him.

They tried to steal his memories from him. They tried to take away what lay ahead of him and determine what his life would be. But he wouldn't let that happen. Little by little, he was crafting that life for himself. The memories were coming with him. They were the beginning, the structure. He built around them.

He spread the newspaper clippings and torn magazine pages out on the table in front of him. Some were aging, the years curling their edges and starting to discolor the paper. Others were new and barely read. One pulled his attention, and he picked it up out of the center. The newspaper image was of two people, stiff and emotionless as they leaned back against a desk.

He knew the room. An office in the FBI headquarters. The article detailed the exceptional work of two agents bringing a particularly intense case to a close. He ran his fingers along the image of Emma. She looked stark and intense, but even with her hair pulled back into a tight bun and wearing a severe suit, she was beautiful.

He looked at the second picture, and his jaw and the back of his throat tingled. The laughter bubbled up inside him, and he couldn't hold it back. It was the last picture take of Emma and Greg together. Looking at them standing beside each other, no one would know they were supposed to be a couple. They looked like they barely wanted to be in the same room together; much less were in a relationship. It wouldn't be long after that picture that their relationship fractured, and they were little more to each other than a memory.

CHAPTER EIGHTEEN

"N o one? You haven't seen anyone near that house at all?"

Jim Corcoran, one of the neighbors from near the end of the street, shakes his head in response to my question.

"No. Not in a long time," he says. "You say there's a young woman moving in there?"

"There was," I answer, trying to ignore the somewhat lecherous note in his voice. "Thanks."

I leave his porch and make my way down the sidewalk and to the next house. A woman I can only remember talking to two or three times since I moved back opens the door slightly. She peers at me hesitantly, her eyes flicking around my feet and behind me like she's trying to suss out why I'm there.

"Hello?" she says.

"Hi. It's Emma. From down the street," I say.

"I know who you are."

"Great. It's Ellen, right?" I ask.

"Yes."

Her eyes keep moving, and she grips the side of her door tighter by the moment. I want to reassure her I'm not there to sell anything and I'm not wielding a petition for her to sign, but I just continue to smile instead. I hope it's the kind of pleasant, unassuming smile that makes people want to be cooperative and puts them at ease. I'm not sure. I don't know if I have one of those smiles in my collection.

"I just have a quick question for you." I twist slightly and point toward the house beside Janet and Paul. "Have you met Ruby? The woman moving into that house?"

Ellen leans slightly out of the door and peers in the direction I'm pointing.

"Ruby? I don't know anybody by that name," she frowns.

"You never even met her?" I ask.

Ellen shakes her head. "No. I never even heard someone was moving in there. Usually, we know when someone new is moving into the neighborhood."

I let out a sigh. "That's so strange."

"Something wrong with her?" she asks in response to my mutter.

I avoid coming right out with the news that she's dead. It would be better for them to know who I'm talking about before they start figuring out how to feel about her death.

"It's just that she said she walked around the neighborhood, introducing herself to the neighbors. That's how I met her. When I came home from a jog, she was standing at my sidewalk. She told me she met the people on this street," I explain.

Ellen shakes her head again. "Maybe someone else, but not me."

"Thank you," I say, feeling weighed down with disappointment.

"I'm sorry I couldn't be more help," she offers.

"It's alright," I sigh. "You have a good day."

The next two houses I visit are largely the same. No one seems to have met Ruby. They are surprised to hear me mention someone moving into the house, much less her telling me she was walking up and down the street, introducing herself to the neighbors. I'm discouraged and even more confused when I finally get the first small bit of information that has anything to do with her.

"I didn't see a woman," Brandon Larsen tells me when I get to the house three doors down from mine on the opposite side. "But I did see a car at that house."

I perk up slightly. "You did? What kind of car?"

"Well, it actually wasn't so much a car. It was a truck. From Davis Landscaping Solutions," he nods.

"Davis Landscaping Solutions? That sounds familiar," I raise an eyebrow.

"It should. They're those boys who come take care of some of the lawns around here. They're up here usually a couple times a week during the summer, a little less around this time of year," he says.

"But why would they be at that house if no one was living there?" I muse, trying to guide him into the realization Ruby had moved in. "She must have hired them to come do some work when she first got here."

"Not necessarily," he counters. "They're up at that house every few weeks to keep up with the lawn so it doesn't get out of control. The company that takes care of the house sends them. I only mention it because they came twice in the same week, and like I said, that's unusual this time of year."

Now that he mentions it, I seem to remember seeing landscapers mowing the grass during the summer. I didn't think anything of it at the time, but now something else he said pops back into my head.

"The company that takes care of the house... is it Lionheart Property Management?" I ask.

"I believe so," he says.

I nod. "Thank you. I appreciate your help."

I hurry down off the porch and rush back to my house. Without even going inside, I hop into my car and head into town. Pamela isn't happy to see me when I burst through the door, but I don't have the time or patience to concern myself with her today.

"I've already told Derrick all about the terrifying rope, Emma," she rolls her eyes. "You don't need to fill him in."

I won't even dignify that with a response. I walk right past her desk and to Derrick's office. He's on the phone, but gestures for me to come in. He finishes the conversation and gives me a pleasant smile.

"Hi, Emma. Always nice to see you. Something going on with the house you need our help with?" he asks.

"I'm not here about my house," I tell him.

"Oh?"

"The woman who moved into the house across the street from mine is... missing. I was wondering if you had any contact information for her so I could make sure she's alright," I say.

Derrick folds his hands on the top of the desk and tilts his head to one side.

"The woman who moved into the house across the street from you?" he asks, sounding confused. "What woman?"

"Ruby." I dig back through my mind to the first time I saw her. "Baker. She moved in just a few days ago."

He turns around in his wheeled chair and pulls his feet like a Flintstones car to get to the file cabinet against the wall.

"You say it's the house across the street from yours?"

"Yes. Next to Janet and Paul Francis. The house with the extra lot as part of their yard and the attached garage. 2021."

He opens one of the drawers in the file cabinet and flips through the folders inside. It's strange to see a company that hasn't gone completely digital, but Derrick follows in the footsteps of his father and his father before him. Finally, he pulls out a folder and wheels his chair back to the desk.

"2021 Candlewood," he muses, opening the folder and scanning the papers inside for a few seconds. His expression changes. "Hmmm. Give me just a second."

He picks up the phone on his desk and hits a button. I hear it ring in the front of the building.

"Can you come in here for a second?"

The voice on the other end of the phone is muffled, so I don't hear it coming through the partially closed door. But the sharp click of the footsteps approaching the office tells me everything I need to know. Those are the clicks of gaudy leopard print heels too high for the office. And I know exactly who's attached to them.

"What do you need?" Pamela asks as she comes into the office.

"Tell me about 2021 Candlewood," Derrick says.

Her expression contorts with confusion.

"What do you mean?" she asks.

"Emma is concerned about a woman who moved into that house."

"What are you talking about?" she asks.

"My new neighbor. She moved in a couple days ago," I explain.

"No, she didn't," Pamela frowns.

"I met her. She's come to my house twice," I say. "I saw her at the house."

"No one was at that house," Pamela insists. "It isn't for rent, it's for sale. There's been no interest."

"Thank you, Pamela," Derrick says.

She leaves, tossing me a glare as she goes. As soon as she leaves, I push the door closed and turn back to Derrick.

"Obviously, there's been some interest. She was there. Her stuff was all over the house," I say.

"Emma, I checked the file on that house. It has been available for quite some time and we haven't shown it to anyone. Pamela is the agent representing that particular property, so I wanted to ask her about it just in case she didn't put the proper notations into the records. That's one drawback to keeping paper records. Sometimes people don't want to keep up with them."

"Derrick, I met this woman. I saw her stuff in the house," I insist.

"The only thing I can think is it was a scam," Derrick says.

"What kind of scam would that even be?"

"I'm sure you've heard of real estate scams during your time in the Bureau."

"Not exactly my department," I tell him.

"Well, there's a fairly common scam involving properties available for sale. Someone presents themselves as the owner or landlord and fraudulently rents the property to a person willing to pay them in cash. Once they have the money, they disappear. The person eventually figures it out and has to leave," he explains.

"So, you're telling me you think I met a woman who was scammed into thinking she rented the house? And she disappeared in the middle of the night because she figured it out?" I ask.

I fight against the compulsion to mention the murder. I still need them to admit she was there in the first place.

"It's an explanation for how something like that could happen," he says. "But the people who do that usually access the property by stealing keys from a lockbox on the outside. We don't use lockboxes or allow potential buyers or renters to tour properties themselves. In order for someone to go into that house, they would need a key, and all the keys to that house are accounted for here."

Derrick stands and walks over to a large cabinet on the wall. He inputs a code into a keypad, and a light flashes green, allowing him to open the door. He picks one out and holds it out at eye level.

"Right here," he says, holding it up to show me the thick plastic identification tag but purposely not letting me touch it. "2021 Candlewood."

CHAPTER NINETEEN

"Do you want to explain to me what happened at the Lionheart office today?" Sam asks as he comes into the kitchen that evening.

"Shit. They called you?" I ask.

"Pamela did," he says, reaching into the pan on the stove to steal out one of the mushrooms I have browning.

"Of course she did. Did she conveniently slip in a note about what she was wearing, too?" I ask.

I walk over to the spice cabinet and start pulling out bottles.

"Leopard heels? Is that a thing?" he asks.

I glare at him over my shoulder, then roll my eyes and finally find the garlic powder.

"It is."

"Good to know, but you're not going to distract me. What happened up there today?"

I feel like somebody tattled on me to the principal. As I sprinkle the garlic into the mushrooms, I nod toward the large pot sitting in the sink.

"Can you fill that up?"

He nods and heads to the sink to put in the water for the pasta. Over the sound of the water, I finally admit it.

"I went around the neighborhood today asking people about Ruby," I tell him.

"Emma," he says, the name drawn out like he wants to pack as much meaning into the sound of it as he possibly can, so he doesn't have to use other words.

"When I first met her, she said she was going up and down the street, introducing herself with the neighbors. I can explain away why she might not have encountered Janet and Paul, but I figured there had to be someone who saw her. Or some sign of her at least," I plunge ahead.

"Alright. And?"

"No one saw her or knew about her or even met her. One did tell me he saw a landscaping truck outside the house. It's Davis Landscaping Solutions, the company Lionheart contracts with to take care of the houses they manage."

"So, a landscaping company that takes care of empty houses was at the house, and you think that's proof she was really there?" he asks.

"They don't just take care of empty houses. They do landscaping for people all around town. But the main point is he saw the truck twice in one week," I say.

"Okay?"

"It's November, Sam," I point out. "Why would a landscaping company need to go to a house twice in November?"

"That is strange, but we don't know exactly what the crew was doing there. One of the ornamental trees could have fallen, or there might have been problems with their equipment the first time they came that week. There could be a lot of explanations."

"Exactly, which is why I decided I needed to find them. So, I went up to talk to Derrick."

"And that's when you had your run-in with Pamela," he says.

"I wouldn't exactly call it a run-in? Just our customary unpleasantness."

"But she did tell you nobody lives in that house," he points out.

"You already knew what happened, and you still had me go through the explanation?" I ask.

"I needed to know what you were going to say about it. She told me you were in their ranting and raving, and no one has gotten anywhere near that house in months except for the landscaping crew," Sam says.

"So, now you think I'm crazy just like she does?"

"That's not what I'm saying. I'm just trying to figure all this out like you are. Pamela is the one who handles the house. She would be the one who would sell it or rent it out, and she hasn't done either."

"I'm telling you, there was a woman in that house. Her name is Ruby Baker. Or, at least it was. Look." I walk over to the counter and pick up the cake stand. "She baked me a cake. This is her cake stand. A few days ago, when you called me in the morning, she was here. She came over to borrow some sugar and spend a little time here talking. Then she came back with the cake the next day. She told me she came to Sherwood because she was running from a really abusive relationship. He was apparently horrible to her, and she was afraid for her life. It looks like that was justified. Only nobody will believe that I saw her, much less that she was killed. So, he's going to get away with it."

"What do you want to do?" he asks. "What would make you feel better about this whole situation?"

"Call Pamela back," I say.

"What? Why would I do that?"

"Because she's the one who directly manages the house. Call her and ask her to let us inside. If we can get into the house, I can show you Ruby was there. Just because you didn't see her, doesn't mean her ex didn't take her body away. Get Pamela to let us inside to search the house."

Sam doesn't look convinced, but he takes out his phone and calls Pamela. He stands in the kitchen while I get the pasta cooking. and I hear him explain to Pamela he wants to do a sweep of the house. He asks for somebody to send over a key, and a few seconds later gets off the phone.

103

"She's going to come over tomorrow and let us inside," he says. "She doesn't let anybody take the key out without her being there."

"Great," I mutter.

I'm not exactly thrilled that she has to come along, but it makes sense. If she's the one responsible for the house, she's the one that's going to take the heat for Ruby being there without Pamela making the proper records. She's going to want to come along and try to talk her way out of the sticky situation.

———

The next day I wait anxiously for Pamela to show up. She slides her dark red Miata up in front of my house five minutes late. I can't help but think it's intentional. She takes her sweet time, sweeping her hair back over her shoulder and adjusting the sunglasses on the bridge of her nose. With an exaggerated flourish, she sends a wry smile across the top of the car toward me on the porch.

"Sorry to be late. I got delayed at a showing for an actual person wanting to buy a house on Bayberry," she says.

I bite my tongue until the retort swelling in my throat finally fades away.

"Thanks for doing this," Sam says. "It shouldn't take long."

"I hope not. You're not going to find anything. No one has even looked at this house in months. I'm not sure why. It's a really cute house. Three bedrooms, two and a half baths. Living room, den, dining room, bonus room. Full basement," Pamela rattles off.

"We aren't looking to buy it," I tell her.

Pamela's eyes slide over to me.

"Maybe it's the neighborhood," she says.

"There has to be an explanation," Sam says. "Emma has reason to believe the woman she met is in severe danger. So, I'm just going to take a look around and see if I can figure anything out."

It's the first moment I feel a small bit of hope. Maybe Sam's right. Maybe when I looked into the window and saw Ruby on the floor, she was just unconscious. Maybe it's possible she is still alive, and we can find her. All that matters is getting into the house and proving she was there so we can put our focus on what happened to her.

Pamela leads us across the street and takes the same key Derrick showed me yesterday out of her pocket. She unlocks the door and steps inside, getting out of the way to let us follow her. My heart squeezes painfully in my chest as soon as I step into the living room.

It's immaculate. It's completely empty, with no sign of any of the boxes or other items I saw there.

"See?" Pamela asks. "We had it cleaned after the last people moved out, and it's been this way since."

The thought of the chocolate cake at the front of my mind, I rush into the kitchen. It's just as clean and stark as the living room, and my eyes lock on the oven. It's brand new, the door still secured shut, and a plastic bag with the owners' manual taped to the front.

"The oven..." I start.

"Is new. Installed after the last people left, just like all the other appliances. None of them have ever been used," Pamela says.

"I'm going to look at the rest of the house," I say, walking past them.

"Be my guest. Just please don't mess anything up. If we ever can catch interest from someone, I'll like the house to still be presentable when I show them," she calls after me.

I rush from room to room, desperate for any small sign Ruby was here. Every room is as empty as the others. Even the garage has nothing in it but a single bucket of paint likely left over from touch-ups done after the last people left.

"How about the basement?" I ask.

Pamela shows me the door, and I hurry down the stairs so fast I almost lose my footing.

"What does she think she's going to find?" Pamela mutters to Sam as they both follow me more slowly.

Sam doesn't respond, but his silence presses in on me almost as much as if he did say something to her. I look around in the faint light of the unfinished basement. Suddenly, I notice something.

"There," I point. "Look."

Sam comes up beside me and follows where I'm pointing.

"What am I looking at?" he asks.

"There are two footprints on the floor," I explain. "Like someone walked in mud and thought they wiped their feet before they came in."

"It could be," Pamela says. "When the landscapers were redoing the backyard in the spring, this door was open so they could come in if they needed to. There's a small bathroom in the back. But the door to the rest of the house was locked. Is that everything? Have you seen enough? Because I really need to be getting back to the office."

"Thanks for doing this," Sam says.

We walk out of the house and back across the street, but I'm not done. I'm not satisfied. Those footprints haven't been there for almost a year. Something is very wrong, and I need to find out what it is.

CHAPTER TWENTY

"I don't understand what's going on over there," I say, storming back into my house. "It doesn't make any sense."

"Emma..." Sam starts.

"She was right here. In my house. We sat at the kitchen table, and she told me all about her ex-boyfriend Frank and what she went through with him after her divorce."

"Emma..."

"She baked me a chocolate cake. Look, I even have some of it left." I go to the refrigerator and pull out the platter with the leftover portion of the cake. Some of the fudge icing peels off when I take off the aluminum foil. "She made a joke about actually borrowing sugar because she brought it back."

Sam walks up to me and takes the platter from my hands. He deliberately sets it down on the counter, then takes me by the upper arms, so I look him in the eye.

"Emma, you need to calm down. We did what you wanted to do. We went over to the house and looked around. We went into all the rooms. You looked at the oven, the garage, the basement. You didn't find anything. It's time to let it go," he says.

I pull away from him. "Let it go? You just want me to... what?

Pretend I conjured the image of a woman on three different occasions, then imagined a murder?"

"I'm not saying that."

"Then what are you saying, Sam? Because it certainly sounds like you think I made it all up."

"Tell me something, Emma. Other than the other night with the confrontation and you thinking you saw her body on the living room floor, have you seen Ruby actually inside the house?" he asks.

I start to answer that obviously I have, but then I stop. I realize I didn't actually see her go into the house or come out of it. Just stand near it.

"No," I tell him. "But her stuff was inside, whole stacks of boxes. And there was a car in the driveway the other night. She said her brother was going to build shelves on the living room wall for her, so I'm guessing that was him."

"Shelves?" he asks, sounding confused.

"Apparently, she has a lot of books."

"There are already shelves on the wall," he says.

"He must have built them."

"No. They've been there. I knew a guy who lived there when we were younger. You probably don't remember him. Allen Mulroney. He was only here for about a year before his father got another new job. But I went to the house, and I remember there being shelves on the wall in the living room. They were actually built into the wall. I noticed them because the family didn't have any books on them, just some candles, and I thought it was strange."

I shake my head. "I don't understand what's going on."

"Look, this is obviously working you up. You haven't been sleeping well. You've got a lot going on. You just need to think about something else. Let's talk about the fundraiser some more," he suggests.

"Every time I think about the fairgrounds, I see that noose. It reminds me of…"

I let my voice drift off, not wanting to bring up any of the bad memories for him.

"Everly Zara?" he asks.

I nod. "It just wasn't what I was expecting to find in there."

"I know. But it was a haunted house. Just a prop. Come on. Let's talk about the kinds of food we'll have."

The enthusiasm in his eyes makes me laugh. Somehow this has gone from a small event he was going to throw together, to something I was going to handle, to sounding like he's planning a giant birthday party for himself. His excitement is adorable, but I only hope it's contagious. I don't want to think about a carnival when my mind won't go far from the house across the street and the woman I know was there.

I try to force myself to think about the plans and listen to Sam's ideas. He still wants me to head up the organization, but his visions are much clearer. Not long after we sit down in the living room to talk, his phone rings. He talks for a second, then looks at me regretfully as he tucks it away.

"This is going to have to wait. I have to go assist with a traffic stop," he tells me.

"People certainly are getting rowdy in Sherwood the last couple of days," I comment.

"Holidays coming up makes people crazy," he shrugs. He leans down and gives me a kiss. "I'll call you later."

He walks out of the house, and I start toward the laundry room. My phone rings, and I go back to answer it, assuming it's Sam calling with a warning to stop thinking about Ruby. Instead, I see Bellamy's name across the screen.

"Hey, B," I answer as I carry the phone with me and start the washer for a load of towels. "How is your research going?"

"I've actually made some good progress. I was doing some more poking and prodding and found the house you and your parents apparently lived in down in Florida."

"You did?" I ask. I wish I could remember more about the house. Even its address. But like so much of my childhood, it's been blurred and blotted away by all the piled-up memories and conflicting stories. "Wait... house? Just one? I thought there were a couple different places."

"As far as I've been able to track, there's only one. There might be another one I haven't found yet, but according to the daughter of the man who owned it then, your family lived here on and off for years. He did a lot of vacation rentals before short term vacation rentals were super popular. Your father would call and tell him when you were going to be around and book it for as long as you'd be there," she says.

"I'm surprised he remembers us that well. Someone who rents a house as a vacation rental has to see a lot of people. It can't be that all that unusual for the same family to come regularly," I point out.

"Well, he's gone now. He died several years ago. But his daughter Christina manages the house now even though she lives in Virginia."

"She lives in Virginia?" I ask, surprised.

"Yes. She wasn't able to give me any details, but I got the feeling they knew each other from something different than just him renting the house in Florida to them. She told me the whole family used to spend half the year in Virginia and half in Florida."

"Wait, did you go to see her?" I ask.

"Of course I did. You think I would find out she was less than two hours away and I wouldn't go talk to her?"

"I would think you would let me know so I could go with you," I say.

"Honestly, I didn't know what she was going to tell me. I didn't want you to get your hopes up and have it be a dead end. What I can tell you is that this man was someone important to them. Christina still has letters and postcards your parents sent to her father. One was from your mother wishing him a happy Easter, but you were in Vermont, so it was a snowman bunny holding a basket of eggs. It was really cute," she chuckles.

"Easter in Vermont?" I frown. "I don't remember that. When was that?"

"April 17, 2003."

I can't speak. My throat tightens, and no matter how hard I try, I can't force any sounds out of my throat.

"Emma?" she tries a few seconds later.

I close my eyes hard and shake my head to get myself out of my thoughts and back into reality.

"That can't be right," I finally manage, shaky but trying to keep my voice steady.

"It is. I wasn't going to tell you because I wanted it to be a surprise, but she gave them to me to bring back to you. She heard about your father and after your mother... she thought you might like them," she explains.

"Yes. That's exactly why that can't be the date on the postcard."

"I don't understand. There's one from your father, too. It's kind of generic. Just a landscape. But it has the same date. April 17th. The Thursday before Easter. Then there's a letter from the 23rd, just a few days after Easter. Christina told me there was a picture in it of the three of you dressed up for Easter. She's going to try to find it so she can send it to you, too."

"Bellamy, my mother couldn't have sent him a postcard from Vermont on April 17th of that year. And there can't be a picture of the three of us on Easter. That's the year I turned twelve. My mother was murdered the Thursday before Easter. In Florida."

I abandon the towels and rush into my bedroom. I clatter down to my knees beside the bed, yanking out the firebox from under it. My hand shakes as I try to put in the combination. It takes me three tries before I manage it. The door pops open, and I reach in for the envelope full of important documents. It's where I keep the deeds to the two houses, insurance information, the letter my father left me, bank account information, and other critical documents.

Including my mother's death certificate.

"Emma, what's going on?" Bellamy asks.

"I'm going to send you a picture. Hold on."

I put the certificate on the bed and snap a picture, making sure all the information on it is clear. I send it through to Bellamy and wait a few seconds.

"Got it," she says.

"See? She died that April," I point out. I am practically trembling, but I'm trying to keep myself steady. "April 17th."

"What do you remember?" she asks softly.

"Not everything. Flashes. Pieces of that night. But I remember we were in Florida. At least, I think I do. There are just so many questions about that night and everything after. And this is a big one. What could this possibly mean?"

"I don't know," she admits. "I'm sorry, Emma."

"Is anything I remember right? Does this mean that the place my mother died is wrong? Or the date? Or both? How could any of that be possible?"

"I don't know," she says again. "But I'll keep digging. I'll find out everything I can. I promise, okay?"

"Thank you," I whisper.

I hang up the phone and sag down to sit on the bed. My hand rests on my mother's birth certificate, covering her name as if I'm trying to protect her now when I couldn't then.

CHAPTER TWENTY-ONE

I spend most of the night hunched over my computer, poring over the information Bellamy emailed me. The scanned image of the postcard stares back at me, tormenting me. I know the handwriting on it. Even with everything else in my childhood either forgotten or clouded behind questions, that's something I won't forget.

I can still see it sweeping my name across the front of my lunch bags, and on the bottom of notes, she wrote me to hide in my coat or my backpack when I went to school. I can still see the grocery lists, the letters, even the bills paid.

My mother definitely wrote out this Easter greeting. But the date doesn't make sense. She couldn't have been in Vermont to send the postcard on that day. She was dead before the sun rose.

I pull up an image of the house, after looking up the address Bellamy sent me. The address doesn't seem familiar. I toss it around in my head, even say it out loud to feel it on my tongue. It doesn't have any meaning. But when the image comes up on the screen, I can feel myself standing there. I remember the sun on my skin and the blissful relief of the breeze. I can smell the flowers that grew in the flowerbeds along the front of the house. Emotion tightens in my throat as I trace the house with my fingertips.

The emptiness left by my parents is always with me. It's as much a part of me as the breath in my lungs and the blood in my veins. It's a constant feeling, lurking under every emotion and thought. It's always there, but I live beyond it. I move past it and keep going like it isn't there. Not because it doesn't hurt, but because most of the time, I don't remember what it feels like to not have it.

But that constant feeling makes the sharp stab of emotion that rushes through me more intense. All the feeling had once been softened and smoothened out by time, but now it rises up and floods over me, crashing like waves of memory to the front of my mind. Those memories shift to thoughts of what could have been, and it's suddenly like I'm drowning.

I've always been told everything that happens affects something else. Nothing is isolated. Nothing is solitary. Even the breaths people take create something else. Ever since my mother's death, a lingering voice in the back of my head has whispered to me, asking the same question.

Am I what caused this? Did she die because of something I did? Or didn't do? Or just because I existed? Did my father disappear because of the same?

I'm an adult now. Questions like that shouldn't impact me anymore. I shouldn't be afraid of what I can't see when the things I can are so much more threatening. But in the latest hours of the night, when the suffocating tension threatens to break into morning, I can't push the thoughts away.

Those first bits of light crack on the horizon and creep through the windows while I'm still staring at the computer. I have to find something. Anything that might help me understand. Bellamy's research abilities aren't significantly better than mine, but she sees things differently, comes up with different angles. It's what makes her especially good at her job as a consultant for the Bureau. It's also what led her to the discrepancy about my mother.

I want to dig deeper. To find out everything I can. My whole life has been overrun with questions. I've never been able to be completely, totally confident in what I remembered. It has always been hazy and jumbled, just out of reach, no matter how I grasp for it. That's not what I want. No matter what the answers are, I need them. I can't live the life ahead of me when the foundation I'm building it on is so unsteady.

Daylight taunts me mercilessly until I finally push the computer away and force myself to lie down. My eyelids drop down over stinging eyes, and my mind goes blank. It's less sleep than it is my body simply shutting off, but I'll take it.

————

I hear something—familiar yet strange, new yet like I've heard it a million times before. A tiny brass bell rings over my head. I'm lying on a red velvet couch in a room I don't recognize. It continues to ring, over and over, but I can't reach it. My mother is there. Her graceful, thin face, her dark hair. No, it's not my mother. It's Ruby Baker.

Why is she here?

I try to ask her if she's safe, but before I can open my mouth, the brass bell looms large right in my face. It rings again and again. Her face flashes. It's my mother again. No, it's Ruby Baker. She smiles and asks how I liked the cake.

Her face is covered in blood.

The bell rings again. Shattering my ears. Finally, the sound breaks through. Dark gives way to light, and I come out of sleep enough to realize it's my phone stuffed under my pillow that I'm hearing.

"Hello?" I mumble into the phone, rubbing my eyes to wake them the rest of the way up.

"Emma? Are you okay?" Sam asks.

"I'm fine. I was just sleeping," I tell him.

"Oh, I'm sorry. Go back to sleep. Get some rest."

"No, what's going on? What do you need?"

"It's nothing," he tells me. "We got a call for a break-in, and one of the guys is out sick today. I thought you might want to get out of the house and come along. But it's fine. Get your sleep while you can."

"Are you sure?" I slur through the phone, trying to will myself awake. "I can come."

"No, really. You sound tired. It's nothing serious. Just an abandoned building. I'll see you when I get off this evening."

"'kay."

I put my phone back under my pillow, but any grasp I had on sleep is gone. After a few minutes of trying to convince myself to rest a little longer, I give up and force myself out of bed. A shower wakes me up, and I call Bellamy as I make coffee to keep the energy rolling.

She immediately rushes into a description of her morning and the man at the coffee shop who she thinks is hitting on her but isn't sure. By the way she's talking about it, it's blatantly clear the man is doing everything he possibly can to get her attention, but she's not absorbing it. It's not that Bellamy is dumb or even particularly dense about the attention she gets from men. She's one of those effortlessly beautiful women who can roll out of bed and go to the grocery store, but still manage to look like she's in a magazine. I suspect there's something else behind her confusion in this situation, and that something else goes by the name of Eric. After years of an almost contentious relationship opposite each other in the dual roles of my best friends, they were forced to spend more time together when I went to Feathered Nest. In the year since then, they've been orbiting around each other, simultaneously relying on each other more and pretending they don't notice each other.

As much as I just want to push them together, I know both of them well enough to know that wouldn't work. They have to figure this out for themselves, one way or the other. When she's finished talking, she lets out a breath, and I know she's had enough of that train of thought. I give her a few vague words of encouragement that don't really mean anything. They don't need to. She just needs to talk things out. Then it's my turn.

"Have you found out anything else? About, um..." I ask. I don't need to clarify what about.

"I haven't been able to confirm anything. There are a couple of things that have popped up, but nothing set in stone," she tells me.

"I appreciate you trying," I say, my voice coming out partially as words and partially as a sigh.

"You know, I've been considering a vacation to Florida for a while now. It just so happens I have some time available," she says.

I brush my fingers back through my hair and shake my head even though she can't see me.

"I can't ask you to do that, B."

"You're not asking. It's an offer. I plan on running away from this almost-winter gloom and absorbing some sunlight. I might as well do some in-person poking around while I'm down there and see if I can confirm anything or get more information."

"That would be incredible. Things are a little complicated here right now, but if they straighten out, maybe I'll meet you down there for a few days," I tell her.

Realizing I haven't had a chance to tell her anything, I fill her in about Ruby. There's a short stretch of silence once I finish the story.

"And no one else has seen her? No one knows who she could be?" she asks.

"No. But I need to find out. Wherever she is, she's in danger."

"Let me know if I can help," she says.

"You're already doing enough. Thank you, though."

After too long, the combination of the coffee and the sugar rush of a leftover cinnamon roll kicks in, making me feel somewhat human again. I start across the street toward Ruby's house, intending to take a look around the outside, but I've only made it halfway before my phone alerts me to a new text. It's from Sam.

I need you. Meet me here.

A second message comes through with an address. I jog back to my house, quickly change my clothes, and get in the car.

Following the directions on my GPS, I head toward the outskirts of town.

CHAPTER TWENTY-TWO

The GPS brings me further out than I expect it to. It's late in the afternoon, and the main part of town is far behind me. Finally, I see an empty sign ahead, marking the entrance to a parking lot, and I turn in. Veins of grass crack through the old, crumbling pavement. What used to be white paint delineating parking spots across the black expanse are now reduced to flecks of white here and there. It's a small lot, likely made to accommodate no more than ten cars.

At the end of the parking lot, a cobblestone walkway weaves through an overgrown lawn up to the sagging front porch of a derelict, abandoned hotel, furnished from what used to be an impressive farmhouse. Modern modifications and additions are evident, but for the most part, the building is as it was when it was built as a home so long ago.

A narrow access road leads around to the back of the building. I assume that's where staff would park, leaving this lot available for guests. The emptiness of the front lot strikes me. I can only guess Sam and the rest of the team have gone back behind the building. I start to drive toward the access road, then hesitate. I take out my phone, pull up his number, and go to call it. Before it can ring, I end the call. If he is inside with a potentially dangerous person, I don't want to alert them to Sam's presence. At the same time, I don't know why he would summon me to a dangerous call without preparation.

Are you here?

I send the text and wait. Only seconds later, my phone alerts.

Yes. Come inside.

With no other cars in the lot, but also no urgency coming from Sam's messages, I'm not sure what to feel. Going against my initial instincts, I call Sam. It rings several times, but he doesn't answer. The back of my neck pricks. I reach under the passenger seat for my stun gun and attach it to my belt with a can of pepper spray. Holding my phone tightly and shining the flashlight from the front, I gingerly walk up the front steps and onto the porch. It feels like it can barely hold my weight. This is dangerous. I know it is, but I can't stop myself from going inside. Sam is here, and I'm not leaving him alone.

The door to the once-beautiful building opens easily. Either it wasn't properly secured in the first place, just abandoned to crumble the way back into the dirt, or it's been breached several times before. I'm more inclined to think the latter. People tend not to abandon the things that matter to them easily. A hotel like this was someone's dream. It took all their time, energy, and resources, and this was a great source of pride for them at some point. Whether it was wrenched away from them because of financial losses or shuttered because the person who dreamed of it died and the rest of the family didn't want to continue with the legacy, its closure was most likely not an easy thing. Even though it was lost, whoever walked out of the hotel last the final day of its operation felt something for this place. They may have held a deep-seated hope that someone else would scoop it up and bring it back to its glory. Or they just wanted to give it the respect it deserved after so many years. Either way, I don't see them just shutting the door and leaving it behind.

They would know the big building would appeal to people looking for mischief. They wouldn't want it damaged or to be where something horrible could happen.

I walk inside. The dank, dusty smell of air trapped within the building for too long nearly chokes me.

"Sam?" I call out.

My voice sounds explosively loud in the silent hotel. Above me, I hear heavy footsteps. I move toward them and feel fear starting to crawl up the back of my spine. My hand moves to my stun gun. I'm ready to pull it out if I need it, but I continue forward. I call for Sam again, but there's no response. The main stairwell in the middle of the entryway leads up to a large hallway. I try to orient myself, figuring out where the footsteps might have come from, and turn to the left. I've never been here, but it's eerily familiar. The memories it brings up of the last time I walked through an abandoned, disintegrating home make me queasy and the memory of heat ripples along my skin.

I take a few more steps down the hallway, then stop. My heart pounding is loud in my ears, and a shiver of disquiet goes down my spine. Taking out my phone, I dial Sam again as I'm heading back out of the hotel with every intention of getting in my car.

But I hear a faint ringing somewhere in the hotel. I keep the call open, letting the ringing guide me back along the hallway in the opposite direction.

"Sam?" I call out again.

This time I hear a groan, and I repeat the call to continue faster toward the sound. It draws me around a corner in the hallway and toward a dark gap in the distance. As I approach, I realize the gap isn't a hole in the wall, but an open elevator shaft. The call ends, and I try to call again, but my phone won't respond.

It takes all I have not to scream in frustration. Ten steps ago I had reception, but now suddenly it can't connect. I back up to call again, but it still won't connect. I continue down the hallway and shine the flashlight beam into the shaft. Footsteps come up behind me, but I don't have a chance to turn around. A hard push makes me stumble. I can't grab onto anything and fall into the shaft.

Pain radiates through my hip and shoulder as I hit the top of the elevator several feet down from the door. Above me, the doors slam closed. Saturated darkness surrounds me. With no power in many years, there are no emergency lights, no glowing buttons, no exit signs. I dropped my phone as I fell, but heard it clang against the metal. Lowering myself carefully to a crouch, I touch the top of the elevator and feel around slowly. Finally, my fingertips find my phone, and I pick it up. The flashlight is off, and the screen is dark. I press the button on the side, but it does nothing.

"Shit. No. No, no, no," I growl.

I shake the phone. It's an idiotic compulsion, but one that pops to mind any time something unexpectedly doesn't work. I press the button again, but it still stays dark. Another profanity puffs out of me, and I hang my head for a second, gathering my thoughts. I have to think. I can't let the terror take over and make me lose control. If I'm going to get out, I need to get a hold of myself and think clearly.

Pushing my phone into my pocket, I reach ahead of me in the darkness until I feel the metal cables holding the elevator. It occurs to me I don't really know how far I fell, or even which direction I'm facing now after crawling around trying to find my phone.

My shoulder and hip still ache, but most of the pain has subsided. I don't feel seriously injured. I take hold of the cables and try to pull myself up onto them. It doesn't take me long to realize that is a futile effort. Even if I was able to scale the metal, the cables are positioned in the center of the elevator, several feet away from the doors. I likely wouldn't even be able to reach the doors, much less have the leverage to push them open. I climb down off the cables and take a step. My foot slides into the gap between the elevator and the shaft wall, making me stumble. I gasp and reach for the cables again.

Once I'm steady, I unwedge my foot and sit down. It somehow seems even darker than it was when the doors first closed. My eyes aren't getting used to the darkness. The air in the shaft is getting colder, sinking through my clothes until I'm shivering.

I try to come up with options. Without my phone, I can't call for help or use any light. The elevator is too far from the doors above me to reach. An instinctive fear in situations like this is that the air will run out. I know logically it's not going to happen, but that doesn't stop the nerves from starting to settle in.

What the hell is going on? Where is Sam?

CHAPTER TWENTY-THREE

Above me, I can hear footsteps again. I shout out to Sam, but my voice only bounces around the shaft and comes back down on me. Seconds later, a tiny sound in the silence sends chills along my skin. It's like fingers drumming on the doors of the elevator. A slow, systematic popping against the metal. That's not Sam. He would never do something like this. I don't know who is in this hotel with me, but they have me trapped.

A sudden wave of vertigo makes me feel like I'm sitting right on the edge of something, ready to fall. I push backward, and my hand slips across a change in the texture of the metal. I feel it again. It's a slight dip, almost like a gap in the top of the elevator. The hatch. Thank the universe for outdated technology. The building has obviously been abandoned long enough that the rules for elevator compliance hadn't updated by the time they closed. Today nobody trapped inside an elevator is wriggling their way up and out of a hatch onto the top of the car to try to get out. But when this elevator was built, it was equipped with a small door leading down into the car.

There's no lock securing the door, and it only takes me a few moments to open the hatch. Stale, sickly smelling air rushes up out of the car. I don't know what's beneath me or what's going to happen when I drop down, but it might be my only chance. The average distance between floors in a building is ten to fifteen feet. Standing up and stretching my arms above me to feel where the elevator doors are tells me there's a very good chance the elevator is either at the bottom floor or very close. I'll take the possibility of getting out over sitting here and waiting for whoever's done this to open those doors and come after me.

I swing my legs over the side of the hatch so that they dip down into the cabin. Just as it is in the elevator shaft, it's complete darkness beneath me, so I have no way to prepare myself for what I might land on.

I take a breath and let go.

This fall is much shorter than the last one. I crumple to the ground and take a second to absorb the shock before climbing to my feet. Holding my hand out in front of me, I feel for the walls of the car. I'm still turned around, not sure which direction I'm facing. Finally, I find the rail weaving around the wall and follow it until I get to the buttons. From there, I run my hand over the door frame until I feel the crack between the car doors. I pry the doors open fairly easy and my heart sinks as I feel stone. The car isn't aligned with the doors to the floor.

Above me, I hear a horrible grinding sound of metal on metal. The doors are opening. Panic rises in me, and I crouch down to the floor, running my hands down the brick. A gasp of relief bursts out of me when I feel the texture and temperature change to cold, smooth metal. The car is still several feet above the station for the first floor, but it's something.

I hunker down to the floor and brace my feet against the back of the elevator. Thankful for my height and my years of strength training, I dig my fingers into the space between the doors and go to work prying them open. I'm running on hope that the elevator is old enough to not have the restrictors in place that would prevent the doors from opening. My fingers ache and strain. I take a deep breath and yank with everything I have. After several long, silent seconds of this, it doesn't feel like the doors are going to move, but finally, they slip and create a small gap.

I listen, waiting for more sound from above. It's gone quiet, but I don't know what that means. I pull up to a crouch for leverage to keep prying. The grinding sound starts above me again at the same time, the doors in front of me pull apart. The cold and darkness amplify my fear. But I have to keep going. If I stay, whoever trapped me in here will find me. Or I could try to escape. Maybe I'll be playing right into their hands. But I don't care. I'm not waiting around like a sitting duck.

It feels like time is sliding by too fast. I can't keep up. I keep having to stop, to catch my breath, and try to pull the doors open more. Just a little more. That's all I need.

With one heaving groan, I pull them apart enough to squeeze through. A small amount of light filters through, and without wasting any further seconds, I stick my legs down through the hole. I push forward and out just as I hear the heavy thud of something hit the top of the elevator car. I hit the floor and feel pain twinge in my ankle. I can't bother with it now. I scramble up, ignoring the pain as I run through the bottom floor of the building. I didn't see this portion when I was first going through the hotel. It takes some time to figure out where the elevator is positioned relative to the front door and the stairs. I hear the grinding of the metal again and run for the first door I see.

It opens out into a kitchen. Several windows high on the wall allow some moonlight into the space, and I can see the shapes of the counter, prep stations, and large refrigerators. At the back of the room, a narrow door likely leads out to the back of the hotel. Like the front door, it's been breached, and for the first time, I'm thankful for the idiocy of vandals. I run out of the back and through the tiny gravel back parking lot toward the access road, coming around the corner just as headlights wash across my face.

Tires squeal as the car slams to a stop.

"Emma!" Sam's voice comes at me through the blinding glare of the lights.

I continue toward him, and he meets me a few yards away, gathering me into a hug.

"Thank god you're here," I gasp, finally allowing my body to catch up with me.

"What are you doing here? What's going on?" he asks.

"There's someone in there. Someone is inside. They pushed me down the elevator shaft."

"What?" he asks. "You have to slow down. What happened?"

"I was in the upstairs hallway, and someone pushed me into the elevator shaft. They were coming after me," I tell him through heavy pants.

Sam's eyes snap to the hotel, and he guides me behind him by my shoulders.

"Go get in the car. Lock the door and don't open it."

He pulls his gun out and heads for the door. As he approaches, he leans toward the radio on his chest to call for backup. I don't want him to go inside alone. I hate the idea of him being in there. As if he can hear my doubts, he turns back over his shoulder.

"Get in the car, Emma," he commands.

I go for his car rather than my own, wanting the comfort of being near him. I sit in the silence, waiting. I don't want to say it this time or admit it's what's going through my mind, but I know I'm waiting for a gunshot. Ten minutes pass before another squad car comes into the lot, filling the space with even more light. Blue beams across the pavement make my eyes ache. Savannah and Daniel, two of the other officers, rush up to Sam's car and peer through the window in at me.

"What's going on, Emma?" Daniel asks.

"Sam is inside," I say. "You need to get in there with him. He shouldn't be alone."

Both officers rush into the building, their hands going for their guns as they do. Savannah steps up behind Daniel, her hand resting on the back of his shoulder as they prepare to enter the unknown. It seems like forever, but all I can do is sit there by myself. At any moment, I'm expecting someone to dash from behind the building to the car and get inside. But I don't see any movement near the dilapidated hotel or the parking lot until the front door opens again and all three officers come out.

I open the door and step out. My ankle feels weaker, and I limp over to see him. He shakes his head.

"There's no one in there," he says.

"What do you mean there's no one in there?" I ask. "Someone was there."

"Emma, we searched every single room. That was no one there. I found the elevator shaft, and I can see where you got in, but I didn't see anyone else there."

CHAPTER TWENTY-FOUR

I'm completely bewildered as Sam sends Savannah and Daniel back to the station, then climbs into the car beside me. I'm back in my own car, my hands gripping the steering wheel even though I'm not going anywhere. I watch the blue light disappear as they head off. There's no more reason to warn anyone. They decided there's no emergency. I finally turn to Sam.

"I heard your phone," I say.

He looks at me strangely.

"My phone?"

"In the hotel. I heard your phone. I got your text messages asking me to come here and meet you, and I went inside. I couldn't find you, so I called your phone. I could hear it ringing. That's why I went down that hallway," I tell him.

"Emma, I wasn't here. I don't know what you heard, but it wasn't my phone. You saw me drive up, and I didn't text you. I tried to call you, but it went straight to voicemail."

"You did text me," I fire back, with more irritation than I mean to. "It said you needed me and gave me the address to come here. Then when I got here, I texted you back and asked if you were here because

131

I didn't see your car. You sent another message that said to come inside. That's why I went in."

He looks at me strangely.

"I didn't text you. I called you earlier to ask if you wanted to come out here with me, but that was it. I responded to the call and didn't see any signs of a break-in. I mean, the doors were unlocked, but I'm sure they've been that way for a long time. Nobody takes care of this place, and people probably go in and out all the time. I swept it and left."

"Who called to report the break-in?" I asked.

"They didn't leave a name. They just called, said there was something going on here, and we needed to respond, then hung up. Stuff like that happens sometimes. Nine times out of ten, it's a prank, but there is always that possibility of a tenth time, so we have to investigate everything. Why didn't you call me?"

"I just told you, I did. I called you a few times, and I could hear the phone ringing, but you never answered. Then I tried to call you again, and my phone wouldn't work. It wouldn't even turn the flashlight on. Why would you text me to come out here if you left?"

"I told you, I didn't text you. Look," he reaches into his pocket and pulls out his phone. He pulls up the ongoing thread of our text message conversation. I'm the type of person who erases my texts at the end of every day, so it's somewhat mind-boggling to see the days and weeks unfolding on his screen. "See? Nothing. No texts to you and no texts back to me. No phone calls from you, either. But you can see I called you."

"I did get a call from you. My phone stopped working, and I haven't been able to get it back on."

"Let me look at it," he says. "I might be able to fix it."

I hand him my phone, and the moment he hits the power button, it pops back on. I stare at the screen, dumbfounded. Snatching it back from him, I flip through the screen.

"It would not turn on when I was inside. I tried over and over again. It just stayed black," I say.

"Show me the messages," he says.

I pull up my texts, but they're blank.

"No. No, that's not right," I say. I turn the phone off and turn it back on, then check the texts again. Nothing. "I don't understand what's happening."

"I'm going to take you home," Sam says. "You can tell me what happened."

My mind won't stop spinning the entire way back to my house. I can't think clearly, much less put anything into words. Sam doesn't push me, but drives silently, occasionally glancing over at me as if to check and see if I'm ready to talk. When we get back to my house, I disappear into the shower. The pain through my body has gotten worse, but the hot water rinsing away the dust and grime makes me feel a little better. Sam is in the kitchen making tea when I get out. Even my thickest sweatsuit isn't enough to take the chill out of my bones, and I curl up in the corner of the couch, wrapping a blanket around myself and holding the tea close.

"How would I know where you were if you didn't send me the address?" I finally ask.

Sam shrugs and shakes his head.

"I must have mentioned it to you when I called," he says.

"No. You didn't. You just said you got a call for a break-in. You didn't mention where it was. I didn't find out until I got the address in that text."

"Emma, I can't explain that. All I can tell you is I didn't send you a text. Not one telling you I needed you, and not one giving you the address to get there. I would have no reason to do that," Sam says.

"Then how did you know where to find me?" I asked.

"The GPS tracker," he tells me.

As soon as he says it, I remember. Shortly after the incident at the cult, Sam insisted on some extra security measures. One was attaching a GPS unit to my car and making me promise to keep the location tracker in my phone activated at all times. That would allow him to find me like it did today.

I run my fingers back through my hair, kind of shaking my head.

"Sam, someone was there. Someone pushed me into that elevator shaft. I didn't just fall. And there was somebody coming after me when I was trying to get out."

"We searched. There was no one. Let me see your ankle. You're limping pretty badly," he says.

"No. You don't believe me. You think I'm making it up," I say.

"I don't think you're making it up. I don't know what happened. You were obviously afraid when I got there, but we didn't find anyone there."

"They could have gotten out through the back the way I did," I point out.

"Daniel went directly to the back door and didn't see anyone. I'll send someone to search the area if it will make you feel better."

"But you think I'm imagining things," I snap. It's a little unfair, but I'm hurting and tired and irritated. It's obvious he's trying, but he can't bring himself to believe what I'm saying. "Don't you?"

"I'm going to send them out to search the area and see if they can find anyone," he says, conveniently ignoring my pointed question.

He steps out of the room to make the call. When he comes back, he reaches for my leg. "Let me see your ankle."

I relent to him checking it and cringe as he presses his fingers into the tender area around the joint.

"Why would I hear your phone ringing?" I ask.

He shakes his head. "I honestly don't know." He lifts my leg and kisses my ankle. "It's not broken. Probably a strain. But if it still hurts in a day or two, you should have it seen to make sure there's no hairline fracture."

"I don't understand what's going on."

"Like I said. You're exhausted. How long has it been since you've had steady sleep? You know as well as anyone how that can impact you. With everything you've been through, the stress you're under, and no sleep…"

"Sam, I know what I experienced. I'm not delusional," I insist.

"I never said you are. I just want to make sure you're taking care of yourself."

"This has something to do with Ruby," I tell him. "I don't know what, but it does."

———

I saw every hour of the night after Sam left. Sleep took over for a handful of minutes at a time, but every time I opened my eyes, I saw the night ticking away a bit at a time.

The morning air smells like snow. I remember what Sam said about the holidays coming. It feels strange in the center of my chest. It doesn't feel like Thanksgiving should be so soon. I can't even imagine Christmas.

It's the quiet time after sunrise. Half the street is still asleep, and the other half has gone to work or school. It leaves the street empty. I haven't seen the man walking down the sidewalk in a while. He used to come just before this time, nearly every day, in a dark sweatshirt that covered his head and his hands stuffed in his pockets. He would make his way down the sidewalk in front of my house without acknowledging anyone or anything.

Until the morning he stopped and looked right into my eyes. Eyes that looked like his reflecting back at him. The thought of that moment still makes my spine tingle, and today I'm glad to not see him.

I'm also glad for no one to see me as I make my way across the street to Ruby's house. My ankle slows me down slightly, but I'm soon behind the house. Following through with the plan I had yesterday, I walk around the house and into the backyard. I look around, then take out my phone and snap a few pictures. There's nothing about this lawn that would require an entire landscaping crew in November. They would be hard-pressed to find enough for the entire crew to do in the middle of spring.

Next, I go to the back porch. Nothing seems out of place until I open the screen door. There's something on the threshold, piled against the door like it spilled and was pushed into a mound when someone closed the main door. I cautiously dip my finger into it and rub it against my thumb.

Is that... sugar?

CHAPTER TWENTY-FIVE

FOUR YEARS AGO

The officers were everywhere now. They didn't think Travis noticed. They thought they could just fade into the world around him, and he wouldn't realize they were following him and tracing his every move. It let him stay a step ahead of them so they would never catch up.

He knew they were suspicious. They started investigating him quite a while ago, but still didn't have the guts to say it to his face. There were always insinuations. Little statements made to seem innocuous, but that concealed threats. They wanted to frighten him into slipping up. If they pushed him off balance or made him feel like they were right behind him, maybe he would do something to lead them in the right direction.

It was a move of desperation. He knew they had nothing to follow and were just grasping at straws with everything they did. Each time they came to the house to speak to him, veiling their questions in checking in on him or giving him updates, they were actually trying to dig inside him. Sure, they spoke to him as if he was the husband of a woman who disappeared, who ran off and had left breadcrumbs behind her that suggested she abandoned him for another life. They comforted him. They consoled him and listened to him. But Travis had learned which of the officers would look at him with sympathy and compassion, and which held disdain and suspicion in their eyes. Which ones still thought of him as the prime suspect. They wanted him to say something that condemned himself. They wanted a hint, a detail he shouldn't know or a subconscious suggestion that would warm up a trail rapidly going cold.

He played his part. He alternated between raging against her doing something so selfish and cruel, and sobbing over the loss of his one great love and the future they should have together.

They never knew what to do with either emotion.

He would never admit it to anyone, but there had been moments in the last few weeks when he thought he might have tripped himself up. Everything he did was so carefully planned out, meticulously placed in order to guide the investigators exactly where he wanted them to go, and away from what he wanted them to miss. But there was a point when they almost overlapped. A bit of surprisingly in-depth investigative work uncovered a piece of land far from anything else they knew he owned. A piece of land not in his name and never used for anything. They managed to trace it to him and sent search teams out in force. They told him it was in hopes of finding his wife. Maybe she went out there to take some time to herself. Maybe she was just trying to find herself and figure out what she wanted in her life.

They pretended he didn't know it had been months since anyone saw her. There was no way she was out there. But they said it with cloying enthusiasm, and he went along with it. Sometimes he didn't know which was worse: the ones on the search team who spoke to him like a child and built up his hopes because it was easier to deal with than facing what would be his real emotion or the ones who genuinely seemed to believe it.

It was the officers who did neither that made him, if just briefly, question himself. He didn't care when they searched the truck that was parked in the driveway the night they first came to hear his frantic story. They combed through it and used every technique they could to examine it. They found the splash of blood from when he cut his hand tying down a rope months before. They found hairs they couldn't say were suspicious because everyone's wife left hairs in their truck. And they could say nothing when that truck broke down for the last time, and he replaced it with the massive new white one he drove around town.

But when they found that land, his palms tingled just slightly. Questions rattled through his brain. He had been holding up steadily, not saying anything suspicious, being careful not to do anything suspicious. But they nearly ruffled him. They asked about the land, waiting for him to lie. He didn't. Yes, he knew the land. Of course he did. He hadn't been there in many years, not since he was young. Of course, they could search it. He knew nothing about the evidence of ground disturbance at the back of the property. Campers had been trespassing on that land his whole life. Maybe they had a burn pit there?

It was large, they told him. And deep.

Of course they could look, he told them.

What else could he say?

CHAPTER TWENTY-SIX

NOW

Could that actually be sugar?

The tiny grains certainly felt like it. There wasn't a huge amount of it, just a small pile as if someone had tossed some out the backdoor without realizing some had fallen to the floor to eventually be swept up by the bottom of the door. I pick up my phone to take a few pictures again. Just as I take one, it starts ringing. I answer it and hold it to my ear with my shoulder as I use my hands to pull me up, so I don't have to put too much pressure on my aching ankle.

"Hey, Bellamy," I say.

It feels like I've talked to her more in the last few days than I have in a couple of weeks, and that makes me feel guilty. I need to do better about keeping up with her and Eric.

"What are you doing?" she asks.

I look around the backyard of the house and contemplate whether to actually tell her. It's not like this is the most outlandish thing she'll have ever heard me describe. I update her on everything that's happened since the last time we spoke. She makes a sound I can only describe as a shudder when I'm finished.

"Yeah, that's about how I feel about it, too," I tell her.

"But you're alright?" she asks. "Other than getting the shit scared out of you, you're alright?"

"My ankle hurts, and I'm sure I'm going to have some lovely bruises, but all considering, I'm fine. I just don't understand what's happening. How could they not find anybody in the hotel? It's not that big and most of it's falling apart. Where could the person have hidden?"

"Sam said he would send people to look in the surrounding area. The person could have gotten out the back and ran," she offers.

"Maybe," I say. "But it just doesn't seem likely. I ran through that place. It was dark and twisty and confusing. I found the kitchen and the back door out of sheer terror and luck. Unless they were already very familiar with that building and knew exactly where to go, I can't see them getting all the way through it, come out the back door, and far enough away to not be seen by the time the officer went outside. It's not like it's surrounded by a bunch of woods or places they can just disappear. It's a massive field. I just don't know. And now I'm sitting here on a back porch trying to figure out if there's a pile of sugar at the door. Maybe I am losing my grip," I sigh.

"Don't say that," Bellamy tells me. "You are not. You are brilliant and badass and capable. I trust you more than anyone else in this world. If you say something is going on, then something is. You've just got to figure out what."

"Thanks, B. I needed to hear that. But enough about me. What's going on with you? What are you doing?" I ask.

"Well, it's eighty degrees out, and I'm standing in front of a giant Christmas tree flanked by massive toy soldiers." I can hear the grin in her tone.

The memories make me laugh. I know exactly where she is. I can still remember the feeling of standing right there and absorbing the atmosphere of beautiful Christmas decorations where spooky Halloween adornments had been just a few weeks before.

"You're already in Florida? That was fast," I comment.

"I was serious about my vacation," she chuckles. "I didn't just make that up to make you feel better. Things have been insane at headquarters, and I had a lot of vacation time coming. It was just convenient I could multitask while here."

"Well, you are nothing if not efficient," I tell her. "Have you found anything yet?"

"Not yet. I just got here late last night. But I have a full schedule planned ahead of me. Interspersed among sprawling at the pool and getting in my recommended daily allowance of tiny cocktail umbrellas, and doing the whole tourist thing, I'm going to a look into what Christina told me. She gave me some more information about the house, so I'm going to go see it, see if I can get my hands on some records, maybe go to the funeral home."

She's doing her best to make these tasks seem mundane, so it takes the disturbing edge away, but I still feel every word deep in my gut.

"How about that company? Did you find out any more about them?" I ask, trying to push past the thoughts of the main reason she was there.

"Spice Enya?" she asks. "I'm still looking. I just can't make sense of it. I might have Eric do some deeper digging, too."

"I can't tell you how much I appreciate what you're doing," I say. "Thank you."

"You don't need to thank me. I've watched you carry this for as long as I've known you. It's time you're able to put it down."

I'm off the phone and walking back across the street when I notice Sam's car parked in front of my house. He climbs out and looks at me questioningly.

"Have you been here long?" I asked.

"No. Just pulled up. What are you doing?" he asks.

"It doesn't matter," I tell him.

"Of course it does," he says. "What were you doing across the street?"

"Sam, it's broad daylight," I point out.

"It's also private property," he counters.

"I didn't try to get inside. I just walked around in the backyard and checked a couple of things out. That's it."

"Alright. but don't make a habit of it. I don't wanna hear about you creeping around over there."

"You won't, I promise. Now, did you just come to scold me?"

"No. I came to check on you, see how your ankle is feeling, and ask if you wanted to meet up for lunch later. I have some meetings that are going to run late tonight, so we can't do dinner," he tells me.

"Lunch sounds good. Our usual? I'm going to be down around that way."

"Pearl's is perfect. Why are you going to be down in town today?" he asks.

"I just have a couple of errands to run. Nothing exciting. Can we make it a little earlier than usual? Noon?"

"I'll see you then," he says with a smile. He leans in for a kiss, then gets back in his car. "I'll meet you there."

I wave as he drives away and then go back into my house to finish up a few things around the house before I leave. I do have some things to do in town, just like I told Sam. But my first stop of the day is an appointment further away. It'll take some time, and I want to make sure I'm back and have everything else done before it's time for lunch.

Sam is already sitting at our usual table when I walk into Pearl's Diner just before noon. Two glasses of sweet tea sit on the table, and I know he's already put in our order. It's an easy, comfortable pattern we've fallen into over the months I've been back here. Every now and then, we glance at the menu just for appearances, but we both know chances are high we're going to end up ordering the same thing we always do. Chicken for me, eggs and bacon for him, and biscuits and gravy for both of us. It's just too good not to.

"Did you get everything done?" he asks when I sit down across from him.

"I did. It was a very successful day," I nod. "How about you?"

"Going well. I'm not really looking forward to the meetings tonight, but there have to be a few parts of my job I don't like."

Neither of us talk about me going across the street this morning. We talk casually for a few seconds, our fingers playing lightly with each other across the table. A few moments after I sit down, Sandy comes up and sets sizzling, delicious-smelling plates in front of us. As always, I steal a bite or two of Sam's bacon, and he nabs a tiny bit of chicken from my plate. It should be enough for our whole meal, but it's not. Both of us will pretend we're impossibly full until she comes back by with slices of pie and cups of coffee.

"Looks like it's a good thing we got here early," he chuckles. "Swarm's coming."

I glance back over my shoulder to where he's looking at the front door and see several groups walking inside. Coming just half an hour earlier than usual has gotten us in right before the massive rush we usually wade through to have our favorite lunch. It's by design. There's another stop I want to make this afternoon and would like as much time there as possible without cutting my lunch with Sam short.

Two more groups walk in, and I catch eyes with Derrick.

"Perfect," I mutter. "Looks like everybody from Lionheart is here."

Sam takes a bite of his biscuit and stretches his neck to check the rest of the people coming in.

"Don't worry. Looks like Pamela is sitting this one out. You can eat in peace."

I laugh. "Good."

We fall back into easy conversation that takes away the prickly tension that's been between us, and my mind and body finally relax. He starts telling me a story about the morning at the station and has me laughing at the depiction of one of the officers dealing with a spider when a gasp from the other side of the restaurant silences him. We look toward the source of the sound and see a man gagging, trying to get out of his seat. Before he can, his wife clutches her napkin to her mouth.

Behind us, another woman groans. I turn to see her wrap her arms around her stomach and fold over on herself. In a matter of seconds, people all around the restaurant are crying out in pain, bending over their napkins, and sinking down to the floor. Sam jumps to his feet.

"Everybody stop eating," he barks. "Don't touch anything else."

He looks over at me. "Go out to my squad car and get on the radio. Get as many ambulances as you can here."

CHAPTER TWENTY-SEVEN

HIM

She was gone again. In the short time he spent away, handling tasks better left to others and yet never managed by anyone but himself, she left. He felt so much better when she was close. When he was able to drive down the street or walk along the alley and possibly get a glimpse of her. Not always. Not every time.

Sometimes he knew where she was but wasn't able to get close enough because the others were around her. Not that he could blame them. They had Emma in their lives. It only made sense they would savor every second of it. He could only imagine what it would be like to have her that close. To be able to pick up a phone and call her, knowing her voice would be on the other end. To be able to go up to her house and have her welcome him in to sit with her, to share food with her, to just be.

One day soon, he wouldn't have to imagine anymore. He would be like them, only more. There would come a time when he wouldn't have to hide away from her gaze just to look at her. When he could just reach out and embrace her when he wanted to. She wouldn't be afraid. She wouldn't wonder or worry.

It was that longing that made it so much harder. And as much as he knew he needed to keep his distance, he wished he didn't have to.

He wanted her home. He wanted her back where she was safe. He wanted to bring her where she belonged. He didn't like the days and weeks that were passing. The longer she stayed in Sherwood, the more attached she became to the life she had there. There was a time in the not too distant past when she'd shed herself completely of that past life. She barely remembered it. At least that's what he told himself. He didn't like to think of a time when she was kept in such a bubble, shielded from everything that was real and true.

Her going back to Sherwood was dangerous. It drew her back in and tempted her with that life. She didn't understand. He had a much better one to give her. It would be more than she could ever imagine. And when the time would finally come to introduce her to it, she would know all he had done for her. Emma would understand everything. All that he had gone through. All that he had sacrificed for her. She would finally know the exact, painstaking effort he took to create that life for her, and she would be convinced it would be right for her.

He hoped he wouldn't have to do much convincing. He hoped she would see what he had for her and know instinctively. She would see it was what she should have always had. What she had always deserved.

He hoped it would be easy to reveal to her all the lies and manipulation that stopped her from fulfilling her true potential and being the person she was meant to be. Every day he had to gently guide her into that understanding. But every day she spent gone was another day he couldn't just live alongside her and experience the world together.

It's why she needed to get out of Sherwood. Achieving all he wanted would be much harder if she was further engrossed in a new life.

He'd taken care of that once. Had made her and Greg nothing more than a distant memory.

It wouldn't be as easy to do again. Not with someone like Sam.

CHAPTER TWENTY-EIGHT

By the time I've called the ambulances, alerted the hospital, and run back into the diner, several more people are sprawled on the floor. I run up to Sam, who is standing near the door, preventing anyone from leaving.

"What's going on?" I ask.

"I don't know," he says. "Not everybody is showing symptoms."

"No, not now. But that doesn't mean they won't," I tell him. "We need to keep everybody here. With something like this, we can't let anyone leave without being seen and documented. We can't risk whatever this was spreading."

"You're right. There could be delayed symptoms, and we'll need as much information as we can," he nods. "Are the ambulances on their way?"

I nod a quick confirmation and head to the kitchen, rolling up my sleeves to wash my hands. For now, all we can do is administer first aid and make them as comfortable as possible.

Sam and I get to work checking in on the people closest to us and recording their information. There really isn't much we can do for any of them. All are complaining of the same symptoms. Severe abdominal pain, cramping, nausea, vomiting. Two have passed out, and I watch as a third stands, trembles, and collapses to the floor. A woman standing a few feet from me immediately rushes toward the man now crumbled to the floor. I follow her, and she looks up at me as she takes his pulse.

"Violet. I'm a nurse," she explains. "I'll help in any way I can."

"Thank you," I say. "Do you have any idea what might be happening?"

She shakes her head. "No. Foodborne infection doesn't generally hit this quickly. Unless there was something very severely compromised about the food, I don't understand how it could happen this extensively, and this quickly."

"The ambulances should be here soon," I tell her.

"Help!"

The scream is chilling. Violet and I both jump to our feet and whip our heads around. A woman is sagging beneath the weight of a younger woman who is crumpled in her arms. The younger woman has a hand pressed to her chest and is gasping for breath. Her eyes are widened with fear, and she's struggling to get to her feet but can't support herself. The woman holding her, who I assume is her mother, slowly drops to her knees and brings her daughter down into her lap. Violet and I run toward them just as the girl takes a wheezing gasp and falls still.

"Help her, please," the woman sobs. "She's not breathing."

"Put her down," the nurse commands.

The woman lowers the girl to the floor. I take her hand to pull her back out of the way. Violet needs to do CPR, and most people are not prepared for how traumatic it can be to witness a loved one getting worked on in that way. The sound of ribs cracking and the violence that seems to go into each compression can be too much. I don't want the woman to interfere and potentially compromise the effect of Violet's efforts.

"I'm Emma," I say to the older woman, trying to get her to focus on me and instead of what's happening on the floor. "What's your name?"

"Jacqueline," she stammers.

I nod encouragingly. "It's nice to meet you."

The words feel slimy and inappropriate on my lips. It's one of those phrases people say, a collection of words that don't really mean what they seem to at face value. The worth is in the transaction, in filling the moments between two people who have little else to pass between them.

"That's my daughter," she sobs. "Nicole."

"How old is she?" I ask.

It really doesn't matter. A child who can't breathe is a child who can't breathe, whether they are a baby in your arms or a grown adult.

"Twenty. She's visiting from college."

Jacqueline's voice cracks as she says it. I rub her arm to try to soothe her. Finally, the ambulance sirens slice through the air, and bright red lights flash through the glass front of the diner.

"Come with me," I tell her, rushing toward the front of the restaurant where Sam has returned. I reach for him and tug on his arm to turn him around. "Jacqueline and her daughter need to go first. Nicole is twenty years old, not breathing. Violet is doing CPR."

Sam nods and runs out to meet the ambulance. Seconds later, legions of EMTs clad in vibrant yellow, carrying heavy medical kits, push through the door into the diner. Sam shouts above the din in his most commanding voice, instructing everyone to move out of the way so the stretcher can get inside. There's just enough space, and Violet relinquishes responsibility for Nicole's heartbeat as she's brought up onto the rolling bed and given an oxygen mask.

The next hour is an intense, frightening blur. Sam and I do what we can to help the paramedics process the scene and get everybody out of the diner. Those who aren't showing any symptoms, or who are mild enough to get to the doctor on their own, give us their names and contact information so we can get in touch with them if we need to. After an exhausting rush, everyone is out, and it's our turn to head to the hospital. Neither of us are showing any symptoms, but we want to be there to tell the doctors everything we can and get any information that's available.

The ride in the squad car from Pearl's is completely silent. We pull up and quickly march into the ER.

Around us, the hospital is in chaos. Nurses and doctors run from bed to bed. Every examination room is filled, sometimes with two or three people in the same family, and affected people have spilled out into the waiting room as well. More wait on the other side just to be seen.

They're so busy, we can't even check in yet. All we can do is stand and wait.

"How could this happen so fast?" Sam finally asks. "What could possibly have caused this?"

"I don't know," I tell him. "Violet says foodborne infections usually don't act like this. Something else is going on."

Just as I say it, Pearl, the owner of the diner, comes toward us. Tears are running down her face, and her hands pull and twist at each other in front of her. She reaches out for us, then pulls her hands back into her chest again.

"What happened?" she asks in somewhere between a stuttering gasp and a whisper. "How could this have happened? I'm so careful. I run a clean place. The health inspector just came last week. There were no issues."

"We don't know what happened," Sam says. "We're trying to figure that out. How about you, Pearl? Do you feel alright?"

"Yes," she says. "Physically, anyway."

"Good," I smile. The diner is all Pearl has. It's been an institution in Sherwood for longer than I've been alive. I can only hope that whatever this was won't ruin her business for good.

"Emma, I want you to go back to the diner and talk to the investigators there. Tell them everything we saw and find out if they know anything. There are going to be people who are curious and try to get in. Make sure the rumor mill stays shut down about this. Understand?" Sam asks.

I give him a nod and start out of the hospital. As I'm leaving, Bianca Hernandez comes toward me, her arms open. She and I aren't the closest of friends, but I've come to trust her ever since she and her daughter helped us out on a case this summer. She has a history with

Sam, too. It's long over now, but if Sam trusts her, that's good enough for me. I give her a hug and pull back to look at her.

"Are you okay?" I ask. "Do you feel sick?"

She shakes her head. "No. I'm fine. Gloria is, too. We just came as a precaution."

"I'm glad. Sam is over there." I nod toward him. "I'm going back to the diner."

She nods and heads over to Sam. As I'm turning back to the door, I see Derrick stumble across the waiting room and drop down into one of the chairs. I rush over to him.

"Hey, Emma," he says, grimacing through pain he clutches in his stomach.

"Have you been seen yet?" I ask.

He shakes his head. "Not yet. I'm not vomiting and I'm still breathing, so I'm low priority."

"They'll get to you soon."

He nods weakly, then opens his eyes more to look at me. "Have you seen Pamela?"

The question strikes me as odd. "Pamela? She wasn't there."

"Yes she was. She had a showing, so she met us there. I lost sight of her in the confusion and don't know how she is."

"I don't know," I sigh. "I have to go back right now, but I'll make sure someone tells you how she is when the doctor sees her."

He nods again, and I stop by the front desk to ask the flustered receptionist if she had heard Pamela's name. She looks at me like she can't fathom why I would be asking her such a question. I ask her to let Derrick know if she does and rush out to my car, feeling thankful the sickness passed over us but worried about all those who weren't so lucky.

CHAPTER TWENTY-NINE

Pearl's is already crawling with people from the health department when I get back. Two officers stand right outside the door, blocking people from going inside. As I walk down the sidewalk, I notice another officer taping up pieces of butcher paper over at the glass of the huge windows making up the front of the diner.

"What's going on?" I ask the officers on guard.

"They don't want people snooping," Cole answers. "We've already had to turn away a bunch of people with their phones out. I'm guessing any minute now the newspaper is going to show up. Sam instructed us to keep the media away and keep the situation as contained as possible."

"That's why I'm here," I nod. "He sent me to make sure everything is locked down and to find out what's going on with the investigation."

"The Health Department's here," Liza, one of the youngest officers in the department, chimes in. "They're picking apart everything, trying to find food that wasn't prepared correctly or that wasn't the right temperature."

She says it in the tone that tells me she puts absolutely no stock in that theory.

"It wouldn't have struck that quickly," I tell her. "It can't just be a normal foodborne pathogen. After the nurse who was here helping told me that, I talked to one of the doctors at the hospital, and he all but confirmed it. There are some instances when a foodborne infection can set in within just a few minutes, but the vast majority of the time, it takes a minimum of two hours. Usually, it's even longer than that. It doesn't make any sense that this many people got sick at the same time."

As we're talking, a severe-looking woman in a dark gray suit steps out of the diner.

"Can I help you?" she asks.

"I'm Emma Griffin. Sheriff Johnson sent me to get any new information," I tell her.

"Annette Rickley. I'm with Sherwood County Public Health, Division of Environmental Health. I'm leading the investigation into this incident," she announces stiffly. She may work for the county, but she's definitely not from around here.

"You got here quickly," I note.

"There's no time to waste when there's a risk to public health. A mass foodborne infection incident like this could indicate severe systematic problems throughout the area," she tells me.

"What's that supposed to mean?" I ask.

"Incidents like these usually point to lax food service supervision and policies. Kitchens get away with breaking rules because they know people, vendors, and suppliers aren't held to high enough standards. It might not seem important when you are looking at it from a narrow perspective, but it compounds. Eventually, it turns into situations like this."

"That might be a problem in other places you have investigated, but not here. This isn't just some random little place roadside shack. This is Pearl's Diner. It's been here for fifty years. And before it was Pearl's, it was Rosie's. Rosie was Pearl's father. He owned it for almost thirty years. It's a beloved establishment for the people of Sherwood, and the staff takes that very seriously. Pearl is stringent with food safety, and she just passed an inspection with flying colors," I argue.

The compulsion to defend Pearl feels like I'm defending the whole town. In the grander scheme of the situation, it might be trivial, but in the moment it feels essential.

"Like I said," Annette says, her mouth curving into a mocking smile, "things get by."

"According to the doctors treating the affected patients, foodborne infections don't occur this quickly," I point out.

"And what is it that you do, Ms. Griffin?" she asks.

"FBI," I tell her simply.

"And are you on this case, Agent Griffin?"

"No," I tell her.

"And do you specialize in foodborne pathogens and their incubation periods?"

"No."

"Then perhaps you should let us do what we specialize in. And when the CDC arrives, let us handle it. We are currently gathering samples of all the food in the diner and will find the source of the problem. If you'll excuse me, I have work to do."

She steps back into the diner. It's a dismissal, and anger twists inside me.

"Has she been like that the whole time?" I ask.

"She's delightful," Cole confirms.

"Well, she can be Satan incarnate if she wants to be. I don't care, as long as she actually does her job and finds out what's really happening. Because I highly doubt more than half the people inside that restaurant were hit by the same infection within ten minutes of each other. It doesn't make sense," I say.

There's nothing new here, so I head back to the hospital. I need to talk to Sam. Obviously, there's something much more going on here than some improperly washed vegetables or a hot dish kept out a bit too long. Something happened to the food, which means someone is responsible.

The main road leading to the hospital is always more crowded, especially at this time of day, so I choose the back road. It's narrower, twisting along the path of the landscape rather than cutting directly through. Even with the slower speed necessary, this way feels faster than having to battle the traffic.

Apparently unsatisfied by my speed, a green sports car comes up beside me and slips ahead. It's one of my biggest pet peeves. I'm already pushing fifteen miles over the speed limit, and this guy wants to head into the oncoming lane, in front of a nearly blind curve, and for what? To save thirty seconds getting to his destination?

The car already in front of me maintains pace for a few seconds, then both speed up and race ahead. They disappear ahead of me.

"Assholes," I mutter.

When I come around a sharp corner, and as the two lanes converge into one, I see the green car that passed me dip dangerously close to the pale gold Saturn in front of me. The Saturn tries to avoid it, but the sports car swerves again, speeding up to force the other car off the road. The Saturn nearly careens wildly off the road, only barely slowing down enough to prevent from crashing headlong into the tree line.

It's shocking. With a burst of exhaust, the green car disappears into the distance. I pull off the road to check on the driver of the Saturn, but before I can open my door, that car's tires squeal and the driver peels off. The bizarre situation locks my attention. What the hell is this about?

I speed up to follow the gold car. At this point in the road, the curves lessen, and the way becomes straighter. It allows me to catch up closer, but I realize I can't see a license plate on the Saturn. Suddenly, the driver takes a sharp turn and disappears down a residential street. I slam on my brakes and back up, but I can't see it anymore. I'm not going to follow it. I need to get back to the hospital. Whatever is happening between those two cars will just have to stay between them.

The parking lot is nearly full, and I have to park in the back row when I get to the hospital. I run across the lot and into the emergency room door. As soon as I see Sam, I rush up to him.

"Sam, something really strange just happened while I was driving back here," I start.

He shakes his head, his bloodshot eyes closing slightly like he's trying to avoid listening to me.

"Emma," he says.

"Just listen. Are there any officers available right now? If so, I think you need to get them out to the Crystal Farms subdivision. You know that one off Orchard? I was driving down it and saw a car run another one off the road," I continue.

"Emma, please," he protests.

I'm too invested in spilling out the bizarre story, I steam right past his interjections.

"When I stopped to make sure the driver was alright, they took off down the road. Drove away from me. There was no license plate on the car, and I couldn't see who was driving. But they went into that subdivision. There might be something really dangerous going on," I tell him.

"Emma, stop," Sam interrupts fiercely, almost aggressively. "I can't listen to any more of your ramblings right now."

I fall silent and for the first time, really look into his face. Seeing it clearly takes away any desire to snap back at him. It's not just drawn from the stress of the whole situation, and his eyes aren't just red from the strain and tiredness. He looks emptied. Devastated. I step up closer to him.

"Sam, what's wrong?" I ask.

"Nicole is dead."

CHAPTER THIRTY

I can't have heard what I think he just said. I close my eyes for a second, then open them to look at Sam again.

"What?" I ask.

"Nicole," he repeats. "She's dead. They got her heart beating again in the ambulance on the way over here, but they couldn't stabilize her. She crashed about twenty minutes ago, and there was nothing they could do."

I put my hand over my mouth, breathing deep. "How could it get that serious? Is anyone else in danger like that?"

"No," Sam says. "In fact, they're getting better. Nobody else got anywhere near as sick as Nicole. Very ill, yes, but nothing extreme and none ever entered critical condition."

"Then what happened with her? I was there when she collapsed. It didn't seem to be anything that made her stand out against the others. Do the doctors have any explanation?"

"No," he says again. "Not really."

"What do you mean, not really?" I asked.

"The doctors said Nicole's symptoms were very strange. They didn't line up with what everyone else at the diner experienced. According to her mother, her onset was right about the same time as

161

everyone else, and she had the same symptoms initially. Stabbing pain in her stomach, nausea. But then it got very serious. She had symptoms nobody else exhibited. It was like she went into anaphylactic shock," Sam tells me.

"Anaphylactic shock?" The revelation doesn't process with everything else.

"Yes," Sam nods. "It's happened before, and she had to be treated, but she was always extremely careful, and she was nowhere near her allergy."

"What was she allergic to?"

"Hazelnuts," he says. "There isn't even anything on the menu at Pearl's that has hazelnuts in them. I've already spoken to her. She doesn't have anything in the kitchen with hazelnuts. Not hazelnut spread. Not even hazelnut coffee."

"Then how did the illness affecting so many other people in the restaurant turn into anaphylactic shock for Nicole?" I muse.

"I don't know, but when you have to sit across from a mother who has put all her hopes and stakes into a team of doctors and tell her they weren't able to save her only child, I don't really think it matters so much," he sighs.

"Of course it matters. You heard the doctors just as well as I did. This isn't a foodborne infection. And now with this happening to Nicole... I can't believe it's a coincidence. Something is wrong, Sam."

"I really can't listen to this right now. You're going too far. This is real, Emma. This is actually happening. A woman just lost her daughter to something senseless, and as of now, unexplained. There are about a hundred people laid up in this hospital trying to get over an illness none of us understand. We're going to have to be dealing with this for a long time. The health department is going to get involved..."

"They already are," I tell him. "When I went down to the diner to find out what was going on, I met the official leading up the investigation," I tell him.

"Fantastic," he mutters, letting out a labored sigh.

I'm stung by the way he's talking to me, but I know he's under an incredible amount of stress, and the sudden death has shaken him. Deciding to put that aside for right now, I take him by his wrist, so he'll look at me again.

"Come on. You need to get some rest. They can deal without you here for a little while."

He doesn't argue but lets me guide him out into the parking lot. As we're walking to my car, I see someone ahead of us. We get closer, and I know it's Pamela. She's getting into a car, but it's not the little red Miata she showed off when she came over to let us into Ruby's house.

It's a gold Saturn.

I take off running, sprinting down the center of the parking lot so she can't pull away. She's backed into the spot, so as soon as I get to her, I slam my hands down on the hood and glare through the windshield at her.

"What the hell are you doing?" she screeches.

"Emma, what's going on?" Sam calls, jogging up to me.

"What were you doing back there?" I demand.

Pamela climbs out of the car and squares off against me.

"In the hospital? Getting treated for the same sickness just about everybody else at Pearl's is getting treated for," she fires back.

"Not in the hospital. On Orchard Road."

"Orchard Road?" she asks, her voice tight with disgust, like it's the most absurd suggestion she's ever heard.

"You know exactly what I'm talking about," I round on her.

"Why don't you enlighten me?" Sam asks.

"This is the car I saw get run off the road," I say, pointing at the Saturn. "A green sports car ran it off the road, and before I could get out to check on the driver—Pamela—she sped off and lost me in a neighborhood."

"Someone here has definitely lost something," Pamela sneers.

"When did you get here?" Sam asks.

"You can't be serious," she answers, then sighs. "I wasn't bad enough for the ambulance to bring me, so I got my car and drove over. I got here right around the time everybody else did."

"Then why couldn't Derrick find you?" I ask.

"What?"

"Derrick. He was in the waiting room, and he said he hadn't seen you since the diner. He was worried about you," I say, crossing my arms. "If you got here when everyone else did, why did he not know where you were? And by the way, you weren't even at Pearl's. I specifically did not see you there."

"Why are you so obsessed with me? What is your deal, Emma?"

"Why couldn't Derrick find you, if you were here the whole time?" I snap, ignoring her question. I swear, I feel like my jaw is clenched so tight my teeth my burst.

"Because he was too busy puking his guts out?" Pamela offers. "If you didn't notice that entire scene was out of control. The group got broken up, and I just got out of there as fast as I could, so I wasn't in the way. I came straight to the hospital. Using the main road. I certainly wasn't out playing tag with a green sports car on Orchard."

"This is the car I saw," I insist.

"You might have seen a gold car, but they aren't that rare," she says.

"It's a Saturn!" I shout. I feel like everyone around me is just refusing to see the obvious answers in front of them. It has been a hell of a day, and I don't have any more patience for this crap, least of all Pamela's. "They don't manufacture them anymore. There can't be that many gold Saturn's in Sherwood. What happened to your red one?"

"My Miata is at the mechanic getting its brakes fixed. This is a rental."

"Who was in the green car?" I ask.

"I don't know because I didn't see a green car." Her eyes slide over to Sam. "Seriously, Sam. Something needs to be done about this. It's getting really worrisome how much Emma is coming up with out of her own mind."

"I'm not imagining things. Don't talk about me like I'm not even here," I say through gritted teeth.

Pamela shrugs, her expression one of feigned innocence. "I'm just thinking about your own well-being. Everybody sees it, Emma. Maybe it's time to be honest with yourself." She trains her puppy-dog eyes on Sam. "Can I go? I'm still not feeling well, and I'd really like to go home and get some rest."

Sam nods, a look close to defeat on his face. He gestures toward the exit of the parking lot.

"Of course," he says. "Go ahead. Feel better."

Pamela opens the car door and smiles at him. "I hope it didn't hit you too hard, Sheriff."

"No. I feel fine. Thanks."

"Well, if you start to feel sick and you need anything, don't hesitate to call me," she says and dips down into the driver's seat.

She brushes her hand in front of her, gesturing for me to move out of her way. Sam tugs me by my arm, and as soon as there's any clearance, Pamela pulls out and drives away. Barely missing me by inches. I follow the back of the car, and a detail settles in.

"There's a license plate now," I mutter, rubbing my fingers against my temples to stem the raging irritation headache that is now only seconds from coming on.

"What?" Sam asks.

"On the car. There's a license plate."

"That's the law," he says.

"I know, but there wasn't one when I saw her on Orchard," I explain.

"She said it wasn't her out there."

"And you're going to just believe Pamela over me?"

"What do you want me to do, Emma? Give her a ticket for getting run off the road by some other car? You don't even know if it was her!"

"Sam, it was her. I know it was." I slow down my swirling thoughts, trying to explain this as best I can. "She didn't seem sick at all, and I didn't see her at the diner, did you? Derrick said she joined them late. But there were just a few minutes between when the rest of the group got there and when everybody got sick. She wouldn't have the time to get there, order food, and eat anything in order to get so sick she would need to see the doctor," I point out.

"Emma, stop," he says.

"You've been telling me that a lot lately," I say, trying to balance somewhere between anger and humor. But it comes out as all anger.

"Maybe I should have started a lot sooner."

"And what's that supposed to mean?"

"I just—"

"Say it, Sam. Don't bullshit me," I snap. "I know what you're thinking. What you've been thinking."

"I agree with Pamela. What's happening with you recently is really worrying me. You're not yourself," he tells me.

"I am myself," I argue.

He shakes his head. "No, Emma. You've always been unpredictable and impulsive. Don't you remember, that's what I said I missed so much about you when we found each other again in college? The spark was gone. You were so subdued and restrained. But that girl I knew has been coming back. And recently that's turned into recklessness. You're suspicious of everything. You're seeing and experiencing things no one else can corroborate. And the thing is, no one can blame you for that. Not after what you've gone through. Maybe because you've started to finally settle in more, stress and anxiety are rising to the surface, and are causing these issues."

"Did I miss when you studied psychology?" I narrow my eyes.

"No. And I didn't. I'm only telling you what I think might be going on. That's why I think you should go talk to someone."

Heat rises up in my cheeks, and my hands clench at my sides. I get enough of this from fucking Creagan. Sam was supposed to have my back through this. Was supposed to be by my side. I didn't ask for a lecture.

"It's already bad enough when people like Pamela decide to make me the target for all their dissatisfaction in life and talk about me behind my back. Trust me, that's not fucking new to me. But it's so much worse when it's someone I thought I could trust."

"You can trust me," he insists. "And that's why I'm telling you this."

"I can trust you, and that's why you're telling me you think I've got a screw loose? That's fantastic. You know, Sam, I didn't have to come here, and I certainly don't have to stay. But I did because you needed me. I really don't appreciate you not doing the same for me when I need you," I tell him.

"I'm here for you, Emma. I always am. That's what I'm trying to do. I care about you so much. I just want you to feel better."

I give a single nod and start toward my car again. "Then I guess I should go home and rest like everyone else. Have a good evening, Sam."

With that, I slam my car door shut and spin out of the parking lot.

CHAPTER THIRTY-ONE

FOUR YEARS AGO

Everything was steady again. The police briefly dangled the threat of the disrupted soil over his head, parading him out to the land to search, never quite bringing him close to where they said the site was. But it didn't take long for them to say the words that put him fully at ease.

"Would you know anything about a round area of disturbed soil?"

As soon as those words came out of Officer Phillips' mouth, all Travis's concerns disappeared. They had taken what he said to them and twisted it around, thinking it was the key to make him give himself away. It was a tactic played out in every detective movie and TV show. Interrogations turned into twisted games of wordplay, with each side bandying for dominance. So often that was what tripped somebody up. They thought they were too smart, that they were the ones manipulating. In the end, they chose a word or gave away a detail without ever realizing they did it. They told a secret on themselves. Some didn't even realize it until it was brought back on them. Presented like on a platter. Then there was nowhere to run. Nothing the suspect could do.

But then there were some who did it on purpose. They dangled little bits of information, tiny details or hints, thinking no one would ever catch on. They thrived on watching the investigators squirm and knowing they held them in their hands.

In a way, Travis felt like that. He was guiding them along, just as he had been since the very first night. They didn't realize he had been crafting the situation since well before that. No one did. No one ever would. There was no trace because he left none. There was nothing to follow because he didn't lead anywhere. Not until he decided to. When he was ready, and only then, he laid the trail in front of them. All they had to do was follow it.

When Officer Phillips mentioned the circular patch of disrupted soil, Travis knew they were losing grip. She wanted desperately to hang on to him. She had been trying to dig hooks into him since the first time she looked at him. There was never sympathy in her eyes. Her words weren't reassuring. She said what she had to, but it wasn't sincere. When she mentioned the circular patch, what small grasp she might have had on him disappeared. She was caught. As much as she had been chasing him, he had been chasing her. He wanted to know what she did and what she was thinking. He wanted to see into her and watch her ideas unravel. Now he knew the thread was gone.

He was the one who mentioned the possibility of a fire pit. Many years before, when the property was more popular, and he had a family who could share the same space for any length of time, they would camp out on that land. They always saw evidence of others who came that way. There were signs, of course. Posted markers boldly declaring that this land was private property and for tres- passers to keep out. Most did. Others didn't. The family rarely knew.

It only became a problem once. Two travelers who thought they left society behind. They walked out onto the land with the thought of nothing else to burden them. They shed the responsibilities and laws they believed held them back and ventured into the unknown. Wild and free, drunk on dreams of glory. But it was not to be. Instead, the alcohol that warmed their veins also quieted their minds and dulled their instincts. They drifted away on it, asleep beside the fire that consumed them.

Travis found their bodies when the snow melted.

But that would mean nothing to the investigators. The burn pit scorched the ground, but it didn't go deep. Those campers didn't know enough to dig out a space for their fire. They'd just let it jump from the wood and onto the grass, where it burned wild and free until the rain stopped it. There could have been so much more damage. Directionless lives seemed like a small price to pay.

Officer Phillips thought she caught him when he mentioned the burn pit. She thought he walked himself right into uncovering the truth. Only she didn't know there was no circle. She didn't know the disrupted soil was far away from that spot. Months ago, it wouldn't have looked only like loose, upturned soil and instead like solid rock. Cracking through the stone was much harder than putting it there, to begin with.

So, now they could find the soil. Now they could find the strange segment of ground that had been dug deep then filled in again. It would mean nothing. They could question him about the burn. They could question him about the land. He was still calm. This would all work out. It wasn't exactly part of the plan as he had it originally, but it was going to be fine.

They knew nothing. They would always know nothing. There was nothing to know.

CHAPTER THIRTY-TWO

NOW

"It's good to see you back," the therapist says with a smile.

Her name is Katherine, but I never call her that. Just referring to her as The Therapist makes me feel less strange about the interaction. When I think of her by her name, it turns her into a person, someone I should be familiar with and have a relationship with beyond the small room where I'm expected to open up to her. This way, while I know she's human and her own entity, I get to pretend she only exists here in the office. If her entire life is centered only on being here and listening, then I don't feel as awkward. I don't become as defensive.

She's still trying to crack me open and find what's inside. Everything she says is another tiny cut, an invisible incision to help her find her way deeper within me where she could find my gears and thoughts, my batteries and blood.

I nod in response to the greeting. I don't really have one to give back to her. It's nice to be back near headquarters, to see the people who got compartmentalized when I shifted my life to Sherwood. It was nice to walk into my house last night and see it just as it was when I left, preserved and protected by Bellamy's regular visits. And I'm looking forward to having lunch with Eric when I finally make it out of here. Good to be back here, in this office, on this couch? I'm not quite at that place.

"It's been a while since we've talked. What made you decide to visit? Not that I'm complaining, of course."

She smiles and tosses her head to the side in that choreographed way that says she's trying to be friendly and casual, to put me at ease. But we don't know each other. It's one thing to be cordial and even friendly with new people, trying to build up a rapport, or even testing what it might be like to be actual friends and see if it fits. Like walking into the Ice Cream Palace in Sherwood and using those little bitty spoons to taste the flavors. It's somehow harder to pretend that sort of comfortable relationship over and over with someone you will never have a true friendship with. Especially when that person knows dark inner details of your life. It's like tasting a layered ice cream, but the spoon is so tiny you only get one of the flavors every time.

She wasn't always this way with me. She's tried out various different ways to talk to me, different mannerisms and attitudes. She's sampling me, too. She wants to figure out which is the one that's going to reach me. As if one of these times she's going to hit on the type of person I need her to be and I'll split like a geode.

"I'm here because Sam thinks I should talk to you," I say.

There's no reason to lie or to shine up the excuse, so it doesn't seem so stark. A therapist's office is nothing if not a place for honesty.

"Sam?" she asks.

"I told you about him when we spoke about Sherwood," I tell her.

Knowing I won't rise to her bait, she nods.

"The sheriff. And how is your relationship with Sam going?" she asks.

"Well enough for him to think I need to be here. I'm hoping knowing I've come back and talked to you will make him back off."

She seems taken aback by the bluntness of the statement.

"Back off?" she asks, wanting clarification.

"He thinks I'm losing touch with reality because I haven't been sleeping well."

"Just because you haven't been sleeping well?"

I look at her. At the woman sitting across from me, her prim legs in semi-sheer black pantyhose folded at the knee, a pen poised at the ready to capture anything interesting I might have to say on the yellow legal pad on her lap. I wonder what sitting here talking to her is supposed to do. What Sam thinks is going to happen if I pour it all out to her.

I guess I have to try.

"Some things have happened in the last few weeks, but no one seems to realize they're happening but me," I start. "Now Sam is getting really wary of me and doesn't believe anything I'm telling him. It's not that he thinks I'm lying. At least, I don't think he's gotten to that point yet. He just thinks my brain is slipping and I'm living in delusions."

"Can you explain that to me a bit better?"

Her fingers almost twitch in anticipation on the pen. It's like they know I'm about to say something they will want to document.

"I'm sure you read about the incident with the cult a couple months ago," I say.

It's not a question. I know she has. Everyone has. Discretion is not Creagan's strong suit when he has something to crow about, and the infiltration and takedown of one of the largest and most dangerous cults in the country by one of his agents had him climbing up on the roost and fluffing his feathers for days. The fact that I wasn't an active agent at the time and was investigating a murder, not the cult itself, didn't seem to take away any of his swagger.

"I did. Would you like to talk about that?" she asks.

"No," I sigh. "But it's a good starting place."

I delve into the story. She listens silently as I tell her about my kidnapping, the way they tried to erase my name and sense of self, and the way I barely escaped. I tell her about Ruby, and her disappearance, and the noose hanging from the door at the fairgrounds. About getting trapped in the hotel and the mysterious illness that left Nicole dead. When I finish, she continues to stare at me for a few seconds as if she's waiting for me to add something. Finally, she speaks.

"And you believe all these things are linked?" she asks.

"I feel like they have to be," I offer. "That's too many coincidences. It's too many things happening, one right after the other, for them to not have something to do with each other. It just seems like I'm the only one who can see that."

"Tell me more about Ruby Baker," she says.

I let out a breath. "What do you want to know?"

"Everything you do," she tells me.

"I really don't know much. I only met her three, maybe four times. She just moved into town after running away from a severely abusive ex-boyfriend. Frank was his name. She got with him after a divorce. Her ex-husband wasn't abusive, but he didn't thrill her, I guess. She was nice, but she seemed, I don't know how to put it... fragile? Like, even when she was smiling and talking to me like everything was fine, that happiness and enthusiasm was a thin layer over her, just ready to shatter at any second. I don't know if that makes any sense. I hoped she would get stronger over time. Maybe being in Sherwood and getting a chance to have a fresh start would make her more confident. As soon as I saw her get attacked through the window, the first thing I thought was her ex. I figure he found her and wanted his revenge for her leaving him."

"And you say no one else met her? None of your neighbors or anyone else in town?" she asks.

"No. The first time we met, she told me she had been going up and down the street meeting everybody, but when I went to talk to them after she disappeared, they said they hadn't seen anybody in that house and no woman had come to their houses to introduce herself. When I spoke to the company that manages the property, they said no one has shown any interest in it for years. She couldn't be renting it because it wasn't for rent, it was for sale. And when we went inside, there was no sign of anybody ever being in there. She baked me a cake, but the oven was brand new and had never been used."

"And what do you think about that?" she encourages.

"I really don't know. I do know I saw her. I met her. She was in my house. I gave her a cup of sugar, and she joked she was really only borrowing it when she came back with the cake. I still have her cake stand. I don't understand what could possibly have happened. But I didn't just make her up like some twisted imaginary friend," I insist.

"But that's what other people think," she says.

"That's certainly what some of the people in Sherwood think. and I think it's what Sam's starting to think, too. And if it was just Ruby, maybe I'd think the same thing. It's a lot easier to explain it away as the stress scrambling my mind," I point out.

"Easier than what?" she asks. "What's the alternative?"

"Admitting something horrible happened? Realizing there's some common thread to all this and no one is willing to believe it's happening, much less help me?"

"And if that's the case?" she asks.

"What do you mean?"

"If there is a continuous thread that links all of these incidents together, but you still can't make anyone believe you, would you still pursue it? Would you be willing to face that scrutiny and judgment in order to find out what was happening and stop it?"

I don't hesitate. My answer doesn't take even a moment of thought.

"Absolutely."

"Just be careful, Emma. Sometimes it's hard to see yourself, and you have to trust that the people around you still can."

CHAPTER THIRTY-THREE

E ric is waiting for me outside the office when my
appointment is over.

"So, what did the doc say?" he asks. "Does she think she
can glue your broken little brain back together?"

I roll my eyes at him as I walk past. A cold wind makes me pull my
coat tighter around myself, the gesture reminding me of Ruby and her
sweaters.

"Let's make jokes about that when all this is over," I mutter.

Eric slings his arm around my shoulders. "Come on, Emma. You
don't think I actually believe you've lost it, do you?"

I sigh. "Hold that thought until you've heard the whole story."

He brings me to lunch at a favorite place of mine, a hole-in-the-
wall spot that serves the most incredible Indian food. The warm, spicy
smell that fills my lungs with my first step into the restaurant feels
like home. It's moments like this when the questions start coming
back, and I wonder about my future. I'm dangling directly over two
lives, both as much mine as the other, both places home in their own
ways.

We sit in one of the cozy booths, and seconds later, a grinning
waiter brings over the bread service I have many times declared I

could live on. A basket of warm naan and onion kulcha sits beside a wooden board with several bowls of various accompaniments. I tear off a piece of the naan and dip it into garlicky pickle dip. It's just as delicious as I remember, and I sink back in my seat just to enjoy a moment of peace.

"You want to tell me what brought you all the way back here to see the therapist you never wanted to talk to in the first place, or should I just start jumping to wild conclusions?" Eric asks after a few seconds.

The waiter comes back to the side of the table, and we order our lunch. When he walks away, I turn back to Eric.

"What did Bellamy tell you?" I ask.

He looks at me like he's going to protest, but then nods, admitting they talked about the situation with Ruby. For some people, knowing their best friends are talking about them behind their back would be upsetting. I'm just glad I don't have to go through the entire story again. I don't want to revisit every little detail and wait for his reaction. Knowing he already has the foundation of the story is reassuring. It not only saves me from the spiel, but it means it's been percolating in his mind. Even if it hasn't taken up the same type of immediate, conscious thought as it has for me, his brilliant brain has pulled it back into its dark recesses and has been dismantling it in the background.

"It wouldn't be the first time someone covered up a murder by making a person simply disappear," he offers through a mouthful. "But I've never heard of someone never existing in the first place. Why would you be the only person she met?"

"I don't know. But there's a reason behind it, and it has to do with everything else that's going on. Someone is trying to tell me something, Eric."

I stare at my fingers drumming on the top of the table for a few seconds, then look up at him again. "Is there a way to remotely control someone's cell phone? I'm not talking tracking it or turning it off during dinner. I mean, can someone actually take over another person's phone without that person knowing it?"

"I'm not sure what you're asking," he tells me.

"Did Bellamy tell you about the hotel?"

"She said you got stuck in an elevator shaft," he frowns.

"That's the Reader's Digest abridged version of it, but we'll go with it. Sam got called for a break-in and asked if I wanted to go, but I stayed home. A little while later, I got a text from him saying he needed me, then another giving me the address. When I went to the address, it was a rundown hotel that's been abandoned past the edge of town for decades. I got more text messages telling me to come inside, then when I was in there, I called him. I swear, I heard his phone ringing. That's when I went to follow the sound and I got pushed into the elevator shaft. But when I tried to call him again, my phone stopped. It wouldn't even turn on. It had a full charge, so there's no reason it should have done that. When Sam finally showed up, he told me he didn't send those messages, and they weren't on his phone or mine anymore. And as soon as I got out of there, my phone worked again. But they were there. And someone was in that hotel with me."

"And you know it wasn't Sam?" he asks.

"Is that one of the wild conclusions you're jumping to, or do you genuinely believe he would do something like this?" I ask.

"I'm just going through the facts."

I think of the thimble tucked far away in the back of a drawer. That thimble represents a time when I lost myself because I didn't want to believe in my heart what my mind already knew. Keeping the memento was promising myself I would never do that again. And I haven't. That's not what's happening this time.

"It couldn't have been Sam. Someone pushed me into that elevator shaft, and I could hear them coming after me. But when I got outside, his car came into the parking lot. There's no way he could have done both. But I knew it wasn't him. I went inside because I thought he was in there alone and might need me. I even started to leave but stayed because I called his phone and heard it ringing deeper in the hotel. It scared me. I thought something might have happened to him. I didn't believe there was any way he could have hurt me, but seeing him come into the parking lot confirmed it. The timing makes it impossible. But those messages. And the phone ringing. I don't understand how that happened. There's no way I would have known to go to that hotel if I didn't get the address. But neither one of our phones have the messages anymore."

"There is technology that can make that possible. There are apps that can disguise phone numbers, so it looks like one person is calling or sending a message when it's actually someone else. And there are others that can be used to brick the phone. It makes it unusable. Essentially, those programs put the phone under the control of whoever is controlling the app."

"But how could that happen? Wouldn't a program like that have to be installed onto my phone in order to work?" I ask.

"Yeah," Eric nods. "Someone would have to install the app in order to use it."

"But I have my phone with me all the time. Nobody has access to it."

"Wasn't it lost for a while?" he asks.

"For about a day," I confirm. "But I was at home the entire time, and the only person who was there with me for any part of it was Ruby."

"There's a connection. Is it possible she could have had anything to do with it?"

"I had it when she was at my house the first time, then found it in my laundry room before she came back," I explain.

"So, you just need to convince Sam your phone was taken and modified by a woman who doesn't exist and who wasn't there to put it back," Eric summarizes. "Simple."

"Exactly." I take a bite of my curry and let my thoughts tumble around as the flavors roll across my tongue. "The thing is, that's the simple part. What does it have to do with Pamela getting run off the road and lying about it? Or Nicole dying?"

"You're sure they're connected?"

"I'm convinced whoever was in that hotel with me killed Ruby and covered it up. Now they're playing a game with me, and I don't know the rules. My therapist told me to be careful and to trust other people to see me when I lost sight of myself. I think that's the problem."

"What do you mean?" Eric asks.

"I've thought so much about the house across the street, and what people did or didn't see there. I think it's time I started to see Ruby instead." I stand up and lean over to hug Eric. "Thank you for lunch. And for the help with the phone. I'll call you."

"You didn't even finish. Where are you going?" he asks, gesturing to my half-full plate.

"I need to get back to Sherwood. It's time to get to know my imaginary friend."

As I move to put my coat on, the bottom of my sweater lifts and Eric's eyes lock on my hip.

"Emma," he starts.

Without a word, I tug my sweater down and walk out of the restaurant. I don't owe him answers. He doesn't need to know I could have just as easily called my therapist rather than driving two hours from Sherwood.

Or that I came into town last night after spending the evening at the range where I trained the first time my father put a gun in my hands.

CHAPTER THIRTY-FOUR

I don't want to be inside the house when I get back to Sherwood. I'm drawn back out onto the porch. Wrapped in a quilt my grandmother made before I was born, I sit cross-legged on a wicker loveseat to one side of my front door with my computer in my lap.

I'm scrolling slowly through results from typing Ruby's name into every search engine there is. The name is there, but none of the images are her.

It's not completely unfathomable that she wouldn't have social media, or that it would be under a fake name. Someone who's gone through what she did would have plenty of reasons to not want to be so easily found. She mentioned her ex-boyfriend Frank isolating her from everyone else around her, which could easily have meant stopping her from having any online presence. Even after she broke away from him, I can imagine her hesitating to open herself up to the murky world of the internet. It's hard to know who you'll find that you can actually trust, or who might find you.

Thinking about her ex reminds me that I never asked if Baker was her married name, or if she took back her maiden name after her divorce. My mind goes back to her sitting in my kitchen, telling me about the life she left behind, trying to remember every detail of our conversation. I remember her telling me her husband's name was James. I type it into the search bar alongside her name, adding the name of her hometown. I'm hoping tossing together as many pieces of her as I can, will finally be what it takes to find her.

No sooner do I hit enter than I realize I'm right. I just wasn't prepared for what finally finding Ruby would mean.

The sound of my phone ringing on the wicker beside me startles me. I just barely catch my computer before it slips off my lap. I'm still staring at my computer screen when I answer the phone.

"Hello?"

"Emma, it's me," Bellamy chirps. "I might have found something, and I wanted to tell you about it. I went to the funeral home today."

The words hit a wall in my brain, bouncing off the screen in front of me and mixing with the words I'm reading off it, so I'm not sure what was actually said.

"Wait, what?" I ask. "I'm sorry. I'm… never mind. Say that again."

"The funeral home, Emma. I told you I was going to ask around at funeral homes about your mother."

"That's right," I say, rubbing my fingers into my eyelids.

"Are you okay? Is something going on?" she asks.

"No. Go ahead. What did you find out?"

"That's the thing. Not much. I went to all the funeral homes in the area around the house where your family lived and just started asking. But I didn't get very far. They were all pretty closed up and didn't want to answer any questions because I'm not next of kin. I tried to convince them it's been so long that it would be alright and that I wasn't looking for any really personal information, but it didn't help. So, I figured I might have skipped a step, and I went backwards. I headed to the newspaper office and looked through old issues from the year you turned twelve. That's the one bit of information we are absolutely sure about," she says.

"Yes," I told her. "I might not remember everything about being young, but I know she died before my twelfth birthday."

"Exactly. So that gave me a narrowed down timeline. I went through all the issues and didn't find anything. Then I found out there was a newspaper during that time that is now defunct. I had to go to the library and see the microfilm. But I found it."

"You did?" I ask, my attention finally pulled away from the computer.

"Yes. And here's the thing. You were right. Her date of death is listed as April 17th, 2003, just as you said. It also mentioned the funeral home where her viewing was being held," she says.

I shake my head, squeezing my eyes against the thought of it.

"She didn't have a viewing," I say. "She was immediately cremated."

"As you've told me. Which intrigued me, so I went back to the funeral home with a copy of the information, hoping that might persuade them a little. But they still wouldn't talk. I figured I was going to need something else and was about to leave, but as soon as the funeral director walked out of the room, another attendant came up to me. He's only been working there for a few months, so he obviously didn't have any information you could give me about your mother, but he told me I was not the first person to come by recently and ask about her."

"Why would somebody else be asking about my mother's funeral?" I frown.

"He didn't know. All he could tell me was a man came by a couple of weeks ago and spoke to the owner. I spoke to the owner, too, but the attendant specifically said that man was in the office with him for much longer than I was, and they kept the door closed the entire time. But that's not the strangest thing about it. Right before he left, the man walked up to that attendant and said he wanted it to sign the condolence book."

"That's an odd request," I note. "Was he there for a viewing or funeral, and just stopped by to ask about my mother?"

"No. He walked in, spoke to the director, then asked to sign the condolence book," Bellamy tells me.

"Did he let you see it?" I asked.

"He did. I looked over every signature in that book around the time he remembered that man coming in, and one name in particular jumped out at me. Gregory Ronald Bailey."

She says each name slowly, enunciating the syllables to make sure it gets through to me. But I didn't need the emphasis. The shock and confusion burst behind my eyes like a blow to the head.

"Greg Bailey," I say. "But his middle name is Ryan, not Ronald."

"I know, but what if that was the point? What if he signed his name wrong on purpose? Who else do you know with that name?" she asks.

It only takes a few seconds for the realization to hit me.

"Ron Murdock." The man who dropped dead on my porch in Feathered Nest a few months ago after delivering a message to me while I was supposed to be undercover.

She makes an affirming sound, and I shake my head. "What the hell is going on?"

"What do you mean?"

It's not Bellamy's voice, but Sam's. I look up and see him walking slowly up the sidewalk toward me.

"B, I've gotta go. Thank you for calling me. Let me know if you find out anything else," I tell her. "Love you."

"I will. There are a few more things I want to check out. Love you too."

I press the button to end the call and set the computer on the small table in front of me, lowering the screen slightly so Sam can't see my research.

"Is it alright that I'm here?" he asks, gesturing at the porch while hesitating with one boot on the bottom step.

"Of course," I nod.

"Was that Bellamy?" he asks. "Is everything okay?"

He walks up the steps and leans against the post.

"Yeah, that was her. Um," I glance down at my phone, then back at Sam, wondering how much to share with him. We haven't spoken since I left the hospital parking lot a few days ago, and I'm not sure he wants to get tossed into the fray with me. "She's actually in Florida looking into my mother's death."

"She is?"

"Remember, I told you she found the person who made the necklaces."

"That seems like a pretty tenuous reason to go all the way to Florida," he points out.

An irrational amount of frustration rushes up inside me.

"You know what? Don't worry about it. Is there something I can do for you?" I ask.

"No. We just haven't talked. I wanted to check on you. I'm sorry that came out like that. Tell me what's going on."

I tell him about the discrepancy with my mother's death and Bellamy's visit to the funeral home. He seems intrigued by the potential link between the strange middle name and Ron Murdock, but not entirely convinced.

"It could be someone with the same name," he offers. "Greg Bailey isn't exactly an outlandish name."

"No, it's not. I'm sure there are plenty of others. There may even be a few right there in the area. But what are the chances someone with the same name as my missing ex-boyfriend would go to the funeral home asking about my mother's death?" I ask.

He gives a relenting nod. "That would be a pretty extraordinary coincidence."

"Yeah. There seem to be a lot of those going around recently," I mutter, adjusting the quilt around my shoulders.

There's a tense silence for too long, and it's finally Sam who breaks it.

"Let's go ahead and say that it really is Greg, and he was trying to send you some kind of message. How would he even know about Ron Murdock?"

I sigh. "That one I can't explain. He had already been missing for almost a year by the time Murdock was killed."

"Do you think Greg could have killed him?" Sam asks. "And didn't you say you don't think Ron Murdock was even the man's actual name?"

"I don't know. I really don't. It's all just... a lot," I tell him. I sigh. "Can we change the subject? How has work been?"

"Well, they finished the official investigation into Nicole's death."

CHAPTER THIRTY-FIVE

"They finished the investigation already?" I ask. "That didn't take long."

"Apparently, it would have been a lot longer if they had to identify a foodborne pathogen. But like you said, that's not what it was," Sam explains. "They tested all the food at Pearl's and all the ingredients still present for a whole host of pathogens but concluded it wasn't any of them. The issue wasn't one of food safety."

"Then what was it?"

"All the victims' symptoms were pretty severe, but they didn't last too long. Most who went into the hospital in apparently bad condition got better within just a couple of hours. The vast majority were recovered and able to go home the next day. Only very few continued to have lingering symptoms. Severe stomach cramps, muscle contractions, vomiting. A couple of the patients showed heartbeat disruptions, and that's what tipped off the doctors. It was the effects of emetine."

"Emetine?" I repeat. "I've heard that before. As in ipecac?"

"One and the same. Some of the food was still around from being tested, so they tested it for emetine, and there it was. Somebody must have thought it was a good idea for a funny joke but didn't realize how severe the effect would be."

"So, not food poisoning. Just good old-fashioned regular poisoning," I say.

"You can put it that way," he says.

"Where was it? What food was it in? Not everybody was affected."

"The only place they were able to find it was in the gravy. Apparently, a lot of people were in the mood for biscuits and gravy that day, which is why so many were people affected."

I look at Sam incredulously.

"A lot of people were in the mood for it, including us. We both ate most of what was on our plates, but neither one of us had any symptoms. Neither did Jacqueline. I saw her table. Both she and Nicole were eating biscuits and gravy, but Jacqueline didn't have any symptoms at all. That still doesn't explain what happened to Nicole. The doctors said she died of anaphylactic shock. How is that possible when there weren't any hazelnuts in the restaurant?"

"I don't know," he shrugs. "We're still hoping to figure that out. I did want to let you know that there's going to be a visitation for her in the morning. I would understand if you don't want to go…"

"I want to go," I interrupt.

"Are you sure?" he asks.

"Sam, I was with her mother while Violet tried to save her life. The least I can do is pay my respects."

"The public hours are early because Jacqueline wants a few private hours just for the family before the closed memorial service tomorrow. If you want to ride with me, I'll bring you."

"Sure," I tell him. "Did you send people back to the hotel?"

The question is awkward, tacked on to the end of the conversation, but he hasn't mentioned the incident, and I need to know. I can't just let him gloss over it and continue to pretend like nothing happened when I know for a fact it did.

"Yes," he tells me. "I told you I would, so I did."

"And?" I asked.

"Nothing. They didn't find anything, Emma. They searched the entire area around the hotel. They made a five-mile radius, far further than a person could have walked in the time between us leaving and the team getting there. There was no sign of anyone who could have done what you described," he tells me.

"Someone was in that hotel," I tell him for what feels like the thousandth time. "I heard footsteps and the phone ringing. And somebody knocked me down into that elevator shaft. There was somebody there. They were chasing me when I got out and found you."

"It's an old, nearly crumbling building," he says. "I'm not going to lie and say there haven't been times when I thought it was downright creepy. Buildings like that play tricks with your head. They can make noise and cast shadows. It's easy to get it confused and think something's happening when it really isn't."

"I don't need you to explain perception to me," I tell him. "This isn't the first time I've been in an abandoned building. And trust me, it wasn't the foundation settling or the walls cracking that was playing tricks with my head."

"They looked, Emma. They searched as far as they could. If there was someone in that hotel who ran, they would have found him. I hate that you went through whatever you did, and I wasn't there to help you. You were obviously scared, but you were also in pain. You know what pain can do to your thoughts. Getting hurt only heightened your fear and made you interpret things wrong."

"I didn't hurt my ankle until I was climbing out of that elevator, and whoever the hell was in there was coming down after me. I didn't need anything to heighten my fear at that point. I was pretty well scared shitless already," I retort, anger flaring back up again.

"Again, I'm sorry you went through what you did. I'm sorry whatever miscommunication happened that led you there and put you in that type of position. I want to believe what you're saying because then there'd be somebody to blame."

"I don't think you do," I say.

"Why would you say that?" he asks, his face shocked.

"Because if you did, you would try harder."

The tension between us is almost tangible. I want it to go away

193

and go back to the way we were. But I'm still struggling with Sam not fully trusting me and believing what I tell him. He comes and sits beside me, turning so he can look into my face.

"Emma, I'm not against you. I'm right here. Right beside you. And that's where I want to be. I'm not trying to push you away or make you feel like I don't care. I'm doing everything I can to help you figure this out, but I'm at a loss. I don't know what you expect me to do," he says.

"I expect you to trust me," I say. "To help me."

"I do trust you, just like I always have. But I can't help you with something I haven't seen or experienced."

"You have experienced it, Sam. You were there when I found the noose. You were there when I barely got out of the hotel. And you were there when everyone got sick."

"You found a prop at an old haunted house. I know you were terrified in that hotel. I still don't understand how you got there, but it was an accident. The incident at Pearl's was a prank. It went wrong, but that's all it was," he says.

"I'm sure Jacqueline agrees it was a hell of a prank," I spit, standing and gathering my things to go back inside.

Sam reaches for my hand as I gather the quilt around me, but I pull away.

"Emma…"

"I'll drive myself to the visitation."

CHAPTER THIRTY-SIX

HIM

"You know, I thought we had an understanding. From the very beginning, I told you exactly what I needed from you, and promised if you just fulfilled those things for me, everything would work out fine. Didn't I?"

The man stretched on the floor in front of him growled through gritted teeth as the hot piece of metal sliced through his skin. It was sharp enough to cut through but kept just dull enough to need pressure.

He called this man Lamb. He was so easily led. Not that he believed it would be very difficult to persuade him. He watched him for weeks, getting accustomed to his patterns and knowing his habits. In that time, he learned there was little change from day to day in his life. He kept to his schedule. He followed the same routes. He ate the same foods. By the second week, he could predict nearly every move Lamb was going to make. There were few surprises. And even when there was a change, when something shifted, or he was forced to contend with something new in his path, Lamb managed it with a steady calm, then went back to his routine.

But there was an exception. He never stepped away from the call of duty. When there was a need, he didn't hesitate. He did as he was told and followed through to the fullest of his ability. And it was those abilities that surprised him most about Lamb. Quiet and unextraordinary on the surface, he hid a brilliant mind and sharp physical skills that made him an asset. He only needed to draw him in. And there was only one way he was going to do that. It was immediately obvious. And immediately effective.

"Yes, I will admit, I deceived you at first. But I didn't really lie. Not fully. I told you exactly who I was, you only thought something else. That's because you didn't know the truth. Just like Emma doesn't. But she will. That's the point of this. Don't you remember that? Don't you want to protect her? Make sure she has a good life? Keep her away from the threats and dangers? She doesn't know. It's up to me to keep her safe, and I entrusted you to help me."

"I did help you," Lamb hissed.

"But then you lied to me."

"No, I didn't."

The metal cut in again, making another notch in already blood-stained skin.

"How did you do it?" he asked.

"I didn't," Lamb protested. "I don't know how it happened."

Another cut. It would be a slow process for Lamb. It didn't have to be that way. It could have been so much simpler. He was willing to honor Lamb, to raise him up above even those who had proven themselves for so long. Once he was away from Emma, there was nothing to hold against Lamb. His skills, knowledge, and abilities would be so helpful, incredibly valuable to the mission. Both his dreams of Emma and the larger mission they followed each day. If only it had been as easy to convince him of the gift as it was to be welcomed into the ranks. Lamb would have earned an outline on his back rather than the row of notches in his skin.

But he would keep trying. He could be forgiving. He knew not everyone came naturally to the mission. Some wouldn't understand the value they could have. They would resist. He didn't give up easily.

He rarely threw his recruited away. And he wouldn't throw Lamb away. There was still worth in him. Still value. He just needed to train him and bring him fully into the fold, so he understood his place and was ready to give himself wholly to the mission.

He had never failed to break a recruit. One way or another.

CHAPTER THIRTY-SEVEN

I can't be on the porch anymore. What felt like freedom when I first got home and took my place on the wicker couch now feels like exposure. I walk into my house, not caring if Sam follows me. He does and closes the front door behind him, turning the lock in place and checking it twice. It's a habit I've noticed he picked up in the last several months. I know for a fact he didn't used to do that. When we were younger, he never locked the door. His mother used to tease him that he felt like he was insulting the people around him if he kept his house secured. Even as a sheriff, he always kept it unlocked, to prove some point to the people that the town was safe.

Now he grapples with me regularly, trying to convince me to add more locks to my doors even after I relented and agreed to an alarm on my windows and back door.

My computer comes with me into my bedroom. I open it the rest of the way and put it on my bed, scanning the screen again. There's no mistaking what I'm seeing. It's not a different woman with the same name. It's not a mistake. It's a picture of Ruby, smiling at the camera from a face surrounded by a cloud of dark curls. She looks over one shoulder with a lovely grin, clad in a cream-colored floral dress. The picture is old, obviously from when she was much younger and hadn't yet had her run-in with Frank, who stole her security, her independence, the flowers on her clothes, and the light in her eyes. I thought he stole her life. But the words on the screen tell me there wasn't one to steal.

She was buried over a year ago.

"Emma, I have to go."

"I'll see you tomorrow," I tell him.

There's silence on the other side of the door. I can almost see him standing there, considering what to say next.

"Alright," he finally says.

I hear him walk away and the door close behind him. I sit down on the bed and pull my computer closer. Another scan through the search results brings up an obituary. Then a memorial page. My stomach turns. They're all there. They're all her. By all signs, I lent sugar to a dead woman.

The more I read, the more the shaking feeling in my chest hardens. The more my blood runs cold. I grab my phone and make a call, but there's no answer. Not willing to wait, I rush out to my car and head into town. As soon as I pull into the Lionheart parking lot, I notice the windows are dark.

It's too early for them to be closed. I sit and wait for half an hour before pulling out of the lot and driving over to Pearl's Diner. It's good to see several people filling the tables. I worried her business would suffer after the scare, but it looks like the people of Sherwood are trickling back. Pearl gives me a weary smile when she sees me come in. She finishes wiping off a table and walks over.

"Hey, there, Emma," she says, her voice softer and less animated than it has always been. "Dinner alone tonight?"

"No, actually. I just wanted to ask you a couple of things," I say.

She looks at me strangely.

"I thought the investigation was over," she frowns.

"Oh, it is," I assure her. "This is just for me."

She nods. "What can I help you with?"

"I've been thinking about Nicole, the girl who died after... what happened the other day."

I want to say it as gently as I can, but there's no careful way to approach it. Pearl nods again. She looks at her hands resting on the counter I'm standing beside and pulls at her towel.

"That poor girl. So sweet. She was doing so well in college and had all these plans," she says.

"You knew her well?" I ask.

"I know everyone in this town, honey. But there was definitely something special about Nikki. She had her whole life ahead of her. She would have done so much."

"I'm so sorry," I say.

"I just don't understand it. Jacqueline told me they say she died of her allergy, but I never have hazelnuts around here. I don't like them, and they're not something anyone has asked for. So, how did she end up with enough to kill her?" Pearl asks.

"They're sure she didn't have an allergy to anything else?" I ask.

"Yes. They had a terrible time when she was younger, trying to figure out all her sensitivities. She has seasonal allergies and topical allergies as well. But nothing that's going to be that serious. I remember Jackie telling me years ago, they tested just about every food you can think of. The only one that causes problems for her was hazelnuts," Pearl explains.

"But you can develop allergies to things you weren't allergic to before," I say.

"It's possible. But there's nothing here she hasn't eaten dozens of times before. She always orders the same thing."

"Biscuits and gravy," I say, nodding.

"Yes. And that's the same recipe my great-grandmother passed down. It hasn't changed."

"Can you do one more thing for me?"

"What's that?"

"Will you show me the kitchen?" I ask.

"The kitchen?" Pearl asks.

"Yes. I just want to see it."

She gives a slight shrug and leads me through the restaurant and into the kitchen.

"It's clean," she says. "I always keep it clean. Inspector has been here three times since that day, and it's always spotless."

"Oh, I know," I tell her. "That wasn't what I wanted to check."

"Then, what were you looking for?" she asks.

"I wanted to see if there was a way someone could get in here without going through the main restaurant."

"There's the back door," Pearl says, gesturing behind the grill to an open storage space and the narrow white door at the far end.

"Do you mind if I look?"

"Go right ahead," she says. "It's just a door. Leads out to the alley. Nothing but a few parking spots for staff and the dumpsters out there."

We walk through the kitchen, and the fast-moving cooks look up with tight smiles. I go to the door and peer out. At first, I only notice a pile of wooden pallets waiting to be picked up by the produce delivery company and the large dumpster to the side. Then a flash of light catches my eye, and I step further out into the gravel alley. I make my way around the dumpster, and there it is. A green sports car. I point at it and glance back over at Pearl.

"Who does that belong to?" I ask.

"That silly little green thing?" she asks. "That's my grandson's. You know Kevin."

He must have heard his grandmother talking about him because a second later I see the tall redhead step out the door and into the November sunlight.

"Hey, Emma," he says.

Kevin is one of those people from Sherwood who I still have locked in a different era in my mind. To me, he's the senior baseball player half the girls in my freshman class had a crush on, then the college player who came home with a broken leg from sliding too hard into a base. In that one day, his entire future shifted. Visions of a career in professional baseball became veterinary school, and now he has a practice doing house calls for pets throughout the town.

"Kevin, I didn't even notice you in there. Does the diner have a furry mascot now who needs tending?" I ask.

He laughs and rubs his wet hands on his white apron.

"No. I'm just here helping Granny out," he says. "I just got here a few minutes ago."

"The diner is getting so busy, and I've been short staffed. Seems a lot of young people these days don't have much interest in sticking around town after high school, so I end up without people to do the dishwashing and short-order cooking. Some of my staff have been with me since before you were born, but I always have a slot or two empty," she says.

"Which means I get to step in," Kevin says, wrapping his arm around her. The tiny woman looks swamped next to her youngest grandson. "In between birthing puppies and splinting sprained tails, I'm here doing dishes and flipping pancakes."

"A man of multiple talents," I smile, then point at the car. "Have you had that car for a while?"

"A few months," he says. "I'm hitting the midlife crisis a little early, so I have the time to pay it off."

We head back into the kitchen, and I start toward the front of the restaurant but notice another small door. It's tucked into the corner off to the side of the dishwashing station.

"What's that?" I ask, pointing at it.

"Staff entrance to the bathroom," Pearl explains. "That way, we don't have to go all the way out."

I nod. "Convenient. Well, thank you for letting me see the kitchen and for answering my questions."

"I hope I helped," Pearl says.

"You did," I assure her.

"If you need anything else, come on back."

"I will."

I climb into my car and head back to Lionheart. The lights are on again, and through the front window, I see Pamela sitting at her desk, scrolling through something on her computer. She looks up, but before she sees me, I pull out of the parking lot, heading home.

CHAPTER THIRTY-EIGHT

FOUR YEARS AGO

"But when?" she asked. "When can we stop sneaking around like this?"

"Soon," Travis told her.

"That's what you've been saying for months. When does soon come?"

"I don't know," he told her. "But it'll be soon. You just need to be patient."

"I have been being patient. I've been waiting this entire time. Haven't said a word. Haven't questioned anything. We should be celebrating. This is exactly what we wanted from the very beginning. Isn't it?"

He looked at Sarah for a hard second, then stepped up to her, cupping his hands around her jaw.

"Of course it is. I just have to be careful. Don't you understand that?"

"No, I don't. Why do you have to be careful? She's the one who left you. Nobody can look badly on you for moving on." She tilted her head to the side and looked at him, searching his face and trying to see beyond his calm exterior. "Unless you're hoping she really does come back. Is that it? Is everything you've been saying to me about finally being together just a lie? You were never going to leave her, and now that she's left you, you still won't move ahead with me."

"No," he said. "That's not it. I promise." He leaned down and kissed her. "You're right. This is a good thing, and we should be celebrating. But you have to understand, there are still people out there who don't know the truth about what happened. They refuse to think Mia just decided to walk away. They think they know her better than I did and are convinced she would never leave her entire life behind."

"I know," Sarah said. "I've seen them on the news. I don't get it. They stand there at that podium and sob and read out these dramatic statements about how much they miss her and want her to come home. But where were they when you had to take care of her because she wouldn't stop drinking? Or the time you had to bail her out of jail? Why didn't they help when she took so many drugs, she miscarried your baby?"

"People like to romanticize about people and things when they aren't around anymore. They spent so much time away from Mia and completely cut her out of their lives and didn't think anything of it. But now that she essentially did the same thing to them, they can't stand it. So, now they have a completely idealized version of her in their heads. They would rather think about her as being some sort of perfect angel, who was cruelly taken away from them, than admit they weren't enough for her to keep trying for. It's much easier to be the tormented family of a missing woman who constantly pleads for her return, than it is to have to admit your child or your sister or your aunt just genuinely doesn't want anything to do with you," he explained.

"But what does that have to do with me? With us?" Sarah asked.

"They want to make me out to be as bad a person as they possibly can. They've been doing it from the beginning. I'm used to it. It doesn't get to me anymore. But I don't want that for you. If they were to find out about you, about us, they would be relentless. You would never be able to walk out of your home even go to work without them hounding you," Travis said.

"Wouldn't you protect me?" she asked.

"Of course I would. I would do anything to protect you. That's what I'm doing right now. I can't be with you every second of the day, and I don't want to think anything's going to happen to you just because you're associated with me. You don't deserve to be dragged through the mud and made a public spectacle just because I love you."

"You do?" she asked.

"Yes," he said. "Of course I do. Why would you even have to ask that?"

"Because you've never said it before?"

Travis wrapped his arms around Sarah and pulled her up closer to him. He leaned down and gave her another soft kiss.

"Well, you're going to be hearing it all the time now. Mia has no idea the gift she gave us," he said.

Sarah laughed and wrapped her arms around his neck.

"Don't tell her. Maybe she'll come back just to spite you," she said.

Travis shook his head. "Don't you worry about that. It isn't going to happen."

He ducked his head down to kiss her again, but a sharp knock on his front door stopped him. Sarah looked at him with widened, frightened eyes, and he pushed her toward the back of the house.

"Who is that?" she hissed.

"Go into the bedroom. Shut the door," he whispered.

As soon as Sarah was out of the room, Travis crossed to the front door and opened it.

"Mr. Burke," Officer Philip said. "I hope this isn't a bad time."

"Not at all. Come on in," he said, gesturing for her to enter as he stepped out of the way.

They walked into the living room as they had done more than a dozen times before and took their customary seats. She stared at him. It's how she started all of these conversations. The length of her silence stretched a little more every time she showed up at the house. Travis stared back at her. He stayed steady. Calm.

"Mr. Burke, we recently uncovered a few things that may indicate your wife has crossed over into Canada. Can you think of any reason why she would want to do that?" the officer asked.

"Canada?" he frowned. He feigned thinking for a few seconds, then shook his head. "No. I have no idea why she would want to go there. I've never heard her mention wanting to travel there, and as far as I know, she doesn't have any family or friends in Canada, either."

The officer nodded. She looked down at her notepad even though she hadn't written anything.

"Alright. Well, thank you for your time," she stood and started for the door.

"That's it?" he asked, following her. "You're not going to tell me anything else? You just come in here saying Mia is in Canada, then drop it and leave?"

"We don't know for certain she is actually in Canada. It's just a lead we're following up on and wanted to get your insights. I don't want to share too much with you and get your hopes up. I assure you, if anything more concrete comes up, or if we have any other questions, we'll get back in touch. Until then, if you think of anything, even if you're not sure it actually has anything to do with it, or if you hear anything, call me immediately," she said.

"I will."

They walked toward the door and just before getting to it, Officer Phillips stopped and pivoted around to look at him. There was a slight smile on her face, but not enough to lift it fully.

"Oh, I wanted to mention to you now, that since there's reason to believe your wife left the state, and possibly the country, the department will be calling in further assistance from the FBI."

CHAPTER THIRTY-NINE

NOW

The parking lot for the funeral home is almost full when I pull in, just minutes after the open hours started. I scan the rows of cars, taking note of them and making as many connections between them and their owners as I recognize. My vigilance has kicked back up. My training to note everything happening around me has my instincts on full alert now. During my time in Sherwood, I tried to push those instincts down, but I'm not suppressing them anymore. As I pull into an open spot, I notice a red Miata parked diagonally from me.

Sam catches my eye from across the room as soon as I step inside. He walks up to me and leans down to kiss my cheek.

"Are you feeling better?" he asks.

"I wasn't feeling bad," I tell him.

"That's not what I meant," he says.

"I know what you meant."

On the other side of the room, I catch sight of Kevin. He's standing alone, nearly up against the wall. His hands grip a paper cup of coffee, and his face looks flushed.

"What are you looking at?" Sam asks.

"Kevin. Pearl's grandson," I whisper.

"What about him?" he asks.

"Does he seem to be acting strangely to you? He's just standing there alone, and he looks really upset."

"He's at a visitation for a funeral," Sam points out. "It's expected to be upset. Especially when the person died in your grandmother's restaurant."

"Possibly after eating something you cooked," I say.

"What?" he asks.

"I went to see Pearl yesterday to see if I could find out anything else."

"I told you the investigation was over," Sam says.

"The investigation into what made everybody sick, yes. But you still don't know who put the ipecac in the food or what caused Nicole's allergic reaction."

"And what did you find out?" he asks.

"Yes, Emma, what did you find out?"

I close my eyes, and my shoulders drop as I try to control the surge of rage that rushes up inside me.

"Pamela, this isn't the time," Sam says.

"I think you're absolutely right, Sam," she says, coming around me so she can stand beside Sam and cut daggers into my eyes. "I definitely think this isn't the time for more of Emma's ridiculous ramblings. We are at a funeral home. You think you can put a lid on your crazy for long enough to show this woman some respect?"

"You're right, Pamela," I relent. "We are at a funeral home. I know why I'm here. But I'm curious. Why did you come?"

She looks at me with an expression that expertly blends incredulity and disgust.

"I'm here because a very young woman died, and I was there when it happened. Normal people like to show support in situations like this," she says.

"You keep saying you were there, but I didn't see you. Derrick told me you showed up, but why is it that I didn't see you come in, and I also didn't see you leave?"

"Emma," Sam warns. "Please don't start."

"I'm not starting anything. I'm asking her a question. She's so wrapped up in being a part of the public mourning, but I can't figure out how she was so easily missed in the whole situation. And by the way, I noticed you have your Miata back. No more of the gold Saturn?"

"I told you," Pamela says. "That was a rental. My car was being worked on."

"For the brakes, right? Why would the brakes need to be worked on?" I ask.

"This is ridiculous," she says. She looks up at Sam. "Can't you do something about this? Obviously, her mind is slipping, and she is causing disruption to everyone."

"I'm not disrupting anything," I hiss, trying to keep my voice low. "But I know."

She looks me up and down, expectation in her eyes.

"You know what?" she asks.

"I know you have something to do with all of this. Just wait."

"Are you threatening me now?" she asks.

"I'm not threatening you," I say.

She crosses her arms over her chest and cocks her hip.

"Right. Like you weren't lurking around outside my office last night? I saw you there."

"Where were you before that?" I fire back.

"I was at work all evening," she says.

"No, you weren't. I went by there less than an hour before, and I waited. You weren't there."

"I don't know what you're talking about, but you can ask Derrick. He and the other agents were on showings and client meetings, so I was the one who had to hold down the fort. I ended up having to work late to catch up."

"You weren't there. You were when I got back from Pearl's, but you weren't when I went the first time," I tell her.

"Pearl's? Now you are tormenting that poor old woman? Don't you think she's been through enough?" Pamela asks.

211

"Who's Ruby?" I ask.

"What?" she gasps, her face dropping slightly and her arms loosening from over her chest.

"Alright. I think that's enough. Come on, Emma," Sam says.

"Who is Ruby Baker, Pamela? I know you know who she is."

"How dare you?" she asks as Sam takes me by the hand and pulls me away.

The cold air from outside hits me, helping to start cooling the burning on my face, but I'm trembling.

"What do you think you're doing?" I ask.

"Emma, I'm done. I am so extremely done with this," he sighs, pressing his finger and thumb into the bridge of his nose. "This is not the time nor the place for you to be doing this."

I rake my fingers back through my hair. "This wasn't my intention. But I couldn't help it."

Suddenly, Pamela comes storming out of the funeral home. I'm expecting to see a wave of people following her, ready to watch the drama, but mercifully, they don't.

"Who the hell do you think you are?" she demands, stomping up to me. There are tears in her eyes, and her jaw shakes as she stares me down. "How dare you come in there and talk to me about Ruby?"

"Pamela, go back inside," he says.

"I'm not going to…"

"Pamela, now," Sam commands.

She glares at me for another intense second, then turns and takes long strides back into the funeral home.

Sam turns exhausted eyes back to me.

"Get in your car and drive home," he says. "I'm going to follow you to make sure you actually go."

"I need to tell you what's going on," I argue.

"You need to go home."

His voice is low and even; simmering just below his normal tone. I get into my car and take one last look at the parking lot as I drive out, catching sight of Kevin's green sports car as I go. True to his word, Sam follows me all the way to my house and pulls into the driveway behind me like he's trying to block me from going anywhere. We get out, and I walk up to him.

"Sam, you need to listen to me. Pamela is involved in all of this."

"Emma, you need to get over this ridiculous feud with her. It's one thing not to get along, but you can't do this. You're crossing a line," he says.

I take out my phone and pull up the same pages I had on my computer the night before. Turning the screen to Sam, I point at it.

"See that woman? That's Ruby Baker," I say.

"That's an obituary," he points out.

"I know that. It says Ruby has been dead for over a year," I tell him. "Domestic violence."

"Are you seriously telling me the woman you supposedly saw moving in across the street is a ghost?" he asks. "That's your story now?"

"No. I don't think she's a ghost. But there's something going on, and Pamela may know what. Look. Read it."

He scans through, muttering as he reads, and I can pinpoint the moment he gets to the significant information because his voice trails off for a second.

"Survived by grandmother Esther Bryan, mother and father Jill and Kody Bryan, uncle Jason Bryan, aunt Celia Akon, brother Michael Bryan, and cousins Lily, Anna, and Burke Akon, and Pamela Bryan."

"And look at this," I say, taking the phone from his hand and shifting to another image. "This is her memorial page. It has pictures from her funeral. There's Pamela, right in the front row of the burial."

"Emma, this doesn't prove anything," he says, handing the phone back to me.

I scoff and push past him, hurrying up the steps onto my porch and walking into the house. He follows close behind me, and I whip around to face him as soon as we are inside.

"What do you think I did, Sam? Do you think I stalked Pamela online until I found some horrific family tragedy, stole the woman's name, and created the entire thing? Just for shits and giggles?" I shout.

"Emma, I don't know what's going on, but it has to stop. For everyone's sake, and for yours. You are losing credibility, and people are getting suspicious of you. You need to stay back and just be quiet for a while. I called Dr. Villa on the way. He's going to come over and bring you something to help you sleep."

"What?" I sputter incredulously. "You convinced a doctor to prescribe me medication?"

"It's just mild sleeping pills. You need to sleep," he says.

The house suddenly feels hot and suffocating. I pull off my long black wool jacket and toss it onto the couch. Sam takes a long step toward me.

"What's that?" he demands.

I loosen the holster from my hip. "I'm sure you recognize it."

"When did you start carrying a gun again?" he asks, his voice rising louder and slightly higher. "You said Creagan took it."

"He did. This is a new one."

"He took your gun because you were going on mental health leave. You're still on leave, Emma. You shouldn't be doing this. First, you're seeing things and coming up with outlandish stories. Now you're carrying a gun again. What is going on?"

I place my gun on the coffee table.

"When I agreed to stay here, I tried to let go. Everyone kept telling me I needed a break and to give my brain a chance to heal. So, that's what I tried to do. I tried to push aside my instincts and let go of my training. To just go about everyday life. Not always thinking about what was around me, not always being primed and ready, analyzing and collecting information, readying myself. I thought maybe that would take me off the edge. Being on leave meant not acting like an agent with every breath. Now I know putting those things aside only made the stress worse. I am a federal agent, Sam. This is who I am. It's why I left, and it didn't change when I came back. It's time I remember my life again."

A knock on the door makes Sam's head snap around. He crosses the room and opens it. Dr. Villa smiles in through the storm door at us, and Sam lets him the rest of the way in.

"Thank you for coming," Sam says. He looks outside, then over at me. "I'm going to go. I haven't forgotten who you are, Emma. And neither have you. Stay home. Stop all this. Get the rest and the help you need."

CHAPTER FORTY

D r. Villa talks to me about my struggles sleeping for a few minutes, then writes out a prescription. He reaches into his old-fashioned black leather bag and pulls out a blister pack with two pills.

"Go ahead and do whatever you need to do to get ready for bed. Take a shower, put on comfortable clothes, put on your favorite TV show. Then take these. They act quickly, so make sure you're ready before you take them. These are stronger than the prescription I just gave you. They'll get you to sleep in a short time so you can start catching up on your rest."

"What are the side effects?" I ask.

"Mild dizziness, headache, nausea. Nothing severe. They're all listed on the information you'll get when you fill the prescription. And trust me, Emma, none of the side effects are worse than what's happening to your body when you're only getting a couple of hours of sleep for a long period of time. Sleep deprivation can have a tremendous impact on your health and well-being. It's important to get yourself back on track and stay that way. I promise you will feel much better soon."

His white hair and round cheeks would make him fit right into a nostalgic painting of the mid-century that never was, and I'm almost expecting him to take out a lollipop to reward me for being a good patient. Instead, he snaps the bag shut and heads to the front door.

"Thank you. I'm sorry Sam had you come out here. I could have just gone to you," I say.

"And yet, you haven't," he points out. "But that's why I still do house calls. Now, you should make it a point to come see me in about two weeks to check in about how these are working for you. We'll decide then if you need to keep taking them or if we should change the dose or anything. Get comfortable and take those pills. I'll see you soon."

I contemplate the pills in my hand as I lock the door behind the doctor and head toward the back of the house. I've never been one to reach for a bottle when I need sleep. Too many experiences watching addicts try to pry themselves out of the grip of whatever substance took has always made me hesitate, even when going for a Tylenol. If there's one thing I can say about my career is that it's exceptional for keeping your life on the straight and narrow. For most people.

In the bathroom, I lean on the counter with both hands and stare into the mirror. Dull eyes stare back at me. My skin has a gray cast, and I can't remember the last time I put on even my customary swipe of mascara. I look down at my phone. It sits on the counter, dark. After Eric described the possibility of the programs controlling the device, I've barely touched it. The next time I go up to the gun range, I'll bring it to him and let him look over it. He might be able to find the program and deactivate it. But that will still leave me with the question of who put it on my phone and why.

The sudden wave of questions and confusion crashing through my brain makes me dizzy. I can't get past the look on Pamela's face when I mentioned Ruby. I expected her to react, of course. It's why I asked about her. I wanted to see the look on her face and hear any explanations she tried to give. But the reaction wasn't what I thought it would be. It wasn't the face of someone shocked to be discovered or anxious about coming up with something to cover up what they did. She looked hurt and even offended. It doesn't tell me anything specific. I can't go on just a few seconds of reaction to determine what was going through her mind, but it makes me pause. It gives the entire situation another level of confusion, and my brain feels drained.

I set the pills down in the center of the counter and undress. A long, blisteringly hot shower makes my muscles feel loose, and it seems to take extra strength just to pull on a pair of stretch pants and a sweatshirt. I carry the pills with me into the kitchen to get a drink and gather a few snacks. Going back into my bedroom, I follow doctor's orders and put on a marathon of one of my favorite shows. The packet of pills flips back and forth across my palm as I continue to consider it.

What if this really is all in my head? Is it possible I could have slipped so far into sleep deprivation and stress that maybe I read the obituary of Pamela's cousin, forgot it, and my brain has crafted the story into a new reality?

I pop both pills out of the packet into my palm.

Maybe the noose really was just a prop. Before Everly Zara, I likely wouldn't have thought anything of it. I'm so far removed from my teenage years that I don't remember hearing stories of kids doing ridiculous things like that. If I'm honest, I can probably come up with a few stories of my own.

The pills go down with a swig of tea.

I can't explain the texts, but that doesn't mean there was someone in the hotel. Like Sam said, it was dark and confusing. The sounds could have been anything. Maybe I'm not remembering well. Maybe I did trip.

I slip beneath the covers and rest back against my pillows. My body melts down into the bed and every part feels heavy, dragged down by impending sleep. I can't focus on the show. My eyelids pull down, and just before I fall completely to sleep, a final thought rushes through my mind.

She called her Nikki.

———

Waking up is a completely disorienting experience. It feels like I haven't moved since I got into bed, and my joints ache from staying in the same position for so long. I have no idea what time it is, but the bright, saturated sunlight coming through the window tells me it's not the pre-dawn hours I usually greet when my eyes open for the first time every day. The TV is still on, and I stare at the screen for a few seconds. It's an odd juxtaposition. Just waking up from a long night of sleep and staring into the middle of an episode on TV that usually burns through the latest hours of the night. It's like I missed something. Like the whole world has gotten started without me, and now I'm going to have to catch up.

I pull myself up and check the clock. It's already mid-morning. The day really has started without me. It's strange to think of the hours churning on and the lives steadily unfolding while I was so deeply asleep. As I walk toward the kitchen for coffee, thoughts start to reformulate in the back of my mind. Something pricks and stings, just past my awareness, like I know it happened and can just barely perceive the memory but can't take hold and drag it up into my consciousness.

The house feels cold around me, like my body still isn't quite awake and every sensation is too intense. A few steps later, what my brain was trying to reach hits me.

A shrill beep in the middle of the night. Sounds I couldn't react to because the sedatives kept my body captive even in the brief moments my mind woke up. A thought flashing through.

They called her Nikki.

The cold air gets sharper. It draws me along the hallway. I walk into the kitchen, the thought swelling bigger and bigger in my head, and see the backdoor standing open by several inches. A cold wind flows in, and I wrap my arms tightly around myself to block the feeling. Now I know I heard the high-pitched beeping while I slept. It was the sound of the alarm as someone opened the back door. I rush across the room and look at the door. It isn't damaged in any way. It wasn't forced or broken open. It was opened with a key.

I close it firmly and turn around to reach for the phone. My gaze hits the kitchen table. I had been so focused on the open door when I got into the room, I didn't even notice there's something sitting in the middle of the table. A plate with a slice of chocolate cake holds down the corner of a piece of paper, weighing it down so it couldn't flutter away in the wind let in by the open door. I look down at it.

Have you figured it out yet?

CHAPTER FORTY-ONE

I get dressed as fast as I can and use the landline in my kitchen to call Eric.

"What number is this?" he asks when he answers.

"It's my landline," I tell him.

"Did you lose your cell again?"

"No. But I can't risk using it. Listen. I need you to get all my case files and send them to me. Everything I've ever worked on. Back from the beginning. I need as much information as you can give me about them, alright?"

"Emma, what's going on?" he asks.

"I can't get into it right now. I just need you to do that for me. When we get off the phone, call Sam for me. Tell him someone was in my house and to look in the kitchen. I've got to go," I say.

Before he can protest, I hang up. I take my phone, compromised even as it is, and snap a photo of the cake and the note.

Just woke up to the back door open and found this on my kitchen table, I send him, attaching the file. The phone tries to send, but the text won't go through. Of course. Just my luck. I'll have to hand it over to show Sam directly when I see him.

I stuff my phone into my pocket and put my gun in its holster.

Throwing on my coat, I run out to my car and head directly for Pearl's Diner. Rather than parking at the curb, I follow along the side street until I find the entrance to the alley. My car bounces slightly as it leaves the pavement and hits the gravel, the tires crunching along until I get to the space behind the restaurant. As I park, the back door to the diner opens and Kevin walks out carrying two large black bags of trash. He tosses them into the dumpster, then turns and looks at me, tenting his hand over his eyes to block out the sunlight.

"Hey, Emma," he calls when I climb out of the car. He takes a few swaggering steps toward me. "Couldn't find a good parking space up front?"

"I actually came to look around back here. I realized when I got home the other day, I couldn't find my bracelet. The clasp on it breaks all the time, so I thought I'd come back here and see if it might have fallen off while I was here."

He glances around at the gravel. It's not deep, and patches of dirt show through where the rocks have worn away. Kevin kicks at one of them, moving individual rocks around in a feeble attempt at searching.

"I haven't seen anything like that around here, but you're welcome to have a look. You know, my wife used to have a bracelet that broke all the time like that. I eventually brought it up to the jeweler and he changed the clasp on it."

"I'll have to look into that," I tell him, bending over like I'm searching the ground for something. "It must be a run of bad luck. I woke up this morning and found my back door standing wide open."

"Standing open?" he asks.

"Yep," I nod. "I walked into the kitchen to make some coffee, and there it was, just standing open."

"Do you think somebody got inside?" he asks.

I stand up straight and walk over closer to the green car parked near the dumpster.

"I don't think so. I have an alarm system, so I would have heard it. Last night, my neighbor came over to chat for a little bit, and I must have just not closed the door all the way when she left. She prefers going to the back door because she says the front is too formal." I force a laugh. "She's new in town, so I think she's pretty eager to make friends."

"New neighbor?" Kevin asks.

I look back over my shoulder at him casually.

"Her name is Ruby Baker. Do you know her?"

Kevin shakes his head.

"Can't say I do."

I shrug. "Like I said, she's pretty new in town. Maybe I'll bring her in here to eat sometime soon. I think the two of you would get along. She's a big animal lover. Well, I don't see my bracelet anywhere. I must have dropped it somewhere else. Thanks for helping me look." I walk back toward my car, then turn back to him. "I forgot to ask. Are you feeling better?"

"What do you mean?" he asks.

"I saw you driving to the hospital when everyone was sick. I figured you must have gotten pretty sick. Having to taste everything you cook, you must have eaten quite a bit of the gravy. I was surprised when I saw you. You drove right past me. Down on Miller's Road?"

He looks at me like he's thinking for a few seconds, then tilts his head back and opens his mouth.

"Oh. Yeah. Yeah. That whole day is so much of a blur. I've never been so sick in my whole life. How are you getting on with your recovery?" he asks.

"Oh, I didn't get sick. Sam and I were fine," I tell him.

He looks briefly bewildered.

"You were fine? Don't you usually come in for lunch at 12:30?" he asks.

I hold back the hint of a smile that tries to make its way onto my lips.

"I do," I confirm. "But not that day. We got there early. Lucky, I guess. Have a good rest of your day."

Turning my car around, I drive away from the back of the diner. Instead of turning onto the street beside it, I cross over and go into the alley behind the small shops on the next block. I drive ahead a few yards and pull into the small alcove of parking spots behind a beauty parlor. There's just enough of my car sitting out from behind the wall that I can look through my back windshield and see the street beside Pearl's Diner. It takes a few minutes, but just as I expected, the green sports car pulls out and drives away.

I wait a few more seconds, so Kevin won't see me in his rearview mirror, and pull out of the alley, heading toward the Lionheart office. Everybody inside falls silent when I walk in. Two of the women have the decency to pretend they don't even notice I'm there. They stare at the paperwork on their desks; occasionally looking up at computer screens I have no doubt are blank or displaying only their email. Another stares at me blatantly, then turns to whisper something into her co-worker's ear. There's only one empty desk. Pamela isn't there.

Not bothering to wait for anyone to greet me or give me permission, I stalk through the office to Derrick's door. It's open a few inches, so I let myself in.

"Emma," he smiles.

"I need my keys," I tell him.

"Your keys?" he frowns. "Did you lock yourself out of your house?"

"No, and I apparently didn't lock anyone else out, either. Someone came into my house last night. They had a key."

Derrick stands and walks over to the large cabinet on the wall. He inputs a code into a keypad, and a light flashes green, allowing him to open the door.

"Nobody used the key we have here, Emma. All the keys to all our properties are kept in this cabinet. As soon as you changed your locks, I replaced the old key with the new one. No one has the access code but me. Even the agents representing the properties being sold or rented have to go through me to get them."

He takes the key down and hands it to me. "I have to admit, I'm surprised to see you here."

I tilt my head at him. "Why is that?"

"I heard about what happened at the funeral home. I wouldn't think you would want to run into Pamela. She hasn't exactly been quiet about her evaluation of you recently."

My spine stiffens, and I draw in a breath.

"Well, I guess I'm lucky. She's not even here. I must have just missed her," I say.

"Actually, she took the day off."

"She took the day off?" I raise an eyebrow. That wasn't what I expected to hear. "You mean she hasn't been here at all today?"

"She came by early this morning to tell me she was going to be out and to reschedule her showings."

"Where is she?" I ask.

He shrugs. "I'm not sure. She said there was just something she had to do today. But she'll be back in tomorrow."

"Do you have a schedule of all the showings? Or does each of the agents handle that individually?" I ask.

"They each have their own schedule, but I keep a master calendar, too. I have to make sure there aren't times when everybody is going to be away from the office for long stretches," he explains.

"Could I take a look at that schedule for the last three weeks?" I ask.

"Sure. It's not confidential or anything. It's posted right out on the wall in the main office," he points out the door, and I nod at him.

"Thanks." I look down at the keys in my hand and toss them back to him. "Hang onto these. They might actually be safer here."

I head over to the large calendar posted on the wall and glance over it. It's a massive white dry-erase board with different colored markers used for each of the agents. Pamela is in purple. My mind scoops up the purple ink, plucking the dates and times from the board and lining them up against other moments, other incidents. When I'm done, I head back out of the office, looking over at Pamela's empty chair as I go.

My phone is ringing when I get into the car, and I answer it cautiously.

"Sam, I can't talk on my phone."

"You need to get back here," he says.

"What?"

"You need to get back to your house. I told you to stay home," he says.

"Are you there? Did you see it?" I ask.

"See what, Emma? There's nothing in the kitchen."

"Shit," I mutter. "Sam, I can't use my phone."

"Get back here. You shouldn't be driving after taking that medication. Not when it's going to affect you like this."

"It's not affecting me. Listen to me. I'm getting off the phone and I'm going to bring it to the station. I'll leave it at the desk for you. Have the guys look through it. Call Eric. He'll explain it."

"Emma, what are you doing?" Sam asks.

"I promise it's not dangerous."

"Emma," he says again. In the exact same tone of voice, he's been using on me a lot lately.

"Please trust me, Sam."

I don't wait for an answer.

I end the call and toss it onto the passenger seat and drive directly to the police station. I bring the phone inside and leave it at the desk with instructions to give it to Sheriff Johnson when he comes back.

I plan to stop at the first Wal-Mart on the drive so I can buy the cheapest version of a smartphone I see. It doesn't have to be complex. Just functional. The drive to Crozet is a little over an hour, and I can't be without any form of contact.

CHAPTER FORTY-TWO

I already confirmed my suspicions by looking up the obituary for Ruby Baker on the burner phone I bought, but it still makes my breath catch in my throat when I pull into at the small cemetery. It doesn't take long for me to find the red Miata parked along a curving stretch of path flanked with trees and bushes that will be in full bloom come spring. The stark emptiness of the November landscape, empty branches, and cold flower beds make the color stand out even more. It's almost difficult to look at. Like she should have chosen a different car to come here. Of course, she shouldn't have. She's here for herself, not anyone else. No one else knows she's here. I'm certainly not supposed to. But I couldn't stay away. I had to be sure.

Pamela sits on her knees by a grave towards the back of the cemetery section. Her head hangs over, and she rocks back and forth slightly. I stop walking toward her, feeling intrusive. I'm not supposed to be here. This isn't a moment I should be witnessing. It's the type of moment that leaves an impression in the entire space around it that sucks in energy and leaves a gaping wound. It doesn't need to be witnessed, to be seen, in order to leave its impact. I only came to confirm my suspicions and to set my mind at ease. I turn to walk away, but a feeling gnawing in the bottom of my stomach stops me. She stands up and faces me just as I start toward the grave again.

There's a brief moment where I see an almost peaceful look on her face as she brushes away a tear. But as soon as she realizes I'm there, her expression darkens. Her eyes narrow and her jaw sets so hard the muscles twitch. She stalks toward me.

"You have got to be fucking kidding me," she growls. "What are you doing here?"

I raise my hands to be as non-threatening as I can be.

"I know I'm the last person you want to see right now. Trust me, if the circumstances were any different, you would be ranking right up there on my list, too. But they're not. I needed to come here."

"Why?" Pamela demands. "Why did you need to come here? Just so that you could mock me more? You could torment me with your ridiculous stories? You know what, Emma? I thought you just cracked. You spent too long chasing after murderers and rapists and terrorists, and finally, all the twisted shit in your past just caught up to you and melted your brain, but now I wonder if you're actually just mean. And to be honest, I don't know which one I would rather it be."

"It's neither," I tell her. "If you'd let me explain what's going on..."

"Why should I?" she wails. "Of all the days for you to shove yourself in my face, it had to be today? Why when I'm going through this, should I have to listen to you at all?"

I take a deep breath and let it out slowly. "Look, I'm sorry, Pamela. I have crossed the line a number of times, and I've said some really hurtful things. But I promise that's not why I'm here. I'm here to visit Ruby, too. Because there's someone out there who is using the same person to torment both of us. Someone I know who at least claims to be Ruby. I didn't know her at all, but you loved her. And you might be able to help me figure out exactly why this is all happening," I say. "I can't tell you how sorry I am for... everything. But I need your help."

She breathes heavily for a few more seconds, eyes darting back and forth as she tries to decide what to do. Finally, she looks over her shoulder back at the grave.

"It's her birthday," she says.

"I know," nod. "I thought I remembered reading that in her obituary but checked on the way here to make sure. Can you tell me about her?"

We walk slowly back to the grave, and I see flowers newly placed at the base of the headstone.

"Ruby is... was my cousin," Pamela sighs. "We grew up together. She was the closest thing to a sister I ever had. I doubt you remember, but I didn't live in Sherwood for several years. I was born there and was there until I was around four, then we moved here to Crozet to be near my extended family. That's when Ruby and I got really close. We spent all our time together. Everybody around here would always say if you found one of us, you would find the other. I was happy here. I was happy with her. I didn't realize we had only come here so we could help take care of my grandfather. Apparently, there were some financial problems in the family that none of us kids knew about, and all the siblings had to band together just to get through. When he died, it fractured the family again. We moved back to Sherwood, and I could only see Ruby occasionally."

"I know what it's like to be away from the people you love," I say. "It's awful, and I'm sorry you had to go through that."

"Yeah, well I'd rather still be feeling that than having to see her here," Pamela says in a strained, tear-filled voice. "I knew that guy wasn't good for her. From the very beginning, when she started talking about him, there was something off. I only met him once, but by then she was already so far in. I just wish she had talked to me more. I wish she'd given me the chance to help her. But she was so desperate for someone to love her. She wanted so much to just have her place in this world and start a family that wouldn't fall apart. Can you imagine that?"

"Yes," I tell her. "Actually, I can."

"Well," she says, trying to put strength back into her voice. "I would have told her I was her family, and she didn't need anyone else to create that for her. It's not completely her fault. It's not like I made myself totally available to her, either. I always told her she could call me anytime. I didn't realize he wouldn't let her. The only way she would have been able to tell me what was happening was if I was here, and I was always too busy. Too wrapped up in my career." She scoffs. "I was planning on coming for her birthday. I was going to surprise her and take her on a whole day of activities we used to do when we were younger. I wanted to show her that her little cousin had really made something out of herself. She was going to be so proud of me, and maybe then I could convince her to come to Sherwood with me. Derrick was going to interview her for a secretary position at the office, then we were going to train her to be an agent one day."

"That would have been amazing for her," I smile, emotions bubbling up in me. I've never seen this side of Pamela before. I never knew what went on in her life. To me, she was always this one-dimensional caricature of some frivolous girl always trying to steal Sam from me. I never even considered she was using that as a defense mechanism to cover the struggles she goes through

I was wrong about Pamela.

"Yes, it would have been. But she didn't make it to her birthday." Pamela crouches down and runs her hand across the name engraved into the stone. "I got a call that she was in the hospital. She had an accident. I thought someone smashed into her when she was coming home from work. She worked at a bar up the way called Fardowners. That was one thing he actually let her do. She brought back money from it, so he didn't care how much she hated it, or that she had to drive home so late at night. I was always afraid some drunk driver would run her down. By the time I got here, she was barely hanging on. That's when I found out it wasn't a car. She had gotten into an accident with Robert's fists. The doctors tried, but there was nothing they could do. He mangled her. She died the next day."

"Robert?" I ask.

"Her boyfriend."

"What happened to him?"

"He's in prison. It won't do Ruby any good, but I hope every day he gets a dose of what he did to her. Not enough to kill him. Just enough to make him suffer for the rest of his life." She looks up at me. "Does that make me a terrible person?"

"No. That makes you human. I had no idea you had gone through any of this," I tell her. "I'm really sorry, Pamela."

"No one knows," she says. "At least no one in Sherwood. I didn't tell anybody there."

"Why not?"

"I didn't want them to judge her. That's what people do. They say they don't. They say to sympathize with the victim and tell her story, not the killer's. But it never works out that way. As soon as the story gets out, people start picking apart the woman who was beaten to a pulp, as if they can lay out all the mistakes she made that made her deserve what happened to her. I didn't want anyone in Sherwood to be able to do that to her. And, the truth is, I didn't want them to do it to me, either. I already blamed myself. I didn't want them to blame me, too."

"You weren't responsible for what happened," I reassure her.

"In a way I was. Everyone who ever met her was. But I didn't want to hear that from anyone who hadn't met her. And I didn't want hollow sympathy and people looking at me differently, so I didn't tell anyone."

"So, why are you telling me?" I ask.

"Because you made her real again. When I didn't talk about her, I told myself I was protecting her. I was keeping her all to myself and not letting anyone near her. But when you talked about her, even if you didn't realize who you were talking about, you brought her back. You made her a part of the world again. I had been pretending for a while that she was just at home, and we would get together sometime when we weren't so busy. You talking about her and making me face this, got me to come here. To see her for her birthday," she tells me.

"I'm sorry, Pamela."

"Emma, I need you to tell me what actually happened," she says.

"I did. A woman told me she was moving in at 2021 Candlewood, and that her name was Ruby Baker. Look."

I pull up the obituary on my burner phone. Pamela draws in a sharp breath when she sees it.

"That's not her. That's not Ruby," she says.

"I know that now. But this is the woman I met. She told me her name was Ruby Baker. She was running from an abusive boyfriend. She was from Crozet. She was nice, and she baked me a cake, and we talked. And I saw..." I trail off, taking in a slow, rattling breath.

"You saw what?" Pamela frowns.

"I saw through her window one night. I saw a man... hurt her. And I saw her body on the floor of the house."

Pamela gasps and trembles. There is no doubt she has played this exact scene in her mind thousands of times. I reach out and give her a hug until she gathers herself back together. We take a couple of deep breaths, and I continue talking.

"But then the next morning, she was gone. No body, no evidence. Not even any boxes from her moving in. That's why I asked you to walk through the house with us. And from what you just told me, she got some of the details wrong. Then after she disappeared, I looked her up, and I found an obituary and a grave locator. A memorial page. They all have pictures of this woman. Not the real Ruby."

"How?" Pamela asks.

"It took someone a lot of time and attention to detail to make sure it was as thorough as it is, but there are hackers who thrive on messed up little games like this. Someone hacked into these websites and edited them with the pictures they wanted me to see. They kept the information but changed the birth year to fit with the woman I saw. Then they just left it out there for me to find."

"So, you would think you were batshit crazy," she completes my thought. "I'm sorry too, Emma."

"It's fine. Me and everyone else," I say.

"But why her?" she asks.

"I don't think it was really about her," I tell her. "There was something else going on. Ruby's memory was just an unfortunate casualty. Like I said, this woman got details wrong. She said Ruby was married before, and that her boyfriend's name was Frank."

"Franklin Robert Guzman," Pamela says. "This other woman must have at least seen his name once. She just didn't bother to find out more."

"Exactly. But that means it wasn't really about her," I point out.

"So, what was it about?" she asks.

"I'm not completely sure, but I need you to do something for me. You don't have any reason to believe me or trust me. I know that. And that's fine. After all this, it's fair game and you can go back to hating me. But for right now, I need you to be extremely careful. Stay put here. Don't go back to Sherwood, and don't see Kevin," I tell her.

"Kevin?" she asks, shocked.

"Pamela, just this once, I need you to believe me."

CHAPTER FORTY-THREE

The email from Eric pops up when I'm halfway back to Sherwood. I want to pull off and read through it, but I don't have the time. I need to get back. It's already late afternoon by the time I pull back into Sherwood. My first stop is the police station, but the receptionist tells me Sam is out on a call and doesn't know when he's going to be back.

"Tell him I'm at the library," I tell her.

The library is in the same complex as the police station. The station itself acts as the face of what is essentially the town square of Sherwood. From Main Street, visitors have to turn down a side road and park before walking into the square of buildings. The library, police station, courthouse, law library, and clerk, along with a few small historic buildings, create a perimeter around a courtyard with brick paths leading to a grassy center. The fountain in the middle of the grass has no water in it now, but when the weather heats up, it will become a popular destination for people hoping to cool off in the mist splashing off the concrete.

Rather than going through the hassle of driving around the block just to walk through the gates, I exit out the side door of the station. This brings me to a cement sidewalk that leads around to the brick walkway bisecting the square. I follow it to the library and hurry inside. There isn't much time before the library closes for the day, and I don't want any of the librarians dissuading me from getting on one of the computers. They are set up in small banks throughout the library, four computers to a desk, so they're positioned back-to-back. Partitions between the computers provide some sense of privacy and separation from the person right beside you.

Nobody seems to be at any of the computers in the far corner of the library, so I claim one and sign on using my library card. I still see the card as a defining moment for my return to Sherwood. Before it, there was still the sense that at any moment I could just pick back up and leave. Like there was still no permanence here, despite the constant tug on my heart. It was the same tug from when I left years ago, only even stronger now. Then one day the weather forecast was rainy for the next week, Janet had brought me a giant container of potato soup, and I needed a couple of books to bring it all together. I walked right into the library, and the next thing I knew, I was holding a library card.

It seems ridiculous that something so small could be more impactful than much more significant events. But sometimes it's the tiny details that stand out against the bigger picture. Like the missing board that can bring down a house. Or the mislaid word that reveals a killer.

I open the email from Eric and find a link to the secure location in the cloud, where he uploaded the scans of all my case files. It reminds me of the mysterious video clip I got from Mary Preston. Another message from a dead girl. The thought of all the questions still hanging over the bombing and Greg's appearance makes my heart clench, but I can't think about that right now. I have to concentrate on what's in front of me.

As the pages scroll on the screen, my suspicions unfold with them. I watch as the intricately woven scheme rises out of the history of my career. There's a thread here somewhere, I just have to find it.

A sudden commotion from the front of the library breaks my concentration. I jump up and run toward the shouted voices. Down a row of stacks ahead of me, I see a man stand and take a few steps. I rush toward him and come around the corner just as the too-loud, startling sound of gunshots ring out, and he collapses to the floor.

Inundated by screams, I take a few more steps to him and drop down to my knees beside the man. Blood spreads out across his clothes, and he lets out a deep groan. I look toward the shooter, and my stomach drops.

Savannah stands just a short distance inside the door to the library, her feet wide apart, and her hands still clutching her police issue firearm. It shakes in her hands as she stares, wide-eyed and clearly stunned at the man she just shot. I get up and start toward her, reaching a hand up to try to encourage her to lower the gun.

"Savannah, what's going on?" I ask.

She keeps staring, not answering me. The shock has settled in, and she's lost touch with what's happening around her. Seconds later, the door to the library bursts open with a sound almost as loud as the gunshot.

"Back up, Emma," Sam shouts.

It's not a suggestion; it's an order. It hits me in the gut, and the feeling only twists harder when I see him pointing his gun at me.

"Sam, what are you doing?" I ask.

"Back up, Emma," he says again. "Get on your knees with your hands on your head."

He won't look directly at me, and there's tension in his jaw that goes beyond just the intensity of the moment. I don't understand what's happening. Everything inside me says to go to him, but this is not the time to do that. I know I've done nothing, but I do exactly as anyone should in the situation. I lower down to my knees and put my hands on my head, clasping my fingers together.

It's a simple truth that so many seem to struggle with, but that saves lives. When the police tell you to do something, you do it. The time to argue is later, once the situation is de-escalated. Cole comes around Sam and takes my hands, pulling them down to behind my back so we can cuff me. Using the chain between the cuffs in one hand and his other on my shoulder, he helps me to my feet and brings me over to a nearby chair.

"What's going on?" I ask.

"He's still breathing," another officer calls out.

"The paramedics should be here any second," Sam says. "Just keep him awake."

"Sam," I say fiercely, and he finally turns his eyes to me. "What is going on?"

"We got a call with an active shooter threat for the library," he says.

"Alright," I say. "Then why am I in handcuffs?" I ask.

"The call came from you," he says.

It feels like every word I could possibly say is sucked out of me, along with my breath and my ability to think. It takes a few seconds for me to process it enough to respond.

"What do you mean it came from me?" I ask. "I didn't do it."

"Calling in a false report of an active shooter in a public place is a crime. It becomes more serious when the police respond with deadly force," he says in a near-monotone, delivering a rendition of the situation rather than speaking directly to me.

"I know that," I tell him, but he keeps talking. "Sam, I understand." Lifting my voice above his stops him. "I know how dangerous this is because I've seen it before. It's another one of my cases. You need to listen to me. This is just like everything else that's been happening." I'm frantic now, trying to get out as many words as I possibly can just so he will listen to me.

"Stop talking, Emma. Stop talking right now. You have the right to remain silent, and I suggest you take that right very seriously. Because as of right now, I have no choice but to arrest you."

I'm devastated as Cole pulls me to my feet again and leads me out of the library, reciting my Miranda Rights as we go. He brings me right back along the same path I followed from the police station and escorts me into an interrogation room. He says nothing to me, but takes off the handcuffs and walks out, leaving the locked door behind him.

CHAPTER FORTY-FOUR

FOUR YEARS AGO

Travis heard the car doors slam and was surprised at how many of them there were. Usually, there was only one. Officer Phillips. Sometimes another officer would come along, depending on why she was coming. It might be a very young officer, new to the force, and just getting his feet wet with such a complicated and extensive investigation. It could be a detective ready to fill him in on the direction of their search. But this time, several doors slammed, one right after the other, the staccato like gunfire.

He went to the door before they knocked and opened it to see Officer Phillips standing next to a young, beautiful woman. She wasn't wearing a police uniform like the three men standing behind her or like Officer Phillips. Instead, she was dressed in a sleek black suit with a black trench coat over it. Her blonde hair was pulled back away from her face in a severe bun. Naturally beautiful, she wore only mascara and a hint of lipstick.

Officer Phillips spoke first.

"Mr. Burke, we have a search warrant," she said, holding out the folded papers to him.

Travis took them, not bothering to look down at them. This wasn't the first time this happened, and most likely, it wouldn't be the last.

Things got moved. People second-guessed themselves and changed hiding spots. The memory of significance on items faded. So they searched. And they searched. And they searched again. They were always looking for what they wouldn't find. He never stopped them. He never even tried. There was no reason to. Just like the very first night when they showed up, and he pleaded with them to find her, he always gave them full access.

"Of course," he nodded, stepping aside and inviting them in. "Officer, you know my home is always open to you. I've told you from the beginning there's nothing that's off-limits. Search anything you want to. If it will help find Mia, I want you to find it."

He wanted to impress the blonde woman, and he seemed to have accomplished it. She gave him a slight smile, stepping toward him with her hands in front of her, one holding onto the wrist of the other.

"That's very generous of you, Mr. Burke," she said. "If only everyone involved in investigations of this manner were as cooperative as you, it would make our jobs so much easier."

It was difficult to tell if there was sincerity in her voice or if her youth had diluted the disdain and softened the edge he could see in her eyes.

"Well, I don't see any reason not to be," he told her. "I can't expect you to find what you're not allowed to search for. So, my home is open. I could show you around if you'd like."

She barely waited for the words to come out of his mouth before shutting him down.

"Thank you for the offer, but that won't be necessary. We aren't here to search the house again." He looked down at the search warrant in his hands, reading it at the same time she told him. "We're here to search your truck."

"That's a new truck," he explained. "They already searched the old one. Of course, they're more than welcome to search it again if they want to. It's in the junkyard, but they could probably find it."

"No, Mr. Burke. We aren't here for your old truck," she said.

"But I didn't even have that truck when Mia left. She'd been gone for months when I got it."

"Gone?" the woman asked.

Shit. He slipped. It was the first time he lost his footing, and he could see in her eyes she knew it.

"Gone from here," he tried to clarify. "She left months before I got that truck. My old one was in terrible condition and ended up breaking down."

The front door opened again, and two more officers appeared. One of them held a thick black leash in one hand. His other hand was looped through a fabric strap attached to the back of the bulletproof vest of a K9 officer.

"Great," the woman said. "You're here. The truck is right outside."

"Why is there a dog?" Travis frowned. "I don't do drugs. I never have."

"That dog isn't trained in sniffing out narcotics," the woman told him. "He detects the presence, past or current, of human remains."

Travis felt sick. He swayed slightly on his feet. He knew he was screwed. Now it was just a matter of time.

The woman started to follow the dog but turned back to him.

"Oh, I forgot to introduce myself. I'm with the FBI." She extended her hand. "Agent Emma Griffin."

CHAPTER FORTY-FIVE

NOW

There's a camera right above my head. I know it's there because I've watched the feed many times before. I have the compulsion to look up at it, to talk to it, and plead with whoever is watching the screen to understand what's going on. But I hold myself back. I need to keep myself calm so that when Sam does come in, I'm able to communicate the situation to him as clearly as I possibly can. There's no time to waste.

But he doesn't seem to know that. Time ticks by. Seconds that seemed so precious blend into minutes. They stretch on and on until I lose track. I can't tell how long I've been sitting here. The room is small and plain, with no windows or clocks. That's all by design. The discomfort and disorientation I'm feeling is the intent. I know exactly what's happening and how the rooms are designed to influence how the people inside them feel and think, yet I'm falling under it. I can understand now how people accused of crimes seem to start crumbling around the edges so quickly.

After what feels like hours, or maybe minutes, Sam comes into the room, and I get to my feet. I want to fold myself into his arms, but this isn't my Sam. This is Sheriff Samuel Johnson, and he's staring at me with suspicion and distrust. I wonder if Liza will come into the room with him. It's not uncommon for there be two officers present during questioning, and I would expect it considering my relationship with Sam. But I'm relieved when she doesn't come in, and he closes the door behind us.

"Have a seat, Emma," he says.

I sit down, and he perches on the edge of the seat across from me.

"Sam, you have to listen to me. There is something very serious going on, and something else is going to happen if we don't figure it out," I tell him.

"What do you mean by that?" he asks.

"Don't talk to me like that," I say. "Don't talk to me like I'm another one of the crazy people who come in here wearing tinfoil hats, trying to recruit soldiers in their war against the Illuminati. Someone is taking cases that I worked and using them to discredit me. It's going backwards."

"That's not what we're here to talk about," he says. "This is about what happened at the library."

"I didn't have anything to do with that," I insist.

"I have a recording of the call," he says.

He pulls out a device and plays a recording of a 911 call. The voice is muffled and whispery, but it's there clear enough. "This is Agent Emma Griffin. There is an active shooter..."

I shake my head. "That's not me. You can't possibly think that's my voice."

"It's too whispered to be able to make a conclusive identification," he says.

"Forget about that," I say. "You tell me. You know my voice as well as anybody else. Do you think that sounds like me?"

"It doesn't matter what I think. It's not just the voice. The call went on long enough to track the number, and it comes up as yours. The 911 call stating there was an active shooter at the library was calling from your phone," he tells me.

I shake my head harder.

"No. That's not possible, Sam."

"Emma, stop arguing. You can't fight with the technology."

"Yes, I can. I'm not asking you to believe me. I'm telling you it's not possible. I didn't have my phone when I was at the library."

"And who did?" he asks.

"You did!"

"What?" he asks, surprise lifting his eyebrows.

"Or I guess your receptionist did. We talked before I left, remember? I told you I was going to bring my phone to the station. I wanted you to have your tech guys look at it and find the program that's operating in the background. I brought it over here just a few minutes after that and left it at the front desk for you. I haven't had it all day."

"At the library you said you knew what was going on. That you had seen it before. What did you mean by that?" he asks, shifting forward on his seat.

"Exactly what I was just trying to tell you. Someone is using my cases to cause all this. A few years ago, I investigated a swatting incident," I explain. "Do you know what that is?"

"I've heard of it," he says. "Why don't you explain it to me?"

He's having me do that for the camera. He wants to record what I have to say so that he can use it against me if he needs to. I don't care. He can record anything he wants to, as long as he lets me say the words.

"Swatting is a seriously messed-up internet trend used by gamers to punish others. They find their target's home address, and then they call the police. They make up some story about severe danger happening at that location. It could be that there's an intruder, or they're being held hostage. Most of the time, it has to be an active shooter or bomb threat. It has to be something very serious and urgent. The police then send the SWAT team to investigate. In some cases, the objective is humiliation, but in others, it could be considered attempted murder. And with any luck, the entire incident is livestreamed out to all the other gamers. And the one who did it gets to feel in control," I tell him.

"And people do this for fun?" he asks.

"Sort of," I say. "Like I said, it's usually used as a form of punishment or social control. The ones who are the most wrapped up in it will try to show their power by staging clear-outs. Essentially the same thing, only there isn't one individual person being targeted. Instead, they try to cause an evacuation of a large public place. So, a school or an office building or shopping mall. They'll call in a bomb threat or announce an active shooter and watch the news and wait for the aftermath."

"How can they possibly get away with that?" he asks.

"The anonymity of the internet," I say. "They're able to hide behind screen names and these personas they've created to share with each other. The people don't actually know who each other are, and very rarely will they take public credit under their real name for these instances. Obviously, swatting causes a lot of issues. It takes up police manpower and resources. It traumatizes the person who's on the receiving end of it. But it can get a lot worse."

I clear my throat and continue.

"I had a case a couple of years ago involving a serial swatter. He was really young and isolated, but then he discovered this online gaming community where he was suddenly admired and respected. He created this entire online life, this identity that was wrapped around the idea of him being a puppet master. He could cause anyone to do anything, according to him. Even within this online community, he kept up several fake personas just to bolster his own status and to effectively pin the blame on others. Anyone who crossed him or who stood up to him would get a visit from the local SWAT team. He staged clear-outs of several different public places and cost unbelievable amounts of money, loss of manpower, and resource damaged. Eric and I were on a task force, and we were able to infiltrate this community and track him down. But before we made the arrests, the perp swatted another teenager who he was angry with for talking inside a game to a girl he liked. He told the police inside there was a man with a gun holding up his family. He gave an address. Unfortunately, it was the wrong one."

"The wrong one?" Sam frowns.

"He got the numbers mixed up. When the police showed up to the address he gave them, it wasn't that kid's house. Them being there startled the man inside, and he stepped out onto the porch. He was holding a lighter, but they thought it was a gun and he was shot dead right in front of his door. Don't you see? This has so many similarities," I say. "Someone orchestrated this to directly remind me of that."

"There is no evidence of that," Sam says. "Emma, you know as well as I do there has to be evidence. There has to be a clear path, and right now, the only clear indicators are pointing right to you. Considering everything that's been happening recently and the shift in how people are seeing you, I can't just let you walk away."

"What's that supposed to mean? Don't you see it?"

"People already know what happened. They know there's a man lying in critical condition in the hospital, fighting for his life because he was shot in the middle of the library three feet away from you. And they know you were arrested. As Sheriff, my responsibility is to the people of my town. They elected me, and they trust me. I can't let them down by turning a blind eye to this just because it's you."

"Are you booking me?" I ask in shock.

"I have to hold you while we look into this. The situation with you is becoming dangerous, and I can't let it keep happening. When we have more information, we'll decide where to go from there."

CHAPTER FORTY-SIX

I t was already well into the evening by the time Sam came into the interrogation room to question me, so there's no hope of me getting out of the cell they book me into before morning. The door closes behind me with a thick clang. It makes me feel like I can't breathe. The walls feel tight, and the light overhead is too much, even in its dimmed state.

They expect me to sleep. They think I will lie down on the thin mattress draped across a piece of metal and rest. As if there's anything in this world that can make me feel relaxed right now.

I think about the doctor coming over and giving me the sedatives that put me to sleep so quickly. The prescription for the rest of the sleeping pills is still at home, sitting on my bedside table waiting for me to come to a conclusion as to whether I'll fill it or not. I wonder how that will play into this. Anyone who finds out I took medication that was completely new to me right before this incident happened will jump to conclusions. There have been so many cases of people taking medications that are meant to help them, only to find out they have horrific unintended consequences. It wasn't too long ago that a man who took sleeping pills to help him combat lifelong insomnia ended up murdering his in-laws in the middle of the night.

I know I didn't do anything. I have nothing to do with what happened to that man in the library, but my inability to sleep and taking medication will become a part of this. I pace the cell throughout the night, trying to remember everything I possibly can about my old cases. They don't seem related. They don't feel like they have anything to do with each other, yet someone chose them. What's more important, they're going to choose another one. There's going to be something else, and the consequences could be dire if I can't stop it before it happens.

The night stretches on. It feels like I've been pacing for days when my legs finally get tired, and I'm forced to lie down on what passes for a mattress. I'm staring up at the ceiling when the cell door opens. I sit upright and see Sam standing at the door. He looks like he hasn't slept, either. His clothes are wrinkled, and his eyes are drawn and red.

"You can go," he says.

"I can?"

"Go home," he says. "Don't stop anywhere else. Don't talk to anybody. Go home. I can't hold you for any longer until there's more evidence, but I also can't let you cause any more trouble. I'm sorry, Emma. I wish it didn't have to be this way. I hate that this is happening to you, but my hands are tied."

I walk past him out of the cell to make my way to the small room where I can collect the belongings they took from me last night.

"Are you coming with me?" I ask. "You look like you need some sleep."

"I have an investigation to run," he says. "I'll catch some sleep in the back when I have a chance."

"Sam, I need to tell you what's going on," I say.

"Right now, we have to hope that man doesn't die and that someone is able to prove you aren't the one who made that phone call," he says. "I don't want to bring charges on you."

"I told you, my phone was here. I couldn't have made that call," I insist.

"Your phone was here. We recovered it and got corroboration from Edna. But that doesn't necessarily prove anything," he says.

"What do you mean?" I ask incredulously.

"I shouldn't be talking to you about this without an attorney present," he sighs.

Anger starts boiling inside me.

"I don't need a fucking attorney. I need you to be straight with me."

"Just because you left your phone here doesn't mean you don't have another one. The phone left here is inoperable. It won't turn on. There is nothing to say you didn't get another phone attached to the same number and have that."

"It's not inoperable. It's bricked. Like I tried to explain to you, it's being controlled by a program someone installed on it. It should be easy to prove I don't have another phone with the same number. Just contact my provider," I say.

"Emma, I know how to do my job. This is an investigation you aren't going to be able to control. We're going to contact the service provider, but it's Saturday. The chances of them getting back to us are slim. It will take time," he says. "You're just lucky I was able to get you out before then. You could have been spending the entire weekend in that cell."

"Yes. I feel so lucky."

I collect my things and walk out to the lobby, but Sam follows me.

"I thought you weren't coming with me," I say.

"I'm not. I just thought I would walk you to your car," he tells me.

It's still waiting where I left it. As I approach, I notice something fluttering in the morning air from under the windshield wiper. My stomach tightens, and I prepare myself, almost hoping for a threatening note, so I have something I can show Sam. Instead, I find a parking ticket.

"Power-hungry son of a bitch," I grumble, snatching the ticket from under the wiper.

"I might know someone who can take care of that for you," Sam says, trying to inject some levity into a moment woefully undeserving of levity. He feels the tension and tries another approach. "There wasn't anything at your house when I went and looked yesterday. But if you're uncomfortable and you don't want to be there, you can always go to my house."

I shake my head. "No. I'm not going to put you in that position. I'm sure it will be fine."

He closes my door, and I drive away, waiting until I know he can't see my reflection in the mirror anymore to let myself cry.

———

I walk around to my backdoor and make sure it's closed, then check every window before I return to the front door and go inside. My house feels quiet and unassuming. There's none of the strange, tingling feeling that comes from something being off within your space. I felt that before. I wait just a few steps inside the still-open door to sense if anything is different, but no matter how long I stand there, nothing changes. Relieved, I close and lock the door. My stomach growls, reminding me I haven't eaten anything since early yesterday. I'm tempted to order a pizza, but the risk of the delivery boys snapping a picture and me ending up on some Community Hall of Shame website stops me. Instead, I settle for a massive bowl of popcorn, promising myself a real meal when I can build up the energy.

I take my place on my couch, open my computer, and pull up the file of cases again. A thought occurs to me, and I get out my burner phone. Realizing my collection of phone numbers I have completely memorized is limited, to say the least, I pull up a new window and search for the phone number to Lionheart Property Management.

"Lionheart Property Management, this is Derrick. How can I help you?"

"Hi, Derrick . This is Emma Griffin. I need a quick favor," I say.

"Emma, are you all right? I heard what happened," he says.

"Well, you heard what people think happened. But that's not the point right now. Did Pamela come into work today?"

"Are you asking that because you're planning on coming up here again?"

"No. I just genuinely need to know if she came into work," I say.

"No, she didn't. I spoke to her this morning she said she had a family emergency she was dealing with," he says. "I'm hoping it works out for her. To tell you the truth, I didn't even know she had a family."

"I hope it works out, too."

"Is there anything else I can help you with?" he asks.

"No. That's all. Actually, can I have her cell phone number? I have something I need to ask her," I tell him.

He gives me the number, and I thank him before hanging up. I dial the number, but it rings several times without answer. Outside, I hear a door slam heavily and an engine rev. I end the call and call again. It rings a few times and goes to voicemail as I walk across the room to the window.

"Pamela, this is Emma. I sure hope you listened. Call me when you get this."

I watch as the garage door to what I thought of as Ruby's house opens and a car I don't recognize slides inside. The door closes, but a moment later opens again, and the car slides back out. I pick up the phone again and call Derrick back.

"I'm going to sound like a broken record here, but humor me," I say. "Did anyone have a showing at 2021 Candlewood today?"

"Yes, actually. It's been getting some new attention thanks to recent events. Several people have called wanting to see it. Without Pamela here, I've had to have other agents step in," he tells me.

"Thanks," I say. "That makes me feel better."

I get off the phone and go back to the couch. People have called me many things during my life, but that's the first I've been referred to as 'recent events'. At least I appreciate his attempt at subtlety. He's one of the few people in town who hasn't either implied or explicitly stated that they think I'm one green cherry short of a fruitcake, and it feels good to at least have that going for me.

And speaking of cake…

I pick up the phone again and look up another number. Pearl answers on the second ring.

"Hi Pearl, it's Emma," I say.

"Emma, child. What is going on? Are you alright? I heard you were arrested. I thought that can't possibly be. Not Emma."

"I was arrested," I tell her flatly.

"On the other hand, you have been known to get yourself into things. What's going on?" she asks.

"Everything's going to be alright. No matter what happens, it's all going to be fine. I can promise you that." The words feel heavy in my throat, but I mean them. Somehow, I'll see them through.

"That's good to hear, Emma. Now, what can I do for you?"

"I just have a question. Did you have chocolate cake at the diner yesterday?"

"I certainly did. It was the special dessert. Dark chocolate with fudge icing. Made with Duke's mayonnaise, so it's moist and tender. It was my Mama's recipe," she tells me.

"Did you have that special a couple weeks ago, too?" I ask.

"Sure did. Why are you asking? Were you wanting some?"

"I was just thinking about chocolate cake. It sounds delicious, but I promised Sam I wouldn't leave the house."

"Well, If I can find my grandson, I'll have him bring you a piece when the lunch rush is over," she offers.

"Find him? You can't find Kevin?" I ask.

"He was supposed to come in today, but I haven't seen him yet. I'm sure there's a gerbil to be splinted, or a rose to be pruned somewhere," she says.

"Rose to be pruned?" I raise an eyebrow.

"Oh, yes. Kevin is nothing if not an ambitious boy. When he's not taking care of the animals or here helping me, he picks up jobs with that landscaping company you see around."

"Davis Landscaping Solutions?" I ask.

"That sounds right. He says he likes the chance to get into the outdoors when he can because he's so cooped up all the time."

"I can understand that," I say.

"Well, it's getting on rush time. I have to run. But I'll get that cake over to you when I can. And keep your chin up, no matter what people are saying about you," she says.

"Thank you, Pearl."

I hang up, shaking my head. That's one of those things that's meant well but does little to conceal the truth. The people of Sherwood have lost faith in me. I have to prove them wrong.

CHAPTER FORTY-SEVEN

The sleepless night in jail catches up with me, and I nod off on the couch at some point in the afternoon. When I snap awake, the light is nearly gone from the house, and the dusky blue of evening has started to set in. I didn't wake up naturally. Something startled me awake, but I'm not sure what it was. I hear it again and realize it's a car. Someone else must be doing a morbid fascination tour of the house across the street. Standing up, I stretch my back and walk over to the window. The car parked in the driveway spikes my interest, and I rush to get my shoes and coat on.

Pamela's little red Miata sits in the middle of the driveway, the exhaust pumping out clouds into the frigid night air. The garage door slides open, and a silhouette dips down under it to go in. She must think my warning is off now. I remember what she said about being so dedicated to her career.

Undoubtedly, Derrick finally got in touch with Pamela and let her know just how many people want to see the house. That would draw her back, but she needs to stay vigilant. I jog across the street to talk to her, calling out her name, but she doesn't respond. I'm almost to the garage when I notice more exhaust is coming out from under the door.

My first thought is whoever is seeing the house must have parked in the garage. But then I realize that doesn't make sense. They wouldn't be able to open the garage door.

"Pamela?" I call out again.

The garage door hitches and struggles, stuck in its position. I dip down under it and immediately notice the dark-haired woman standing at the controls, jostling the buttons back and forth to make it act like it wasn't working. I start to move toward her, but she drops to the floor and rolls under the door into the night. Before I can do the same, the door slams down onto the concrete drive with a sickening thud. There's a sound of metal against metal, and I try desperately to yank the door back up, but it's no use. She's locked it from the outside.

With the garage door closed, the small space fills with exhaust quickly. It's warmer in here, so the cloud of fumes isn't as dense and visible, but that doesn't mean anything. it's not the appearance of the exhaust that matters. It's not even the elements that make my eyes sting and choke my throat and lungs that I have to worry about. Those are disruptive. I don't want to be exposed to them for any longer than I have to, but because I can see and smell and taste them, I'm not as concerned. It's what I know is building up around me, odorless, colorless, and tasteless, that makes me frantic.

Carbon monoxide.

The truck looks familiar. It's not exactly right. There are a few slight differences, but I know I've seen a truck very much like this before. My mind is already starting to get foggy. I reach for my phone but realize I took it out and put it beside my computer when I was sitting on the couch. I didn't think to grab it when I was crossing the street with the intention of talking to Pamela.

Running up to the front door of the truck, I tug on it, but it's locked. I run around to the other side and find that one locked as well. I climb up into the bed of the truck and try to open the back window, but I realize it's not the type that slides open. Jumping down again, I bound up the four steps leading to the door to go inside the house. It's also locked, and I remember how thick it is and the two locking mechanisms on the other side. There's no way I'm going to be able to kick it in. My only choice is to somehow get inside the truck and stop it.

I climb into the bed again and kick at the back window, hoping to pop it out of place. I'm quickly getting disoriented as the carbon monoxide replaces the oxygen in my blood. I'm feeling sleepy, and everything inside me begs to just lie down and rest. I can't. I know I can't. If I take even a second to rest, it'll be over for me. I have to keep trying.

I climb down from the truck, looking around for anything I might be able to use. I remember the can of paint sitting up on the shelf and look for it. Relief washes over me when I see it. I scramble up a step stool and reach up for the can. It's nearly empty, but the small amount of paint left in there gives the can enough heft that it just might work.

I hold the can firmly and swing it back, then smash it forward into the glass at the driver's side window. It doesn't do anything.

I hit it again and again. Each hit is more difficult as I get short of breath and weak.

Finally, I notice a chip in the window, then a series of cracks weaving their way along the surface. I use it to give me a second wind and hit the window again. It finally shatters, and I scrape away the pieces of broken glass so I can unlock the door and climb in. As soon as I do, my heart sinks. There's no key. There's no button to end the ignition. There's nothing. Somebody rigged the truck to keep running even without the key.

I try revving the engine, maybe driving back out of this and crushing the door, but it won't take. The gas pedal has been cut. This truck isn't going anywhere.

Coming back out of the truck, I run up to the door and slam my hands on it, screaming at the top of my lungs. It's only when I see my bloody handprints on the cream-colored paint that I realize I cut myself on the window. The pain hasn't set in yet. I know it will, but for now, my brain is blocking it out.

I'm so tired. I'm completely exhausted like there's nothing left in me. I use everything I can to pound on the door again and let out another scream to whoever might be on the other side. To any of my neighbors who might be able to hear me. But I honestly don't even know how loud my voice is. I feel like it's a whisper. No matter how much energy and power I try to force into it, it comes through my lips like a murmur.

I drag myself back over to the truck and try to lift the hood. It won't move. I slam the bottom of my hands against it again, trying to force it up and out of the way, but it won't. I trace my fingertips along the seam between the hood and the rest of the body and discover it's been welded shut. There's no way to access the engine so I can cut it off.

I go back to the door and crouch down near the ground. I want to lie down. Even though the smooth cement floor in the garage is icy, the rest of my body is already freezing. It doesn't seem it would make much difference. I could just stretch out and close my eyes. I could just relax.

I feel my eyelids drooping, and I snap them back awake. I can't let that happen. Ducking my head down, I get as close to the floor as I can and try to breathe in fresh air from outside. It's useless. The door is firmly flush against the ground, and no discernible fresh air comes in. I resort to kicking the bottom of the door as I continue to pound on it with my fists.

Finally, there's no energy left in me. But I'm not just going to sit down. I will go down fighting, even if that's fighting against the very functioning of my body.

There is only one idea left. I open the truck door, lean inside the truck, release the emergency brake, and put it in Neutral. Then I walk around to the front and brace myself with my back against the workbench. Gripping it on either side with both hands, I lift my feet and start pushing against the front of the truck. If I can get some momentum up, I might be able to guide the truck backward and hit the door with enough force to at least bend it. It might not get me out, but it will make someone notice.

I push as hard as I can, using every bit of my slipping strength and body weight to try to move the truck. Slowly, barely, it starts rocking. It's only slight, but it's happening. I keep going, holding the rough wood harder with my cut hands and forcing my feet against it. When it feels like it's rocking enough, I get down and run to the open door, so I can try to push the truck backward.

The truck barely budges. It's too heavy. I use the last of my strength and put everything I can into it. Slowly, I feel the wheels going. Slowly, I feel the truck backing up.

But it might be too late.

My eyes close and my body sinks down to the floor just as I hear a deafening crash.

CHAPTER FORTY-EIGHT

"Emma!"

I think I can hear Sam's voice in the distance. But I can't lift my head or open my eyes to look for him. I hear it again, him calling my name, and it's the most wonderful sound I've ever heard. I'm glad it's the last one I hear. The next time I hear it, I feel strong arms scoop me up off the cold floor. Then they're carrying me, and the suffocating smell of the exhaust starts to go away. I'm bouncing, jostling around, and my face hits something hard. I realize it's Sam's shoulder. He's cradling me in his arms and running across the street to my house.

He lays me down, and I feel something soft but still cold. He has stretched me out in the grass and now lifts my head up, shaking it back and forth as he yells my name down into my face. Sharp stings follow quick smacks on either cheek.

"Emma, come on. Open your eyes. Come on, Emma. Open your eyes. You're fine. Take a deep breath. Open your eyes," he pleads.

I try to tell him I'm doing the best I can. I'm trying so hard to open my eyes. I want nothing more than to be able to see him.

"Open your eyes, Emma. Come on, baby, look at me."

Finally, enough fresh air has gotten to me that I'm able to open my eyes and look at him. The world still spins around me, but I'm aware of my body in the grass and my head in his hands. I'm alive.

"Sam," I smile softly.

"Emma. Oh, my god, I thought I lost you."

He drops his head down to rest on my chest.

"You found me," I say.

"Of course I did," he says.

"How?" I ask, still trying to flutter my eyes open. "I didn't have my phone to call you."

"Your neighbors did," he replies with a laugh. "You are very loud."

"Remind me to be offended by that later," I tell him.

He smiles at me and leans down for a kiss. An ambulance pulls up to the curb, red and yellow lights swirling around and slashing over houses trying to sleep. I recognized some of the EMTs as first responders to Pearl's Diner the day everyone was sick.

"What happened?" one of them calls over.

"Carbon monoxide," Sam tells them. "She was locked inside a garage."

"For how long?" she asks.

I shake my head. "I don't know. Long enough."

"Why couldn't you get out? Was the door jammed?" she asks.

"It was locked," Sam says. "From the outside."

I look over at him. "So, this time, you know I'm not making it up?"

"I'm so sorry," he says. "I'm so sorry I didn't believe you sooner."

The medic adjusts an oxygen mask over my face and encourages me to take deep breaths. It will take hours for me to breathe all the carbon monoxide out of my body, but the more oxygen I can force back in now, the better.

"Let's get her loaded up and head to the hospital," she says.

I shake my head. "No. I'm not going to the hospital."

"Emma, carbon monoxide exposure can be extremely dangerous. You need to get checked out," Sam says.

"I will later, I promise. Right now, there are much more important things that need to be done."

I take a few more breaths of the oxygen, then peel away the mask and head over to the head EMT.

"Are you sure you don't want to go to the hospital? There could be significant side effects you aren't aware of right now," he says.

"I'll take the risk," I say.

There's nothing they can do, and they pack up to drive away as Sam helps me up and toward my house.

"Why would you take such a risk?" he asks as I drop down onto the couch in front of my computer.

"Because something else is going to happen. The only reason I went across the street without my phone is because I saw Pamela's car sitting in the driveway. No one had heard from her today, and I left her a message. Yesterday I warned her to stay away because I knew something was going to happen, and I figured she just wasn't listening to me. So, I went over to talk to her and tell her what I'd uncovered. But it wasn't her. But it was definitely her car. Which means she's somewhere, and we have to figure out what's going to happen next in order to save her."

I start going through my files again, waiting for something to jump out at me, waiting for the little bit of inspiration I need, so I know what comes next.

"Explain it to me again," Sam says. "Tell me what's going on."

"It's based on my cases," I tell him, speaking at rapid speed as my mind still struggles to put words in the correct order. "The dark-haired woman, the one I was calling Ruby, she's the one who locked me in that garage. She's behind all this, and it involves other people, too. We just need to figure out how and why."

"Alright, then start at the beginning," he says.

"I think it's the ending actually. The cases are working back-wards. They're building up on each other, getting worse and worse as they go. She is trying to make me look insane, and she might have succeeded in actually making it happen. It started with the noose at the fairgrounds. That represented Everly. Then the hotel. It was aban-doned and crumbling, and I got trapped, just like Jake's house in Feathered Nest," I say.

"You were right about your phone, by the way. The tech finally got into it, and he did find a program controlling it. The app is able to completely take control of your phone, turn it on and off at a whim, stop phone calls or texts from going out or coming in, it's pretty extensive. I explained to them what you said about the text messages, and they said it would be very easy to use a masking app to make it look like a text came from someone else's phone come even if they didn't have access to that phone."

"Exactly," I nod. "So, they were able to make it seem like you were trying to get me into the hotel. Then I got trapped, and I ended up having to climb out and basically fall to escape, just like I did there. After the hotel was everybody getting sick at Pearl's. It sank in when I heard Pearl refer to Nicole as Nikki. I was part of a case with a girl named Nikki, who was kidnapped. The kidnappers inadvertently killed her by feeding her a meal that had a food she was allergic to, mixed in with the rest. They didn't know about the allergy, so they couldn't help her."

"So, you believe she was targeted."

"Yes. But the hazelnuts weren't in the gravy. Other people would notice the difference in flavor. I bet if someone had thought to check her utensils, they would have found powdered hazelnuts on the fork in her biscuits and gravy."

"And everyone else getting sick was just a distraction," he muses. "Meant to confuse everybody."

"Not everybody," I point out. "Me. Then after that was the swatting. All through there, all along, there was the constant thread of Ruby Baker. Tonight, the carbon monoxide was in reference to a case I had where a man died in his office at home. Nobody could figure out what happened to him. There was no sign of trauma, no evident wounds or illness. Nothing. Then they discovered a business rival had hooked up a generator to a small tube and was feeding carbon monoxide into his office at a slow but steady rate. Because the effect is cumulative and can last for hours, it eventually put him to sleep, and he died. There are only a few cases before that one that we can consider. But that truck means something. It didn't have anything to do with the carbon monoxide case. They used Pamela's car to get me across the street without being wary of anything, but that truck wasn't an accident. They didn't just randomly choose it."

Suddenly, it occurs to me. Bits and pieces fall into place, and I search frantically through my files until I get to the right one.

"What did you figure out?" Sam asks.

"Pearl's grandson Kevin is married, yes?"

"Yes. But I've never met her. She's apparently not very social. There have been some rumors that their relationship isn't the best," he says.

"Which is why Pamela always seems to be coming out of the bathroom when the rest of the office arrives for lunch," I say, finally getting confirmation of what I've suspected since I saw that door.

"What?" Sam asks.

"What's the date?" I ask. "The date of today. What is it?"

"November 29th."

My skin prickles.

I pull up a picture of a courtroom from my very first case as an agent. I look over it carefully and see exactly what I was looking for. I grab my phone and pull up the same image. I rush to my bedroom and come back, hooking my harness into place.

"We need to move fast," I tell him. "I know what's going to happen next."

CHAPTER FORTY-NINE

I wrench off my seatbelt before the engine is off. Throwing myself out of the car, I run across the damp, uneven ground. My ankle twinges where the injury hasn't fully healed, but I ignore it. The light from the flashlight on my phone isn't much, but I don't want it to be. I don't want to make our arrival known too soon. The steady thud of Sam's boots behind me catch up, and he looks down at me.

"I have officers positioned around the perimeter. She won't be able to get out if she runs," he says softly.

I nod in acknowledgement, and we hurry on. The cemetery is difficult to navigate in the darkness, but it's not much further. I take only a few more steps when I start to hear voices. Following them, I finally see a figure in the moonlight. We get closer, and I can see red hair.

"It's Kevin."

He's leaning forward, speaking in a desperate tone. We get closer, remaining concealed behind a thick old tree.

"You promised no one was going to get hurt," he's saying. "You said this was just about making a fool out of Emma."

"Sometimes plans change," a woman's voice responds. "It seems

Emma Griffin is more resilient than I thought. She didn't care what people thought about her and wouldn't back down, so we had to work harder. It was fun at first. I waited a long time to see her squirm. But then it got tiresome. I had to do something else, something that would make more of an impact."

"But why did I have to be involved?" Kevin asks.

Holding my gun poised, I can't just stand there any longer. I rush out toward them. Kevin gasps and stumbles back a few steps. Ahead of me, I see the dark-haired woman I knew as Ruby. She's crouched down on the ground and is holding a terrified Pamela against her. The blade of a knife presses against her throat.

"You had to be involved because you were having an affair with Pamela," I say. "Isn't that right, Kevin?"

He looks at me, his eyes widened.

"How did you find out?" he asks. "The only reason she knew is because she saw us."

"No she didn't," I tell him. "She's not from Sherwood. She's not from anywhere around here. She's from New York. At least, that's where the trial was. She didn't know you were having an affair. She could tell by looking at you, and she pounced on your vulnerability. I watched Pamela's movements. I knew when she was supposed to be at the office and then she wasn't. I noticed when she would have arrived at different places and when you would arrive. But what really got me was the day you poisoned everyone at Pearl's Diner. Your grandmother trusted you, and you betrayed her."

"Kevin?" Pamela murmurs. The woman holds her tighter and presses the knife deeper against her throat, so Pamela gasps and closes her eyes briefly.

"I'm sorry," Kevin says. "It wasn't meant to be that way. No one was supposed to die. Did you know? How did you know if I had anything to do with it?"

"Sam and I were sitting close to the front of the restaurant. We could see every person who walked in. We watched the rest of the people from Lionheart come in but didn't see Pamela. Then everyone got sick, and later at the hospital, Derrick asked where she was. He said she was there. But we never saw her come in. Which means she came in later. The only way she could have done that without anyone noticing is to go through the kitchen. Only she wouldn't want anybody to see her coming through the kitchen doors. So, she used the door beside your dishwashing station, so if anybody looked, it was just as if she was coming out of the bathroom and not into the restaurant."

"But what did that tell you about the poisoning?" he asks.

"You wouldn't want to make her sick but were hoping to get to me. Later, when I asked you if you were feeling better, I said I saw you driving down Miller's Road to the hospital. I never saw that, but you agreed. You were trying to convince me you had gotten sick by tasting the food you supposedly didn't know was tainted. But of course, you knew not to eat it so you wouldn't get sick. You were surprised to find out Sam and I hadn't gotten sick, but it's the question you asked me that clinched it. You asked if Sam and I usually go to lunch at 12:30. Why would you ask that?"

"Curiosity," Kevin says.

"No," I say. "You timed it. You knew what time you thought we were coming in. So, you made the gravy, then waited until you figured we would be there to add in the ipecac. But we were already there. We had been there and ordered. So, we got the gravy that hadn't been tampered with. The one thing you did time correctly was giving Nicole the hazelnuts."

"I didn't know she was that allergic to them," he says. "She and my grandmother were close, but I didn't know her very well. I just thought it would make her uncomfortable."

"And you never asked why?" I ask.

"No," he says.

"Why, Kevin?" Pamela whispers. "Why would you do any of this?"

"To protect you," Kevin says. "Sarah told me if I went along with her plans, she would keep our secret safe. But if I didn't, she would tell my wife about us. She would tell my grandmother. Everyone would find out."

"And I wasn't worth people finding out about?" Pamela asks.

Ruby—or more properly, Sarah—gives another yank on her head. I see a small trickle of blood starting to form on Pamela's neck.

"You need to let her go now," I say. "Put the knife down, and let Pamela go."

"No," Sarah says. The face I had once thought of as a potential friend is now twisted in rage. "She doesn't understand. He so desperately doesn't want anybody to know about his relationship with her, he would do anything. He would do anything to stop his precious wifey from knowing he's been sleeping with her for two years because he never has any intention of not being married. But that meant I could dangle it over his head for as long as I wanted to."

"So, this is about me having an affair?" Kevin asks. "This whole time, you weren't just using that as leverage, it was your motivation?"

"No," I say. "That's not what it is. Is it, Sarah? This is about Travis, isn't it?"

Sarah makes a sobbing sound, and the knife slips slightly against Pamela's throat. I aim my gun, but I don't have a clear shot. The two women are too entangled for me to be sure I would hit Sarah and not Pamela.

"You don't get to talk about him," she says through gritted teeth.

I take a step closer.

"Why not? Isn't that why we're here? Shouldn't everybody know about him?" I ask. "You did all this and came this far so that today we could be standing here. Because it's not any random day. You chose today. It's been your intention all along."

"Yes," she says.

Sam inches up closer behind me and Sarah tightens her grip again. I take one hand off my gun to wave him back.

"Let her go," Sam calls. "Lower your weapon."

"Lower yours," Sarah replies with a sneer.

"Sam, back up. She wants me. Don't put anyone else at risk."

"Why you?" Kevin asks.

"She never told you?"

"Blackmail isn't a friendly transaction," Sarah sneers. "We didn't take much time to get to know each other."

"I sent her boyfriend to prison," I tell him. "On this date, four years ago. Only, no one even knew there was a girlfriend at the time."

"Because he loved me," Sarah snaps, her expression getting more contorted and painful. "He took care of me. He still does. That's why I'm here. No one should have believed you. No one should have ever listened to you. And after this, they'll realize how wrong they were. Travis did nothing wrong. His wife left him. She broke his heart. What happened to her after that was her fault. But you made everyone believe it was him."

"It was him," I counter. "And no amount of trying to discredit me is going to change that. He murdered his wife. Then he dug her up and moved her."

"No," she insists, shaking her head. "And when everyone sees just how unhinged you are, they'll give him a new trial, and he'll come home. He'll come back to me, and we'll be able to have the life we always planned."

"You seriously think you were special to him? That in all the world, you are the one unique being who understood him and who saved him from the dredges of an unhappy marriage?" I'm not able to keep the taunt out of my voice.

"Yes. We loved each other. What we had was rare and beautiful. We shared something we had never experienced with anyone else."

Her knife presses deeper into Pamela's neck, and I shift my weight, subtly gesturing to Sam to start moving around to the back so he could help her. He sinks back, getting out of Sarah's sight, so she focuses completely on me.

"Really?" I ask. "Tell me something, Sarah, who do you think helped him make the phone calls?"

She looks confused, and I notice the grip on Pamela lessens slightly.

"What phone calls?" she asks.

"When Travis was pretending Mia ran off, he made sure the police believed it by staging phone calls and text messages. You know very well you can manipulate the number that shows up when someone calls or even control a phone remotely. You might even realize there are ways you can prevent a phone from being tracked. One thing you can't fake is the location of the phone when calls are made and received. It's on your phone bills. Travis knew this, so he faked them. He brought Mia's phone out into the woods near his family's cabin, then in some unused land they owned, then in a car glove compartment sent to Canada. He made calls and sent texts, then they got responses from his phone, tracked directly to his phone. He obviously couldn't be in two places at once. Someone was on the other end of that phone sending the calls and texts, and someone drove the car to Canada. Who do you think it was?"

Sarah lets out a furious growl and draws the knife across Pamela's throat in a tight slash before shoving her into the shallow grave she dug. She lunges at me with the knife, and I pull the trigger.

CHAPTER FIFTY

"It was my first case as an agent," I say. "Travis Burke reported his wife missing a few months after I officially joined the Bureau. According to him, she just disappeared one day. Everything was going along normally, and they were fine, then when he came home from work one day, she was just gone. He couldn't find her and didn't have any trace of where she might be. The police were suspicious, but there was nothing they could do.

"There was no evidence of anything happening to her. Everything lined up. He said that she liked to spend a lot of her time in her art studio, which was actually a small apartment. He said she would go there for days at a time to work on her new projects and that it never bothered him because he knew it was an outlet for her. That's how he covered it. He killed her days before he reported her missing, but no one could track it because she had a routine of going to her studio and being there for several days without talking to anyone. He planned everything meticulously. He made sure to get rid of her clothes and toiletries discreetly and then said they were missing. Of course, the police searched the house and her studio and didn't find the things that were missing. So, to anyone looking in, it looked like she just left."

"Why would he do that?" Sam asks. "What was the motivation behind killing her?"

"That's the thing. Nobody could figure out why he would want to kill her. It all came down to life insurance. People believe that he killed her to collect on the policy they took out on each other when they got married. But Burke was already wealthy. There would be no reason for him to go through all that effort just to collect on such a comparatively small amount of money. Besides, if he wanted the life insurance, why would he pretend she left? Life insurance isn't to ensure the type of life you expect to have. You can't file a claim because your wife walks out on you, and so the life you knew was over. He would only be able to collect the money if she was dead and they could produce a body. One that didn't look like it was murdered," I explained. "That's why when Creagan put me on the case, I knew something was going on."

"Why did he choose you? You just said it was your first case. You were brand new. Why would he put you on something like this?" Sam asks.

"He didn't think much of it, to be honest. It wasn't like it was a serial killer or a mass theft. It was fascinating, in that this woman seems to have just left and was leaving a trail for people to follow. I was intrigued by the idea of a man crafting the idea of his wife leaving him, not to cover up the murder he had already committed accidentally, but to prepare for one. But that was nothing.

"The police had already investigated so extensively, and he never tripped up. Burke was cold, in a way I don't even know how to fully describe. It was like someone had taken a real person and preserved just the first few outer layers so they could wrap it around a core of ice. He looked friendly and even attractive. He was able to smile and charm people. He was so open and cooperative. But not too much. Sometimes people are too cooperative. They offer themselves up, and it turns suspicion onto themselves. That's not the way it was with him. He didn't offer his house to be searched until the police brought him a search warrant. The same with his truck. He didn't offer to bring them out to any of his properties until the police told him they uncovered the properties. Everything was done on their terms, but with him going along.

"It was a masterful plan. People trusted him. He seemed honest and genuine. Even more than that, he seemed like a man broken by the idea of the wife he loved so desperately being gone."

Sam crosses his arms and scratches his neck. "So, what you're saying is he didn't think you were going to figure it out."

"Or, he didn't think there was anything to figure out. To this day, I partially think Creagan wanted to believe Burke. He got charmed by him too. He was everything Creagan would want to be. Young, dynamic, wealthy. There was no way Creagan wanted to admit that he would do something horrible. So, it became my challenge. One of the first things that came to mind was that he was doing this for a reason, and it was so much more than life insurance or not wanting to be with his wife anymore. He had plenty of money and would have been just fine. But he wanted to craft this disappearance to cover up murdering her for a specific reason.

"That's when I started to think there had to be a girlfriend. If he had another woman to impress. Or another few women to impress, he wouldn't want his wife around. But he's also not going to risk going to prison. So, he did what wealthy, entitled men do, and came up with a story. One that seems possible. But we couldn't find any sign of a girlfriend. There was no unusual credit card activity. There were no surveillance videos of him going into hotels or motels with anyone. All the ways we would usually track an affair, he cleared right through."

"What is it about the truck? You said as soon as you saw it in the garage, you knew it had some sort of significance," Sam says.

"Yes, the truck," I nod. "One of the big parts of the investigation was searching his truck. Which, of course, was the truck he had at the time his wife disappeared. The police in charge of the investigation scoured that truck over and over to the best of their ability. They used dogs and luminol. They went over it with tweezers. They did absolutely everything to find anything suspicious. But there wasn't anything there. By the time I became a part of the case, he had a new truck. He got it almost a year after his wife disappeared, so none of the investigators put any thought into searching it.

But there were so many things that did not add up to me. Ground disturbances and tire patterns and just details I couldn't put together. So, I went back to thinking about his new truck. Just because something's been hidden doesn't mean it can't be hidden again. The truck was searched by cadaver dogs who were able to alert on the smell of human remains. From there, he just started to crumble. We eventually learned he had been putting these plans into place for quite a long time. When he was ready, he slit her throat, put her in a large storage container, and encased her in concrete at the edge of a piece of land his family-owned."

"Jesus," Sam mutters under his breath.

"He left her there for months. Then, he decided to move her. He didn't want to call too much attention, and he knew investigators were closing in on his properties. So, he used his new truck to bring tools that would break through the concrete, then hauled her out. He wanted to go somewhere he didn't think anybody would try to find her. So, he buried her in a shallow grave in the family plot on his family's land."

"How did you realize it was Sarah?" Sam asks.

"I knew everything had to be connected. There was just no way so many things were happening just coincidentally. But that meant it had to be somebody who knew about my cases. And in order to do that, you have to put in some research. I figured out they were doing my cases, and the truck struck a chord. That's not his truck. His truck was confiscated and impounded. But it's similar. Similar enough to almost look like it. It made me think about Burke and what he said about criminals being overconfident. During one of his interviews, he told me criminals always slip up. All that matters is if the police officer is smart enough to find it. And usually, it's because they went too far.

"Her creating those fake death documents was going too far. I'll admit they were convincing, but they were too splashy. It gave me visual confirmation of who I thought was Ruby Baker. Evidence I could show other people. When I found the picture of the courtroom from Travis's trial, I saw her in the background. I'd never noticed her before. Not any of the times I looked at the pictures, and not when I was there. They didn't speak to each other. They didn't look at each other. It was like she had just wandered in and was listening. She looks different now, significantly. But I knew her."

"You're incredible," Sam mutters, shaking his head.

"Not enough to save Nicole. Or Arnold Brown. If I figured it out faster, they would still be here. Caleb and Eva and Gloria would have been safe. Kevin wouldn't have had to go through it."

"You saved us," a powdery voice from the bed between me and Sam says. "Nobody else could have done that."

I look down to see Pamela. The hospital bed supports her head, and all the tubes and bandages around her neck make me want to quiet her and tell her to just keep sleeping. But I'm also glad to see her awake.

"How are you feeling?" I ask.

"It hurts," she says. "But it's getting better. I'm just thankful it wasn't any deeper."

"Me, too," I smile.

Pamela was able to shift just in time to prevent the bulk of the knife blade from cutting into her throat. It's sliced cleanly through her skin, which bled gruesomely, but she's been recovering well.

"How is Kevin?" she asks.

"He had his first hearing," Sam says. "He explained everything and is completely willing to cooperate. I think he has a good chance."

"I don't understand, Pamela. Why have an affair with him? Why not find a relationship of your own?"

"He was exciting and made me feel good," she says. "When you're with somebody for a long time, it's easy to get into a pattern. You lose those butterflies. You don't always want to touch each other anymore. But that's not how it was with Kevin. Because we couldn't be together all the time, that excitement stayed. He's handsome and kind and always treated me nicely. We were always excited to see each other; we were always thrilled when we got to be near each other. We got butterflies."

"But he's married," I say. "It could never be real."

"I know," she says. "But I never let myself think about that. I just kept riding the wave, and I figured one day, it would drop me. I didn't realize just how hard that drop was going to be."

"Why did you lie about being driven off the road?" I ask.

"Because I didn't know what was going on. I saw the car and automatically assumed it was Kevin. And it started acting so erratically, and I was afraid. When we went into that neighborhood, I realized it was that woman. Then I had to think about why she was in his car. It was just too much, and I didn't want to open up about it."

I nod. "That makes sense. The relationship was already so fraught and secretive, you couldn't risk letting anyone in on it."

"I think it was in part because of Ruby. I could never fully trust anyone. My marriage went up in flames. It was horrible. Then after her death, I just couldn't imagine feeling any more pain even close to that. So I chose a man who I would never get fully invested in because he would never be fully mine to have. I tried to improve things and ended up making them so much worse."

"That's not true. This isn't your fault," I say.

"I brought Sarah in," she points out. "Why do you think she chose Ruby? I think of all the things she could have done to mess with your head and make you look like you were slipping into oblivion, why did she have to choose Ruby?"

"I think it fit into her narrative," I offer. "She read about her death, and it seemed like a plausible story. Since she was already blackmailing Kevin, including you, was just an added layer. The tragedy of Ruby appealed to her. It was easy to make somebody accept her when she was presenting such a terrible story. And she already knew that Kevin worked with Davis Landscaping Solutions and was with you. Derrick keeps the keys to the properties in the cupboard, but that doesn't mean they can't be copied when they are out. So Kevin could access the property across the street from me and make it look like she lived there without anyone noticing. It also gave him access to my house. The two of them worked together. Whether he knew what he was doing or not, he had a major hand in it. I'm sorry you ended up being dragged into this."

"It's not your fault," Pamela says. "I'm just glad you stopped her before she could have gone any further."

"I took too long. There wouldn't have been any further, because that was my first case. I'm glad she didn't succeed in killing you, but there's really not much more she could have done."

"Not her," Pamela says. "Her big vision might have been to use your cases against you, but she lost herself in twisting your reality. She would have just kept going. But you didn't back down, even when it seemed like there was no way. You saved a lot of people."

"Thank you," I say.

Sam laughs. "I never thought I'd see the day."

"Have I told you recently how beautiful you are and how happy I am to have you in my life?" Sam asks.

I look over my shoulder at him and laugh as I close the cabinet.

"Are you talking to me or to the cinnamon roll?"

"Is it wrong if I say both?" he asks.

"Not at all. I feel pretty happy to have them in my life, too."

Sam gets up and comes over to me. He wraps one arm around me and feeds me a chunk of a cinnamon roll with the other hand.

"And I am extremely happy to have you in my life," he grins. "I don't know if I can ever tell you that enough."

"Well, I don't mind hearing it. You can say it as much as you'd like."

"I am extremely happy to have you in my life," he whispers again.

I smile and kiss him. It's been two months since Sarah's reign of terror, and Sam and I are still clinging to each other, recovering from almost being torn apart. We both agree my temporary leave from the FBI isn't really a leave anymore. I'm not just in Sherwood to visit or until I've gotten over everything. I never will get over it all. This is my life and it will continue to affect me for the rest of my life.

I adore my work with the Bureau and don't want to give it up completely, but right now, this is where I need to be. Working more with the Sherwood Police Department is giving me the fulfillment I'm looking for, and Creagan still knows he can call me if he needs me. All I know is whatever the day brings me, I want to talk it over with Sam at the end of it. And whatever else needs figuring out, I know that we can do it together.

He's slowly backing me toward the hallway to the bedroom when the doorbell stops him. He looks at me strangely.

"Are you expecting someone?" he asks.

"No," I frown.

He opens the door and I see him stoop down to scoop something out from the porch. He looks down at it, then looks back and forth up and down the street.

"This is all that's out there," he tells me, looking slightly mystified.

My breath catches slightly when I read the return address.

"It's from Feathered Nest," I tell him.

"What is it?" he asks.

I open the envelope and pull out a piece of paper folded once down the middle.

Emma, it's urgent I see you. I'll meet you at the station when you arrive.

I reach back into the envelope and pull out what's left. I hold it up for Sam to see.

"It's a train ticket."

The End

———

"Dear Reader,

Wow, we made it to the fourth book. I appreciate your continued support! No worries if this is the first book you read, you can checkout the rest by clicking here it will take you to my author page on Amazon and they can all be read as standalones.

If you enjoyed this book, please leave me a review on Amazon. Your reviews allow me to get the validation to keep this series going and also helps attract new readers.

Just a moment of your time is all that is needed.

I promise to always do my best to bring you thrilling adventures.

Yours,

A.J. Rivers

P.S. Checkout the next book in the series The Girl And The Deadly Express!

P.S.S. If for some reason you didn't like this book or found typos or other errors, please let me know personally. I do my best to read and respond to every email at aj@riversthrillers.com

Type the link below in your internet browser now to join my mailing list and get your free copy of Edge Of The Woods.

STAYING IN TOUCH WITH A.J.

https://dl.bookfunnel.com/ze03jzd3e4

MORE EMMA GRIFFIN FBI MYSTERIES

Emma Griffin's FBI Mysteries is the new addictive best-selling series by A.J. Rivers. Make sure to get them all below!

Visit my author page on Amazon to order your missing copies now! Now available in paperback!